Masks

NATALY RESTOKIAN

Tellwell Talent
www.tellwell.ca

ISBN
978-1-77370-810-2 (Hardcover)
978-1-77370-809-6 (Paperback)
978-1-77370-811-9 (eBook)

Dedication

This novel is dedicated to the love of my life, Nidal El Ghorayeb, my husband, my best friend, and my soul mate, whose unconditional love and encouragement ultimately made the writing of this novel possible. My husband more than any other person has enabled me to recognize my potential.

Without your faith in me, Nidal, I would never have been able to complete this work.

Your care, support, and sacrifice were the critical ingredients in providing me the strength and persistence to make this dream come true.

You inspired and taught me that with the power of true and selfless love in life, incredible miracles happen.

I will always love and cherish you, till death do us part.

Contents

Preface

Society. Tradition. Religion. All dictating rules, urging you to wear a mask, repressing your strength, courage, passion. Emerge from the crowd and surround yourself with the few who know your true face. Remove the mask and taste freedom. Remove it for a chance at absolute happiness.

Masks

One in a Million

CHAPTER 1

Anna was standing in front of a floor-length mirror in a hotel room in Los Angeles.

She was staring at herself, naked but for a pair of bright fuchsia heels.

Anna smiled. She still had the physical charm to attract men. Being able to use her looks to reach her goals and fulfill her desires was gratifying. She enjoyed looking at herself in the mirror.

The woman who had never been beautiful or attractive in her younger years—a nerd who'd been bullied in school—was now a beautiful, famous, and much-loved public figure throughout the Middle East.

Anna had smooth fair skin, a tall, slim, and symmetrical body with a narrow waist, average-sized breasts, and long arms and legs.

She knew that her oval-shaped face with high cheekbones, brown almond-shaped eyes, and arched eyebrows stunned men.

Anna had believed in herself when no one around her did, and she had made her way into the domain of the rich and famous in the Arab world. She had confidence, perseverance, and beauty.

Fame! Power! Money! She had it all. However, at what price?

Anna was married to Vasag, an attractive thirty-four-year-old guy who—thanks to Anna—was always well-groomed and stylishly dressed. He accompanied her to all her public functions and social appearances. The media ate them up; they were the perfect embodiment of a happily married couple, and that protected Anna from gossip and scandal.

She also had a lover, Abbas, an influential Lebanese realtor and developer she had met three years earlier when she had attended an Arab business conference in Düsseldorf, Germany. He had been unofficially and fraudulently sharing her life and her bed ever since.

Tonight, Anna was indulging in yet another immoral affair—this time with a man named Joe who had her all to himself for this one night. She was betraying both men in her life, men who had already broken her spirit with their egos and their needs.

Now she was checking in the mirror if Joe had left any marks on her neck when he appeared behind her, wrapped his arms around her, and rested his chin on her shoulder.

"Don't we look good together?" he asked. "I mean! Just look at us."

Seductively, she tossed her cascading mass of blond hair that crashed below her shoulders and smiled with her voluminous lips, showing luminous white teeth.

They were both naked. Like Adam and Eve, they were two sinners in the Garden.

His tone was so innocent that she could hardly believe this was the same voice that had made her moan in pleasure only moments earlier with naughty expressions and expert skills. The man who had just given Anna the most erotic night of her life was now admiring her in the mirror with an angelic smile. After six hours of relentless lovemaking, he still desired her.

"Let's go back to bed," he whispered.

Anna followed him.

They had met only recently and were already infatuated.

Anna and Joe had been chatting online and over the phone for three days. They started exchanging erotic messages as she grew more aroused by their relationship, physically and emotionally. No longer able to control her desires, she had given in to her vulnerability and asked him to fly across the world for one night of passion.

Before she'd even seen him, her mind had wanted him as much as her body.

Anna had never craved anyone in her bed. She had not known it was possible to feel the way she now did. She was obsessed.

Her fantasy had become a reality the minute they entered the room. She slowly took off her clothes and stood naked in front of him.

"Hey… Come here. I did not kiss you yet!" were his first words as she stood there wearing nothing but a matching set of pink lingerie and a pair of fuchsia heels.

Anna was perfectly at ease. She had imagined and repeatedly rehearsed this moment over the past three days while she touched herself as he spoke tenderly on the phone.

He continued smelling her skin, kissing every inch of her body from head to toe.

Messy. Noisy. Loud.

Passion.

They never wanted to leave that room.

Their bodies moved in harmony, taking turns enjoying each other. As he faced Anna and lowered his body on top of hers, she screamed. He stopped immediately and looked down.

"You are bleeding! Are you a virgin?" he asked in a panicked voice.

"No way! Are you crazy? I am married!"

Anna looked under the sheets. There was indeed blood between her thighs.

"Wait… Are you married? I had no idea!" he said, moving away from her.

"Stay," she whispered, pulling him toward her.

They were lying on their backs, barely touching each other. After a beat, Anna sat up, covering her breasts with the sheet like in the movies.

"So, what?" she said defensively.

She was a little embarrassed. She did not know why it had happened. Had they been too rough, or did she need to take a trip to the pharmacy?

Either way, his comment about her virginity felt strangely apt. She had the feeling of a young girl who'd been deflowered.

Joe moved toward Anna and placed his mouth on her neck tenderly; her neck, ears, lips, breasts, and thighs all tingled enigmatically at his touch.

He whispered in her ears, stimulating both her body and her mind, as if his touch were a magic spell, making her body float amid waves of passionate energy in some vault of heaven.

Anna knew it was for one night only.

She was aware she was living an enchanted erotic dream. This man knew every inch of her naked body and yet did not know who she was in the real world, dressed-up and made-up.

The night was a mystery, an adventure, a lie!

She felt as though her brain had shut down. It was the only explanation. Had it been functioning normally, it would have prevented her from being in a foreign country, alone, surrendering her body and emotions.

Joe was behaving like he was being paid to respond to her sexual desires. The look in his eyes, however, told the story of a man in love.

He was turning all Anna's thoughts that had captivated her imagination to reality. He was making love to her, not only with his body but also with his eyes, his words, and even his breath.

Anna had lost all sense of reason and logic. In fact, her self-awareness had been lost the moment she had hooked up with him on that chat site. They began speaking on the phone, and three days later he was talking to her between the sheets.

With his shaved head, goatee, and hazel eyes, he immediately took Anna's breath away. He made her feel both vulnerable and safe. He could have turned out to be a psychopath or a rapist, yet strangely, she felt neither fear nor doubt.

They did not ask much about each other's lives, content to experience the passionate collision of their bodies.

In her entire life, Anna had never experienced such a night. As a public figure, she'd always been careful not to damage her reputation. However, tonight, she was free. She could talk about anything without fear of judgment. She could be whoever she wanted to be. He did not know who Anna was.

When they'd first spoken three days earlier, he had asked her to show him a picture of herself. Because her laptop did not have a camera, she could not, so they had shifted to talking on the phone. It was in the early 2000s when video chat applications were still quite limited. Still, he would not stop asking for a photo.

"Why don't you come see me in person and be done with it?" she'd finally snapped.

"Calm down. Stop pretending to be so mean," he said, giggling. "I just want to see your face."

"But I am mean! If you want to see me, you're going to have to fly over here!"

"Are you kidding me? It would cost me the same amount of time and money as a trip to Lebanon," he said.

"Well, if you don't want to spend the money to come and see me, you don't deserve me!" she replied.

Such a stupid guy! She thought, but only for a moment. Her mind then drifted to their innuendo-filled conversations. She knew then that she needed to see him in the flesh.

"If you come," she began softly, "I will spend the night with you…"

It was a challenge, filled with curiosity, arousal, and defiance.

She had apparently hurt his pride, but he said nothing.

Two days later was his birthday, so on October 11 he decided to indulge himself, and he boarded a plane heading south to meet Anna. He was going to meet this girl, whoever she was, spend the night with her, then disappear without a goodbye.

Neither of them was going in with good intentions, but their curiosity had gotten the best of them and had overshadowed their instincts.

No one knows me here. No one will find out, Anna thought.

If she had been aware of the horror stories that ensue from online dating gone wrong, she might have felt differently. In her glamorous world, online dating and cybersex did not exist. She had had neither the opportunity nor the time to experience them.

Anna had lied and told him that she worked in an office. All he knew about this thirty-two-year-old was the hot and bothered voice on the other side of the line. He was clueless about her life. Her husband. Her lover. Everything.

Neither had stopped to consider the potential consequences of their plan. After all, these things happened in movies all the time, and so they treated the situation like a game.

Three days later, they met up at this hotel near LAX. They were infatuated the moment they laid eyes on each other.

They lay there in the hotel room, naked in each other's arms, and neither expected that this meeting would make them forget everyone else in their lives.

He was a single guy, already dating three other women, none of whom had Anna's charm and beauty. Anna had two men in her life, and neither had the ability to captivate her the way this stranger could with nothing but his voice and his touch!

"I never expected you to be so beautiful," he said.

"Thank you."

I wish I could make you mine, he thought. *That would be my lifetime trophy, showing everyone in my family how to choose the perfect wife: lovely! Sexy! Intelligent!*

"Well, I never expected you to be so charming and good in bed," Anna replied playfully.

"You are one in a million."

"That's a song!" Anna giggled.

"I didn't know; I meant that you're too perfect! You're everything any man could wish to have in a wife."

A wife? Anna was surprised by that word.

"You're a dream come true."

"A dream?"

"You are my dream come true," he said, draping his right hand on her flat stomach while supporting his head with the other. He changed the subject. "You're thin…"

"What do you mean? Are you saying I look sick?"

She sat up, covering her naked body with the sheet as if he had not already seen it all.

"No! I mean you look great! Don't you ever eat?"

"You don't want to see me eat!" Anna sighed and laid her head back on the pillow. "I have quite the appetite. I had never touched a shaved head before."

"There's a first time for everything," he replied.

They both laughed.

"So, how did you know I was Lebanese?" he asked.

"Well, we've been speaking in Arabic since we started talking, and I recognize the accent."

"You're Lebanese, too, aren't you?" he asked.

"I am, but my family is Armenian," she added with the pride and arrogance of a young princess talking to her servant.

Joe did not react.

She studied his face for a moment and noticed a few scars on the side of his head and above his eyebrow.

Charismatic, she thought.

The young man next to her was a year older than her. He had olive skin, a muscular body, bright eyes, a defined jawline, and perfectly shaped lips and nose. He was dashing, with a bright smile and a compelling voice. In Anna's imagination, the scars were those of an epic warrior.

Anna interrupted the silence.

"So, what are the scars on your face?"

"They're from a car accident I had many years ago."

"I like them."

Anna was so overwhelmed by him that everything about him turned her on.

"So where do you work?" he asked.

"To be honest, I don't work in an office... I host a TV show," Anna replied.

She already felt she could say anything to him; she felt comfortable and safe.

"Really?" he said, looking puzzled. "You mean you are on the screen? People recognize you over there?"

"Listen," Anna continued, feeling flattered, "let's just live this moment together. Here and now."

She felt safe with him as if she had known him from another lifetime and their souls had recognized each other the second they met.

All I need from you is sex! I do not want to talk about my life; I want to forget about it, Anna was aching to say.

She changed the subject. "Is that your real nose?"

"What do you mean?" he said and giggled. "What kind of a question is that? Do you think I borrowed somebody else's nose before I came over?"

"No, I mean, your nose is perfect." She touched it, adding, "Mine is not real." She moved her head, so he could see her nose from the side. "I've had other enhancements done, too."

His eyes shifted from her nose to her full lips.

His life was so different from hers. In his world, people only got surgery for medical reasons.

They both lay quietly for a moment. It was his turn to break the silence.

"Why did you choose me? I am wondering."

"I did not. I had already chosen a path in my life; I have a husband, a career, a life. I must go back to Lebanon."

So, what is she doing here? He wondered but kept quiet.

"So being on TV," he said. "How does it feel? Do people recognize you in the streets?"

The questions were starting to bother her. She had hoped to forget her life for a while. He fell silent. He did not wait for her to verbalize the thought; he must have seen the sadness on her face.

"Why don't you come and visit me in Canada?" he said.

He did not hear me when I said I was married? She wanted to feel outraged, but she could not miss the tenderness and care in his voice.

"Canada? Are you kidding me? I don't even know your last name!" she said, stunned.

"I've been waiting for you all my life, Anna," he whispered.

She didn't reply.

The white sheets were wrinkled around their bodies; they were both twirling with desire. For a moment, Anna had an inkling that this steamy infatuation might soon lead her along a dangerous path, to a challenge that could change her life forever.

You don't even know me, she thought, but said nothing; her heart was beating like a young girl who was being touched for the first time by her teenage boyfriend. His touch made her skin tingle; she felt her blood pumping and pounding through every muscle and skin cell.

She had never felt such passion in her life. After years of focusing on nothing but her ambitions, she had changed. This simple, handsome man knew nothing of her world, of her pain and deceit. To him, she was astonishing.

Anna remembered all their naughty conversations on the phone. Now he was whispering the same words in her ears, and she was enjoying it with reckless abandon.

She was not thinking of the consequences; she only wanted to enjoy the present. She had nothing to hide from this man. She was out of his reach, with no strings attached. He was her toy boy for one night, her listener and her secret.

He broke the silence.

"I wish you would come with me to Canada."

She did not respond. The phrase "I wish you would" never made any sense to Anna, but at that moment, it sounded like an incantation.

What if fairy godmothers existed and Anna could call on one right now, spin around and start the whole night over? What if she could leave everything behind and follow Joe to Canada? What if she could stop the clock and live this night forever? She was overwhelmed with his masculine arms, his charming look, his innocent smile, and she wished she could give back everything she had been given to stall the hands of time. She tried to shake the thoughts away. *Your body is controlling you now, Anna. Don't think, don't think!* She repeated in her head. *Just enjoy the moment.*

His eyes surveyed her body. He smiled at her candy-red nails.

"You're so dolled up!" he said, laughing.

Anna responded with a giggle.

Joe was in bed with a celebrity. Her dress, her moves, even her perfume was different from any other girl he had ever seen before. He felt like a child being beckoned to the land of youth, full of free-spirited imagination, magic, and wonder. He had taken flight and was heading for Annaland.

In his mind, her life was a fairy tale.

However, he did not realize that there were pirates and thieves, and evil people in stories. Fairy tales are deceiving; villains sometimes do win.

Anna told Joe about how she had worked in various media outlets, from magazines to television, while sparing him the embarrassing details of particular situations in which she had found herself.

When joe mentioned her husband, she circumvented the question. He did not need to know that the man she had made her vows to was aware of an affair she had had in the past, and was okay with it, as long as she continued to provide him with luxury and comfort. She did, however, spill the beans about how he had cheated on her, this time sparing no details—from the STDs he had caught to his pathetic excuses. She told Joe about the times she had been forced to push back while he tried to hit her.

Anna was surprised at herself.

It was probably the first time she had ever felt she could be honest about her past. She did not tell him everything, but for once there were no lies in what she had revealed. She had been in denial for so long that telling the stories felt strange. Anna had gotten used to carrying this emotional baggage with her everywhere she went. At first, the conversation was irritating, but she soon began to feel relief as she poured her heart out to this man who was giving her his undivided attention. Anna was unaccustomed to kindness, so up went her defenses.

"I am not a victim, I know what choices I've made!" she yelled, scowling and running her hand through her long hair as she caught a glimpse of sympathy in his eyes.

"My life is like one of those soap operas," she said.

Anna's eyes were twinkling with tears that were threatening to come cascading down her cheeks. The girl who had lectured him and been so rude hours earlier was now helpless before him.

"Let's go sit in the tub," he suggested.

"Yeah... Why not?"

Anna wanted to go back to her dreamy mood. She had not planned for such a serious conversation.

They stood up, naked, and as they were walking to the bathroom, she stopped once again in front of the long mirror in the hallway to check her eyes. *Why do I have to be such a mess? Inside and out.* Then she saw him looking at her and slowly approaching from behind.

"let's go".

She gave him a half smile, walked to the tub, and stepped in. She submerged herself in hot water as he followed her in and began kissing her neck.

"I love your freckles..." he whispered as he kissed her. She moaned softly; his hands and mouth were all over her. He caressed her gently, down her legs, and then his hands dove deeper into the water. Anna responded with a louder moan, aroused by the firm touch on her breasts. She slowly emerged from the water and sat at the edge of the tub, her legs parted. He grabbed both her knees and tasted her. A few moments passed, and she pulled him up, kissing him furiously, diving her tongue into his mouth, biting his lips.

"What do you want?" he whispered.

"I want you…" Anna answered, her body welcoming him.

"Is this how you imagined it?" He kept on whispered as they felt their bodies uniting.

She did not answer; she was too busy enjoying this scene worthy of an erotica novel, an experience that was only going to last another few hours. She assumed her voice, her breathing, and her hands clawing at his back were enough for him to understand that this had far surpassed her expectations!

They were so taken with each other that questions such as why, what, and how did not cross their minds. Like, two teenagers, they were overwhelmed and did not want to snap back to reality. After all, it was just for one night. Why would she deprive herself of living the fantasy? Was it too much to ask when the life she had to go back to was so bitter? They enjoyed every second with abandon until they were breathless.

Later that night, they were both resting in the water, facing each other. He turned the hot water knob, and Anna shivered, unaware that her body temperature had dropped.

"He stole my jewelry," she suddenly said, breaking the silence.

"Who?"

"My husband."

Their eyes met, but she was the first to break contact.

"You are living with a thief, then… Why? Leave him."

Anna had many secrets, and everything in her life was complicated. *I wish I never said anything.* The pain had become part of the burden she carried each day, and she knew that leaving her husband was not going to solve anything.

"So, is Anna your real name, or did you lie about that, too?"

"I didn't. The rest was on a need-to-know basis; I was scared."

"Scared? You came here, met me, we did all of... this, and you were scared? I wonder what you're like when you're *not* scared ..." he said and smiled.

Anna hesitated before she answered him.

"My name is Anna. I didn't tell you about my real job, who I am in my world because I wanted, just once, to do whatever I felt like doing, without worrying about the consequences of spilling my secrets to a stranger."

"You still consider me a stranger?" he replied. Then he thought for a moment. "You're right." Disappointment permeated his every syllable.

Fame and fortune were not part of his vocabulary. He had led a simple life and was allowing himself to dream of something more. Anna, on the other hand, carried burdens of pain and suffering that her actual laughter and glamour could only hide for so long.

"I am so happy that we're spending the night together. I've never done this before... Meeting online and then, well, you know," Anna said brightly.

"No kidding. Few women would endanger themselves as you did. Do you even know what could have happened?"

A ringtone burst their bubble. Joe reached for his phone, disturbing the calmness of the water.

"Hello?"

"Hi! It is Trivia. Is Anna there? She gave me your number to check on her."

Trivia was Anna's younger sister.

As the saying goes, if you can't fight them...

"Yup. She's right here." He handed Anna a towel and the phone over the edge of the tub.

"Hey, Trivia, I'm okay. I'll call you later. Don't worry about me."

Anna was always the warrior, the villain, and the hero in the family story. No one else indeed played much of a role in her life.

Tonight's story had begun four days earlier when Anna had been sick in bed after a long week of family parties.

Anna was passing the time, surfing from site to site online, when Trivia suggested she check out some chat sites.

"At least you'll talk to people," trivia had told her.

"That's a good idea. Maybe I'll have some fun and mess with some guy," said Anna, playfully.

"Go ahead and make yourself an account."

"I don't know how. You do it for me!" Anna demanded.

"Fine. Stop yelling! Oh my God, you are always so loud!"

Moments later, Trivia was showing her older sister where and how to log into an R-rated site.

Five years younger than Anna, Trivia was unlike her sister, inside and out. Anna's loud, high-pitched voice irritated her, as did her untamable ambition and energy. Trivia was a beautiful woman in her late twenties with piercing black eyes, thin lips, rounded eyebrows, a button-nose, and a pointed chin. Her round face and long red hair matched her glowing white skin perfectly. She was a few inches shorter than Anna, with feminine curves. While Trivia was very quiet and kept her distance, Anna had always made an effort to bridge the gap between them, but she could never find a way into her sister's heart.

Anna was used to her sister's moodiness. She ignored it, only wanting the week to end without any arguments. Anna always spoke her mind and freely expressed herself: by shouting, clapping, jumping, and laughing without hesitation, usually irritating the people around her.

No one ever bothered adjusting his or her behavior for Anna, so why should she? Her mind bounced enthusiastically from place to place, and everyone around her could tell this from the way she interrupted one idea with the next.

Trivia was married with three children.

When does she even find the time to go to these websites? Moreover, why? Anna wondered although she was in no position to judge; her marriage was far from holy. Anna was careful this time to choose her words wisely with Trivia because she was tired of arguments and misunderstandings.

"Okay, it's done. Enjoy!" Trivia logged in. "All right, I'm just going to write a brief bio for you. No pictures or anything. Do not ever use the web camera. It's broken anyway. Good luck! Enjoy!"

Once done, she left.

Anna browsed the pages of the site for a while, fascinated.

"This is cool," she said out loud. "It's like being out in a bar but with a mask on. No one knows who I am. I love it!"

Her mom brought Anna a cup of tea. She responded with a smile.

"Why don't you come and sit with your dad and me?"

"I'm all right."

"Trivia left with the kids, and her husband isn't home."

"No thanks, Mom. I'm fine here," she insisted.

Melineh, her mother, turned on her heels and walked away.

Soon after, however, Anna had forgotten all about her fever, her aching body, and her sore throat. She was clicking on pictures, chatting away. Messages were popping on the screen.

Hello, beautiful!

Hey, sexy!

Do you want to talk?

It was her new favorite game. A girl who used the computer for nothing more than typing articles, marketing plans, and checking email and fan mail was now using it for an entirely different purpose, taking her away from reality. It was her magic lamp, and with every stroke of her hand, she got closer and closer to having a wish fulfilled.

Who would think Anna could have wishes? All her dreams had come true, until the twist in the plot that had turned them into nightmares. She did not even know what she was looking for but knew she had a need that had to be fulfilled. Could anything ever fill the void inside her? Would she ever find her way through the labyrinth?

She was chatting here and there until one guy caught her attention. Not just because he seemed to be a believer—as demonstrated by his use of the cross as his profile picture—but also because of the way he spoke to her. Half an hour into their conversation, she had blocked all the other chat windows and was typing her fingers off talking about everything with this one guy. One conversation led to another until somehow it resulted in dirty talk.

Anna was having fun! His words aroused her. While it was very apparently her first time in a chat room, it was not the case for him. He was an expert in talking in a way to hook Anna. After asking questions like "What are you wearing, and what do you look like?" he took it up a notch and asked for her number.

"Don't you want to hear my voice?" he asked suggestively.

Anna paused for a minute and decided to give him her sister's home number. What harm could come from a chat and a phone number? She had suffered so much disappointment and had been hurt by so many people that she decided to dive right into the fantasy.

Ten minutes later, the phone rang. Anna was alone, and she had told her parents she was expecting an urgent call. The first hello from him was enough to break what little self-control she had left. He showed no hesitation jumping straight into dirty talk after hearing her voice. Expert as he was, Anna needed no man present to enjoy the fantasy; his words alone sufficed to make her moan with pleasure. His voice and heavy breathing at the other end of the line aroused her.

She did as she was told—closed her eyes and used her imagination to picture the stranger's hand on her body.

"What are you wearing, Anna?" he asked in a husky voice.

"A sexy nightie…" she said in a sultry voice while looking down at her cotton pajamas.

"Describe your body to me. Where is your hand?"

"I'm holding the phone, of course," she said, knowing it was not the answer he was looking for.

"Touch yourself with your other hand. Let me hear your breathing. How does it feel?"

As he spoke the words, his voice began to drift away, and an image came into focus in her mind. She remembered the first time she was asked by a stranger to touch herself. She was inexperienced, in need of money, and dreaming of fame.

It was during the early years of her career. There was a casting call for a major role in a television drama. Anna was in the casting room, reading for the role alone in front of the assistant director.

"Try with a different voice. It's a daring character," Salim said, abruptly.

Anna froze, confused. She started over, injecting more emotion into her tone.

He interrupted her again. "No, no, no! It's still not right!"

"How will I do that?"

He took a breath.

"I will leave you alone to read for a while. Try touching yourself first. I'll be back in a while to see how you sound then."

Anna was struck dumb with fear. It finally hit her, what this man was asking of her.

However, she knew better; doing such a thing had no professional value whatsoever unless of course she was sitting on a casting couch and did not know it. The man had left the room, and Anna sat there baffled. Time passed—she didn't know how long—and she did not move until he all but kicked the door open.

"I'm sorry, I can't!" she cried out. She stood, grabbed her bag, and headed for the door. "You were right. The role needs a sexy voice. I don't have it. I could neither touch myself here nor in front of the cameras for thirty episodes!"

The man was corpulent, unshaven, and smelled like tobacco. Rather than looking embarrassed, he laughed, his belly shaking like a bowl of jelly. He was apparently trying to cover up for the unprofessional—not to say vulgar—request. The disrespectful man explained that he had been testing her to see how far she was willing to go for the part. She stared back at him. He responded to her stare with a shrug and called her young and naive.

"I want this role," she interjected. "I would have worked for free, with my dignity!"

"Really? Well, it's a deal, then!"

Anna was taken aback. She realized at that moment that the many faces on the screen, big and small, were likely to have been confronted with situations like this one, and no one would ever know. Anna had overcome it. She had prevailed and was ready for the next step. He brought the papers in, she signed them, and he sent her on her way.

She took a taxi home that day, barely able to afford the fare. As she paid the driver, she thought about the contract she had just signed. Five hundred dollars for a role worth over fifteen times that. She'd never asked for a copy, and maybe she should have.

It's too late now, she thought and shrugged it off as she stepped out of the car and started walking home. The show would be shot all over the region and would take up to six months—six months of having to be available, anytime, anywhere, and unable to take another job. It was going to air on international television. It was worth it, she kept telling herself. She knew she would be exhausted and sleep deprived, but determined as she was, Anna played her role perfectly.

Her eyes flew open, and she was staring at her ceiling light, blinded. Her body was trembling with desire, she was frustrated and excited, and she still remembered how she played her role perfectly on the phone with Joe, hoping he would never hang up. She was at his mercy, her hand moving between her thighs, responding to his every word. She felt her body arching and trembling, and her heart was pounding as she climaxed. She turned to her side and sighed, feeling relaxed and satisfied.

A voice interrupted her daydream in the tub.

"Anna. Aren't you cold?" It was Joe.

She was staring blankly at the wall.

"Anna…"

She blinked, and their eyes locked. Here she was, a mere three days after her cyber fling, meeting the man who had made her toes curl then, and who was continuing to blow her mind. Any hesitation or fear was now long gone.

"You know I told my sister to wait in the car for me to check you out? I was ready to leave if—"

"If what?"

"If you weren't cute!" she admitted.

"You had a getaway driver. Good call! You stayed, though, so I'm out of the woods, aren't I?"

He was teasing her, and she liked it. Smiles lit up both their faces. They talked for hours. They were completely lost in each other. They finally stepped out of the tub, and he wrapped her naked body in a towel. They went back to bed and ordered room service.

Anna was still talking; it seemed she had forgotten that the guy in the room was neither her best friend nor her therapist. She continued to vent to him, disclosing stories and feelings that were usually kept locked up inside. She treated him like a vault, a diary, a church within which one spews truths, knowing that is where they will stay. They cuddled. She cried. They kissed. She held on to him like a lifeline.

He sat quietly, listening, thinking. His face was like an open book. She saw shock, sadness, happiness, and surprise, depending on what part of her story she was telling.

How had he ended up with a girl who had everything he was looking for and more?

However, the girl of his dreams was a total mess.

"How did you find all the strength, Anna? What gave you the power to fight back?" he asked her, after one of her stories.

She looked at him, startled, then shrugged.

"I was alone. I had no choice. When you are alone, you find courage. We ought to fight our battles."

"But yours are wars," he said.

"I know," she sighed.

"Anna. Please give me your cell phone number in Lebanon," he pleaded.

"Why? We will never see each other again, and I do not have time to talk on the phone."

"I want to send you messages from time to time."

"Fine," Anna said after some hesitation. She tore a page from the hotel notepad, wrote the eight digits of her Lebanese cellular number on it, and handed it to him.

They drifted into a deep slumber. She had not slept this well in a while. Something interrupted her sleep. Anna felt his hands all over her. He had already removed her satin nightdress with sexy side lace trim and was softly kissing her skin. All she could think of was how, despite everything she had, her life was empty of this kind of excitement.

Anna had been missing out on desire, chemistry, attraction—things that were inexplicably present between two people who seemed to have discovered their senses for the first time.

"Come here, you married virgin," he said while kissing every inch of her body.

"Stop it! Don't call me that!" Anna yelled furiously.

"I'm sorry..." he whispered and sealed his apology with a deep kiss.

Sleep was now out of the question. Time passed, and the clock was ticking. He had to fly back to Quebec, and she was going back to her hectic life. She watched him pack, thinking about how she had spent the night talking, judging, blaming, and laughing, and had enjoyed every moment of it.

Anna had intended to have a discreet affair, far from prying eyes, and Joe had come to challenge the girl who thought he would not go any extra mile to meet her. Both proved to be immature and reckless but thanked their lucky stars, as they were parting with beautiful memories.

Two taxis were waiting for them outside the lobby. Anna was returning to her sister's house in Los Angeles, while Joe had to catch a plane back to Canada. He wrapped her in his arms for a final hug, and Anna could not hold back the tears. It was as if a part of her heart was being torn away. She smelled his neck, his skin, afraid to let him go. He held her tight, and she felt as though those two arms could protect her from the world, as though their hearts beat as one. Could this be true love? Afraid to succumb to her weakness, the feeling that maybe lust was giving her the illusion of love, she began to pull away.

"You take good care of yourself, my star," he whispered.

His eyes were glistening with tears. Anna always wondered why men considered tears a sign of weakness. In her mind, they were a symbol of humanity and love.

I am going to miss your beautiful hazel eyes, your body against mine, your hands, Anna thought, but kept quiet. She was about to fall apart, so she hurried to her taxi and slammed the door as he waved.

Fate had put them in each other's paths at the wrong time and under the wrong circumstances. Destiny was playing a trick on Anna.

The next day, on the plane taking her back to Beirut, Anna delved deep into her thoughts. Would she be willing to declare war on the fate she had so far been subjected to? She had freely surrendered her body and soul to a stranger. It felt strange thinking of him as such. After all, something inside her had stirred when their eyes locked. Why him, she did not know. Perhaps it was a twist of fate. Maybe the stars would finally align. She felt an inherent sadness, though. She had left her heart in that room in Los Angeles.

Get a grip! You don't even know him!

But we have chemistry. We shared. It was more than sex!

No. It was lust. Love doesn't just fall out of the sky!

She was arguing with herself, barely noticing the passage of time. The food trays had come and gone, and they were landing.

A few minutes later, while stepping out of the terminal, she switched on her phone. The messages flowed in, one at a time. An unknown number with a Canadian area code caught her attention, and she read:

> Do not let him touch you. I want to marry you. I am in love with you! Joe

She barely had time to read it when Vasag appeared with a bouquet of flowers. Anna was frozen in place but managed to force a smile and respond to his hug with a quick kiss.

The whole way home, Vasag talked about work and other topics of little importance to her. Then, suddenly, he was talking directly to Anna.

"How was Los Angeles?" he inquired.

"Um… yeah. LA was beautiful," Anna replied distractedly. She figured she could blame it on jet lag.

She was still shaken by the text message, which she had deleted. As Vasag drove, she called her lawyer, who explained to her that Vasag—despite his assurances to Anna that he would not seek out the services of hookers ever again—had been hanging out at his old spot. The firm had hired a private investigator on Anna's behalf. She needed to know that, after everything he had done, he could at least be trusted not to taint her reputation any further. She slammed the phone shut.

"You were out again, weren't you?" she snapped.

"I didn't want to go, but it was my friend's bachelor party, so I had to!" He was so startled that he hadn't even had time to invent a name for his imaginary friend.

"Fine. Say no more!"

That night, Anna slept on the floor. She wanted neither to kick him out of the room nor sleep in the guest room.

While Vasag slept carelessly, presumably thinking he had gotten away with it, Anna was writing a message in the dark.

Hey, Joe. It's Anna. I am sleeping on the floor. I did not let him touch me.

I love you.

She then deleted both messages and went to sleep, thinking that behind every mistake there is a reason, and behind every heartbreak, there is a justification.

The next morning, Anna went to her office to take care of some paperwork. She lingered there until it was time to drive over to the studio, where she would put on a happy face.

The show had to go on, after all.

The Beauty and Her Two New Besties

CHAPTER 2

"You're late, Anna! I do not have all day! You are not the only one on the screen!" Jamal screamed.

"I'm sorry! I got stuck in traffic near the bridge," she said, panting. "They closed it, remember? For renovations?" Anna tried explaining again while he stared at her indifferently.

"That's not my problem," he finally muttered.

"But I called you twice on my way here. You never pick up the phone!"

"Please do not talk and stay still! I am trying to work on your eyes!"

She immediately closed her eyes and stopped talking.

Driving in Lebanon was always an adventure. Random blocked roads and bridges, and construction workers everywhere were an everyday occurrence. The media had its hands full of political chaos, so there was no time to follow up on road projects. Politicians were celebrities, in their own version of Hollywood. Lebanon had been this way for three decades, a massive circus since the seventies.

Ringmasters controlled the fate of the country with the help of human puppets who served at their pleasure. This is what was considered patriotism.

Beirut, the capital, was like an innocent child whose joy could never be taken away, who would find a way to have fun, no matter what. The city neither slept nor took a break from its pain.

While the major religious and political parties lusted after power, manipulation, and money, the people had one love: life. The Lebanese population woke up every morning with a leap of hope for change. Those whose poverty had deprived them of access to a decent lifestyle retained the most hope in their hearts for a better future. What choice did they have?

Fashion, music, traditional cuisine, and the best nightlife on the planet regularly stole the hearts of visitors. Lebanon's free-spirited citizens would not surrender to their fear of the country's gloomy, mysterious future.

The universe had granted the people two qualities to help overcome pain: optimism and amnesia. Secret remedies to help them continue living in a country where life was filled with complex and varied stresses.

In the television studio, the conversation between Anna and her makeup artist continued.

"I am sorry!" repeated Anna, feeling uncomfortable, her stomach clenched as usual.

"You beautiful women think you own the world. I do not work for you! I am not your personal makeup artist. I work for the TV station!"

The unusually talented artist allowed himself to speak freely to any celebrity who walked through the door. No one dared defy him or question his bad manners; they were at Jamal's mercy on that makeup chair. Anna avoided arguments at work, but Jamal's attitude got to her a little more every time, always right before going on air for her live television show.

Next day after this unusual conversation, Jamal called Anna while she was waiting for him in the studio.

"I am going to be late today. Get dressed, get your hair done, and leave the makeup for last. I'm grabbing a bite with some friends."

Anna groaned. Sure, Jamal had a life, but it was not an excuse to be late for work. *So negligent!* She thought. He was supposed to be in the studio for her, and makeup was always the first thing on the schedule. She let an hour pass and called him back.

"I will be there!" he promised.

The moment she snapped her phone shut angrily and opened her mouth to complain, her assistant interjected.

"You get so upset over simple matters. Relax!" Omar said.

She had no guests that night. The episode was an exclusive on a scandal, and she would be receiving phone calls from nine female contestants in a talent show. A stranger promising them success had offered the girls the chance to sing live in an open-air concert in Egypt alongside several famous singers. Without thinking or asking for any more information, they had agreed. Once they arrived in Cairo, they were locked up in a house in the middle of nowhere. Their passports were taken from them, and they were forced into prostitution. One of the girls finally had the chance to escape, with the help of a client who had come to use their services not knowing they were unwilling participants. They were back and safe with their families, and the man behind this horror was still in Cairo, denying everything to the local police. As he was still under investigation, he wanted to justify himself on Anna's show.

It was two minutes to the start of the show, and Anna entered her studio. She had no makeup on.

The crew stood there, shocked. She nodded her head to start rolling. With the high studio light, Anna looked like a ghost.

"Good evening! Welcome to my show!" She was still fixing her earpiece. "Let me begin by making a personal statement. My face tonight is the result of my patience and good manners toward people who do not respect their professional responsibilities. I am sure that my dear viewers watch this show because we give priority to the topics we discuss and not the way I look." She emanated confidence. "Let my appearance today be a lesson to you all. I advise you all to not rely too much on the people around you. They may let you down, and you need to be prepared, or you might find yourselves in a situation like mine."

The phone started ringing as her viewers began calling to show their love and support. The show ended, and Jamal never came.

No television host had ever dared to show her bare face on an Arab TV channel before. She was challenging the trend with a type of honesty no one was accustomed to. Anna always thanked and publicly acknowledged the people who supported her in the business, especially her friend and plastic surgeon Dr. Richy, one of the best in the Middle East. His treatments made her face glow. She never ceased telling him he was the best. Even on the air, she was honest about her plastic surgeries. At the time, not many owned up to their surgeries, even when they were plain as day.

It was not the first time that Jamal had left her in this awkward situation. She had solved the problem many times by applying her own makeup, but covering up for Jamal had gone unappreciated, and he had taken her for granted once too often.

On the other side of town, while Anna's show was still on air, in a luxurious clinic, Dr. Richy was busy reviewing documents at his desk.

The doctor's phone rang.

"Turn on your TV," Dr. Elias said to Dr. Richy. "Anna's lost her mind!"

Dr. Elias was Anna's dentist and a close friend of her surgeon.

Dr. Richy rarely missed Anna's show. He always observed her, examining her face to check if any adjustments were needed. She was the public face of Dr. Richy's expertise, his handiwork.

He was reviewing the paperwork for an international medical conference he had been invited to attend, where he would represent Lebanon while outlining his latest achievements in face lifting.

"Hold on a minute," replied Dr. Richy, rushing to the living room. "What is wrong with her?" He stared at Anna's pale face, transfixed.

"She looks like a ghost. She's whiter than her teeth!" Dr. Elias said, laughing.

"Well, I'm sure she knows what she's doing."

"We'll see…"

Meanwhile, Anna was concluding her show. After bidding her viewers a good night, Anna rushed off the stage to the dressing room and called Dr. Richy.

"I want my own makeup artist. I can't take it anymore! What are we going to do on Friday night?"

"Don't you trust me?"

"Yes, I do. I want my makeup artist, to stay with me until I end my show."

Anna was worried because Friday was Awards night. Several makeup artists wished to do her makeup, but she wanted someone she could trust. It was a delicate matter.

"Go home and rest. It is after midnight. I'll call you tomorrow," Dr. Richy said. His tone comforted her.

On Thursday afternoon, she was drinking cappuccino in a tiny upscale coffee shop with her driver Hashem when her phone rang. It was Dr. Richy.

"Don't worry about makeup or attire. Everything's been taken care of."

"But I have a designer."

"I know!"

"Fine. We'll do it your way."

"For Friday night, you need silver sandals and silver earrings. No necklace."

"Okay!" Anna smiled. He had never let her down.

"Be at my clinic at three p.m. tomorrow. The designer said not to have your hair down."

"I'll tell my hairdresser to put it up."

Next day, she arrived at the clinic at two. She waited impatiently in the sitting room with her coffee. The secretary, seeing her fidget, told her the doctor was in surgery and would be out soon. Another half hour passed, and two people walked in. They marched over to her immediately, with smiles on their faces.

"Hey, I am Rida," said one of them, in a slightly feminine voice. "I am your personal makeup artist."

"And I am Paul," said the other.

Rida was skinny with long, straight hair and full lips. He was wearing tight jeans and a tight pink blouse. He sported an angelic smile. Paul, on the other hand, had dark hair and piercing black eyes.

"I am so excited to work with you!" Paul exclaimed. "I love your taste. I've never dressed a TV host before!"

"I love your designs, Paul. I've noticed many singers and actresses wearing them during shows. But you are young! So very young."

"Thank you. We're both big fans of your show! And yes, I am only nineteen," replied Paul.

"Wow. And you, Rida?" Anna was curious.

"I'm not that young. I'm twenty-two."

They all laughed.

"Don't worry," said Rida, "I know your face by heart. You have lovely features. Perfect for makeup."

"I'm flattered." She smiled, her cheeks warm.

"This way," said Rida, gesturing for them to follow him into one of Dr. Richy's empty examination rooms. The clinic was huge, and the rooms looked like they belonged in a spa. "By the way," Rida blurted as soon as the door was closed, "I want you to know from the start: I'm gay."

"So?" Anna shrugged, turning around to look at him. "Your sex life isn't my concern. What you do to my face is."

"I just wanted to... settle the matter," Rida said, looking taken aback.

"You do not need to settle anything. I have always worked with gay men, and they tend to be good to me. Usually, at least..." She remembered Jamal's fits and flamboyantly diva-like behavior.

From the bag, Paul produced one of the most beautiful dresses Anna had ever seen. It was a long, baby-blue, silk-and-organza gown with an open back, and it shimmered with tiny crystals. It was perfect. It even looked the right size.

"Is it... my size?" Anna asked.

"It should be. I didn't put in much effort to know your size, and it's obvious, look at you!" Paul replied.

She was flattered. Paul had been in business only two years, but he was already becoming a household name. Anna could tell from his demeanor and expressions that he was gay too, but he did not mention it.

"Please, sit down. Let's start your makeup."

"Not yet. How about some coffee?" Anna suggested. "If you guys aren't busy."

"Not at all. Today we are all yours."

She opened the door and asked Sandra, the receptionist, to bring them cappuccinos. She left the door open and sat back down with her new friends. Sandra arrived with the coffee while they talked about fashion, about television, about society, about their lives, and the conversation led right back to Anna's show.

"I love how daring you are," Rida said. "You are fierce and bold. Just like me! No wonder your fans love you."

"Fans love seeing parts of themselves in celebrities," Anna replied. "People look for something from their own character in their beloved public figures. My fans often share some of my traits or see the world from the same point of view as I do."

They chatted for a while longer, sipping their cappuccinos, until Rida and Paul steered the conversation back to Anna's clothes and makeup.

"What do you think, Paul? Blue? Then gold? With a shimmery orange? No! Too bold!" He seemed to be talking to himself. "Her sandals are silver, not gold, and she has blond hair. I prefer the colors of these palettes." Paul pointed to one of Rida's makeup boxes.

"Yup. Okay," Paul continued, turning to Anna who was sitting in the post-op chair, waiting for them to finish debating. "Take off your blouse. Don't be shy; we're like sisters."

Rida laughed.

"I don't mind." Anna removed her shirt, knowing that foundation had to be applied all the way to her neck and ears. "Could I please have a mirror?"

"No, you cannot!" Rida snapped. "My God! You are all the same! Why do all women ask me for the mirror? Let me finish!" He smiled, trying to make up for the outburst.

"But... I just want to see the color of the foundation you'll be using!"

"Sweetie, trust me, I know my job as much as you do yours. You can look when I am done."

"If you make me look cute, I'm going to make you famous, I swear," Anna said.

"You are pretty! Be satisfied with the results, and that'll be enough for me," said Rida with confidence. "I've got you covered. Dr. Richy told me your show is broadcasted live every weekend. Don't worry. I'll be there."

"How much do you charge?"

"Are you crazy? It is an honor for me to work with you. No charge. I just don't want anyone else touching your face."

"Me too," Paul added. "All I want is for you to wear my designs. Even for your show."

"We have a contract for the show with a shop. I can't let them down. However, on special occasions, I will wear from your collection," Anna promised him.

"Maybe your wedding dress too, then?"

"Sure! For my next wedding!" Anna joked thinking about Joe. Her laughter was hiding a secret hope for a new white dress for a new beginning. She sighed and stopped talking. It was nothing but a dream.

"Well, if a guy proposes to you, I will know whether he'll make a good husband or not. "said Rida.

"You're too late. I am already married."

"Whatever," Rida continued "From now on, Paul and I are going to be with you all the time. Even for shopping."

"Why not? It'll be fun!"

Someone so passionate about his lifestyle couldn't be less passionate about his job, Anna thought.

As they worked, Paul looked at his mobile and smiled.

"Yes! Yes! Yes!" he shouted.

"I don't care about everyone else's opinion of me," Rida said, ignoring Paul's outburst. "Close your eyes, Anna. I am going to apply the lashes. As I was saying, what they think about me is their problem. They can either accept me for who I am or get out of my face. I don't like to hide. I did not choose to be born like this."

"You are so brave to say it out loud, in this society," said Anna. "Not everyone dares to."

"I'm doing nothing wrong. Why is loving someone of the same sex considered a crime?"

Anna was unsure if the question was rhetorical, so she said nothing.

"Do you know how many people from your television studio hang out at gay bars after hours?" Rida continued. "Some even show up with a face full of makeup and their partner on their arm."

"Good for them," Anna replied. "Who am I to judge? No one else should either. No religious or social rules justify this mentality. It's so hypocritical. The majority around us declare Jesus to be their Lord and Savior, who sat and ate with thieves, liars, and prostitutes. Some people think they are better than the Jesus they claim to love and follow."

A few moments of silence descended; all they could hear were the keystrokes of Paul's phone.

"Still on your mobile talking to your boyfriend?" Rida asked.

"Yes, do you mind?" Paul answered, blushing like a bride.

"What do you think about all this?" Anna asked Paul.

"I know gay people who have married someone of the opposite sex just to satisfy their parents and society. They are even bringing kids into the world with IVF and living double lives." He glanced at her, and something about her expression seemed to give him courage. "I have loved the same person since I was a child. We love each other, and I have never been with anyone else. He is seven years older, and he looks after me. We do not go to nightclubs in Lebanon. We are careful not to catch anyone's attention. We only have fun—go out together freely holding hands, party and dance—when we go to Europe. When Dr. Richy asked if we could be your private makeup artist and designer, we agreed because of your courage and your views."

Their admiration made her feel good, but they didn't know that Anna had endured her share of disgrace and humiliation during the steep climb to the top. She wore a permanent mask to hide her secrets. Anna smiled at them and nodded.

"We must go shop together next week," she said.

"Done!" replied Paul instantly.

"And done here, too! Now you can look," added Rida, handing her a small mirror.

"This is beautiful! You're an artist! Rida, I love it." She hugged him, the mirror still in her hand.

A moment later, they were helping her into the dress and shoes. Rida peeked through the door and asked a passing nurse to call Dr. Richy. He looked back at Anna with approval; she knew she looked stunning. Not wanting to wait a minute longer, she rushed into the corridor, holding the dress up with Paul and Rida trying to catch up to her.

"Wait, Anna, you're going to fall. Don't run! Your heels might tear the dress."

Anna was not listening. Dr. Richy, no doubt hearing the sound of her heels in the hallway, opened his office door. A smile lit up his face instantly.

"You look amazing, my friend," Dr. Richy said.

"Thank you! Rida and Paul did this!"

"Well, you have the package, Anna." Dr. Richy smiled.

That night Anna and Dr. Richy went to the event together. Vasag was already the shadow of a thought in her mind, while a man oceans away ruled her emotions. She breezed through the night, charming the room as she walked and talked, glowing with beauty and style. The evening ended.

A few weeks later, Anna was sitting in Rida's salon.

Rida was becoming a very successful makeup artist and was soon going to be running his own company. Anna's pictures would no doubt adorn the walls. This was all thanks to her support. The media had finally acknowledged his talent.

"I believe in God, Anna. I do. I hope God doesn't punish me because I am stuck in this body. I even believe in Jesus Christ, but as a prophet, not as the son of God."

He blamed genetics. He was born different, just like one of his uncles, who had disappeared after his grandparents threw him out of the house, twenty years back. Anna hugged Rida as he wiped his tears with his sleeve.

"Gross! Use a napkin," said Anna, trying to lighten the mood. "Don't feel guilty for something you cannot control, Rida. You are only responsible for the way you treat others. Be happy! You are a wonderful person. Use your anger as a shield of power to shine with your talent!"

"That's what I try to do."

"And I am so proud of you! Now let's do my eyebrows."

"Yes. Let's. Anna, I love you so much. Thanks for being such a good listener. Thanks for your support, I might become famous. I owe you."

"No, you owe me nothing. You were there for me when I needed you. I believed in you, but it's your talent that brought you success."

Anna's religion was her conscience. Her faith was shown in the way she treated others. No one was without sin, and she was definitely not worthy of casting the first stone.

She grew close to Rida and Paul, and she could not care less about the way people looked at her when she was with them. They were breaking the rules of society and religion, and neither pass was ready to accept homosexuality. In her eyes, though, they were two good people with unique talents who had chosen to live a lifestyle that matched who they were. Paul and Rida were being persecuted, hated and criticized by society, treated by some as if they were cannibals, murderers, or prostitutes. All they wanted was to live without fear, without shame, and without guilt weighing them down.

The world was full of savage humans, of beasts killing and slaughtering people in the name of God, and nearly no one blinked an eye. Meanwhile, Paul and Rida were struggling to be accepted for who they were, to have the chance to live.

Anna embraced her friends, regardless of their choices, with their God-given desires and tendencies. Did they belong in hell? No. They belonged in her life, and in the life of anyone with a conscience. A real king not only punishes but also forgives. A true leader does not only talk about bravery but also leads battles. Anna wanted to be the one guiding them through life, teaching them to have no fear. It was naive to believe that they would go to hell for life choices, and yet society never ceased to persecute them. Nature runs its course in perfect harmony if we let it. Why not embrace all that has been created by it? How can we let something as petty as religion and social rules disrupt the delicate balance of life?

Jamal never greeted Anna again at the television station. He gave her dirty looks every time he happened to cross her path. It annoyed her, but she had decided not to waste time and emotions on people who let her down.

Her life was changed entirely. Her entire world now revolved around a man she had met under the most unlikely circumstances. She did not even know much about him. She had no idea if he was hiding anything, but he had captured her heart. He was Joe, from Quebec, Canada.

That's all she knew.

Bread in Her Hands and Tears in Her Eyes

CHAPTER 3

While Anna was living in luxury, her mother Melineh was working at Anna's father's tiny restaurant, nestled in the heart of the Armenian neighborhood. Melineh was in her mid-sixties, her face wrinkled by the passage of time. Despite the signs of hardship, she had once been a beautiful young woman with a strong character and hope for the future, always thankful that fate had at least granted her wish to be the wife of her beloved Asbed.

Asbed was in his early sixties too. He stood tall and vigorous and had features typical of an Armenian man: big black eyes and an imposing beard. He had never studied the culinary arts, yet had inherited the cooking talents of his father, Hovsep, who had spent years as the private cook of a well-known French army lieutenant during the French occupation of Lebanon.

Since the beginning of the civil war in 1978, many people were down on their luck, losing their jobs, homes, lives. Asbed, like many others, had to take on several jobs to support his family. Anna's family lived the horror of war, poverty, insecurity, and fear. Anna and Trivia had changed schools countless times, every time they were displaced. They were consistently in fear; the war was a horror. The sound of the missiles zooming over their heads or bursting nearby, the sight of destroyed buildings, the pungent odor of burning flesh, and the smell of smoke slowly faded away in Anna's mind as she grew up.

Every time the bombings started, Anna's family along with others on the block rushed into the underground shelter—an abandoned leather warehouse—carrying only essentials. Each family carried a satchel containing legal documents and valuables, along with rations of cookies, jams, nuts, canned goods, powdered milk and coffee, a couple of items of clothing, and a large bottle of rubbing alcohol. The things usually people pack while going on a family road trip.

Years after the war, the smell of ethanol still reminded Anna of the tingling feeling on her palms after washing her hands each time in an underground place. It was a space of around five hundred square feet filled to capacity with people of all ages, and from all walks of life. Sick and healthy, young and old, all shared food, sleeping spaces, laughter, and tears. They sat on the bare ground, listening intently to the radio while playing cards. At night, they laid out blankets on the cold cement, hoping to wake the next day and witness the awakening of conscience in the politicians. They were like fireflies trapped in a jar, flapping their wings trying to escape, going in circles. The place was a warehouse that had no working ventilation system, but there was a door at the top of the fifteen-step stairway. They periodically opened it to let in some air, a time during which the men took advantage to sneak a smoke or two while keeping their eyes and ears open for fired shots or bomb pieces.

The children were fearless and carefree. For them, it was an adventure. Even the commotion and the ear-piercing noise of the bombs did not frighten them. It merely made them curious. Shouting, talking, murmuring, toddlers crying, children playing, men discussing politics, women chatting and arranging blankets, girls and boys flirting.

There was no running water, so they carried water into the shelter in gallons, using it sparingly for drinking and washing up. There was no electricity either, so oil lamps and candles filled the place with a warm yet eerie glow. Young Anna was unafraid because the word *death* meant nothing to her; she barely understood her own existence—perhaps the only advantage of being a child living in a war zone. Schools were closed, and there were children everywhere for her to play with. Now and then, her mother or aunt gave her a piece of chocolate or a cookie to divert her attention from the situation they were in, but young Anna and the other children were so full of life, vitality, and bliss that any trepidation toward death was defeated by their innocence.

Unimaginable amounts of innocent blood were spilled in the streets during the years of war from 1975 to 1990. In those days, neither YouTube nor Facebook existed to show the world the unbelievable torment of the Lebanese people living in fear, hunger, pain, and destruction. The war broke many hearts. Many mothers lost children. What a miracle it had been to survive at all! Anna was one of those with the power to suppress those memories and adjust quickly to daily life. Was it survival instinct or strength of will? She never cared to find out. Today, even an ant crawling on a table or a chipped nail irritated Anna, as if she had never shared a bunker with rats and cockroaches without taking so much as a shower.

That day, the war survivor Anna, now famous and arrogant had finished her work and was in the car heading home when she decided to drop by to say hello to her parents. She arrived on the crowded street with her driver. As always, there was no parking anywhere near the restaurant.

"I will double park here and wait until you are done," Hashem suggested.

"I won't be long. Just a quick hello!" Anna promised.

"Take your time. No need to rush."

Anna refused to be addressed as Mrs. or Madam by anyone who worked for her. She always said, "I am simply Anna."

She hurried to the shop. Her father was at the counter making sandwiches for clients. Anna greeted him and rushed to see her mom in the kitchen. Melineh was cleaning parsley; she heard Anna's footsteps, looked up and welcomed her daughter with a smile.

"I am in a rush! Hashem is waiting outside. I am so exhausted... I need to go home, take a shower, and rest. I have an early meeting in the morning."

She opened her purse, took out some money, and put it in her mother's apron pocket. She saw the embarrassment in her mother's eyes. She rarely dropped by and gave Melineh money and was always greeted with the same reaction.

"It is nothing! It's just in case you see something you like. Don't you ever get upset that you don't have a son? I am here for you, Mom!"

Vasag, who was not the breadwinner of the household, was not a big supporter of Anna's simple gesture. His world revolved only around him. Anna made sure her mother never found out about that particular aspect of his personality.

She kissed her mom. "I'm going now."

"Sit down, Anna!"

Anna was maintaining a strategic distance from Melineh's scolding gaze, knowing that her mom was not a naive, simple-minded mother who does not understand her daughter. She sat on a wooden chair and sent a text message to Hashem saying she would be staying a little while longer.

"Let go of your cell phone for one second, Anna!"

I am waiting for a call from Joe. I miss him already, even after two weeks. I need to hear his voice, she wanted to shout out, but she knew she should not, so she obeyed Melineh.

"You are always in such a hurry!"

"Sorry! I am just texting my driver. He doubled parked my car!"

"Your driver..." Melineh repeated sarcastically.

Why are you so judgmental? Anna wanted to say but kept quiet.

Melineh brought some Lebanese coffee, which Anna was not a fan of. She grabbed a cup, though, hoping to avoid a lecture.

"Remember when your father and I used to leave Trivia and you with your aunt every day and went to work?"

Anna was busy looking at her nail, uninterested in the topic. *I have no time for another lesson,* she thought.

"I'm talking to you!"

"How am I supposed to remember that? And what does this have to do with me visiting you today?" Anna was suddenly very irritated.

"Don't take that tone with me. Respect your mother!"

"I'm sorry, Mom." Anna took a sip of the cold, sugarless coffee. She sat up straight, leaned forward with both elbows on the table, and feigned interest in the conversation.

Anna was pure of heart and held no grudges, but her vivid personality and apparent inattentiveness made her seem remorseless and callous. She was almost at the peak of her success, but she was never able to express her pain or even her joy to her parents. She wanted all those who scorned her to see her as the lucky, glamorous person she had become.

Her parents always spoke to her as if she was a guilty, insensitive, and careless child. Anna hid her pain, fearing that it would bring them sorrow. They were focused on their younger daughter who always complained about her life and still needed her parents' help in every single way. Trivia had found a way to win her parents' hearts by playing the victim. She was very good at being Snow White lost in the woods, which made Anna look like the evil queen admiring herself in the mirror. Anna never learned Trivia's methods of lies and drama. Instead, she chose to be the wounded warrior on the battlefield and not the princess locked in the palace, afraid of life itself. Unfortunately, the image was unclear to their parents.

Anna was the black sheep of the family.

Although Anna's parents were hardworking, honest, and persistent, they were never able to afford a comfortable life. They had somehow managed to send their children to university and had given them a good life, all while depriving themselves of their own needs.

To Anna, the similarities between humans and animals outweighed their differences. Most people she saw living precisely like other creatures— people working to provide food; animals preying to survive. People sleeping to rest; animals sleeping to relax. Couples lying in bed only to produce children; animals mating to multiply. People following their religious faith without questioning; animals following their instincts without hesitation.

Anna was a member of this global human jungle. She did not dare break through its fences and jump out to see the world from a unique perspective; she hid behind her mask and obeyed the shallow mundane rules, with all her secrets.

Anna's mom was still going on about Trivia and their youth, and Anna was barely listening.

"No, I don't remember that. Sorry."

"We were looking for a way to make more money. We were ready for a job, and your uncle Gary introduced us to a bakery owner. The guy agreed to give your father every morning fifty bags of pita on consignment."

"Could you make a long story short, Mom? I am going to get stuck in traffic."

"One day, when I'm gone, you're going to regret not spending every possible moment with me."

Her mother knew how to put fear in Anna's heart. Those words always won the battle against any argument or demand. Anna was avoiding the conversation because she knew that the sad story was going to be followed by a lecture, and she was uninterested.

"Sorry, Mom! Yes, go on, please."

"I couldn't let your dad go alone, so I went with him. We filled the car with the bread bags and drove out." She paused to give Anna an intense look. "Yes, Anna. Your mother and father, despite their education and reputation, did not hesitate a single second to sell bread on the streets to bring food to our table."

Suddenly, Melineh's voice changed. She began to talk slowly, taking a deep breath with each sentence. She was looking up at the ceiling, as though the words she was looking for were written there. Anna observed her mother and realized she was trying to hold back tears.

"We were both petrified," Melineh continued. "We weren't safe in the streets. We weren't safe anywhere. The sight of all those closed-down shops terrified me, and at any time a bullet or bomb could have taken our lives. We didn't know when the bombing would resume, but we had no choice! We had our families to take care of. So, we drove until we could park the car in a crowded neighborhood. The car was loaded with bread, but no one came for it. The streets were deserted."

Melineh went on with her story, attempting to hide the torment and dismay in her voice as she revisited a not-so-distant past when she stood tall and beautiful, bright-eyed and proud, with her beloved Asbed by her side.

"Your father," she continued with a faltering voice, "was standing there, like a superhero, unwavering, but in his eyes, I could see sadness and despair. So. I made up my mind. The clock was ticking. We were tired, hot, hungry, and all we had were two bottles of water and a couple of cheese sandwiches in the car. I turned my back to your dad and started shouting. 'Fresh bread! Who wants to buy bread? Come and get them fresh!' There was no way I was going to let him see the tears streaming down my face. None of it was his fault, but I wanted to protect his ego, and I knew he would feel guilty for the situation I was in. Slowly, people appeared on balconies and carefully opened their doors. We started selling the bags. Your father, the intellectual man, was selling bread in the war-torn streets of the city. It was a bittersweet victory."

Anna was in shock. Tears were now running down her cheeks, and she could not speak.

"Do not misunderstand me! I was not embarrassed. We have always worked hard and taught you there is no shame in any work. No. This bewilderment and astonishment were at how much our lives had changed... at how life can, at any moment, take a turn. We didn't have much time to dwell, though. I looked over at the end of the street, as the last few customers were picking and paying for the bread and saw the apartment towers. There was no way they could had heard us. So, I gathered all the courage I had in me and started walking down the empty street, all the way to the building, and started going door to door, from floor to floor in the darkened hallways and stairways. The power grid was out, of course, so progress was slow, but the bakeries in the area were all closed, and nearly everyone welcomed the offer with open arms. They no longer needed to leave their homes to feed their families."

Melineh swallowed hard and sighed. Her lower lip began to quiver, eyebrows angled upward as she looked down.

"A few doors down, and a couple of floors up, a joyful smile greeted me. 'How can it be? Miss Melineh? Is that you? It has been so long! Do you remember me? It's me, Kevork! You were my teacher!'" She looked Anna dead in the eyes. "I did not remember him. I taught for twenty years and had countless students. But that isn't what bothered me. Children have memories like sponges. I just smiled and nodded, neither acknowledging nor denying his greeting. I asked him if he wanted to buy bread. I was speechless beyond the phrase that I had been repeating for hours, and the fake smile was emblazoned on my face. 'Of course,' he said to me. He would buy all the bread I wanted to sell him. 'Out of respect and love,' he said. But that was when it hit me. My former student was now buying bread from me. Instead of imparting knowledge, I was selling bread door to door. I all but threw the bags at him, took the money without counting it, and sprinted down the stairs. The rest was a blur..."

Melineh now held her head between her palms. They were both crying silently. Anna got up and hugged her mother. She always smelled so sweet, like jasmine and roses. Even in that kitchen that smelled of sandwiches, her mother smelled so lovely. Anna handed her a glass of water, which seemed to calm her down. They wiped their tears, and Melineh cleared her throat.

"Do you know why I told you this story? Not to impress you, or to make you feel that you owe us. I just wanted to show you that when we needed money, we didn't ask our friends or relatives, we did not beg or steal. As the Armenian saying goes, we made money out of stone. We worked hard. We kept our dignity."

Anna was unsure whether her mom was questioning the source of her income or trying to teach her a lesson. In any case, one thing was clear to Anna, and it was that the moment Kevork opened that door, her mom was no longer a woman selling bread. She was his teacher once again, and she was teaching him the most important lesson in life—live and earn your living with honor and dignity.

Asbed and Melineh had sold bread in the streets, worked in a factory, sold shoes on sidewalks in a village where they had found shelter from the war, and their last business endeavor was the restaurant, which had become Asbed's permanent occupation. They worked so much that they barely had time to spend with their daughters. Yet, they sat down on weekends with them—even after long, hectic days —and spent hours till the sun was up, giving them advice, listening to them, and teaching them how to be strong in life.

Anna remembered her early teenage years, and how her parents stayed up waiting for their daughters to return from parties until the wee hours of the morning, before getting dressed and going to work.

Anna and Trivia always had an excuse for being late. It was not customary for young ladies to be out so late in those days, and the teenagers still had a game plan ready before reaching the door, their heels in one hand and their sexy miniskirts hidden beneath a coat. The two sisters partied like there was no tomorrow. Their parents were strict and tolerant, all at once. Anna never knew how to behave or what to expect, and this resounded in her life as she grew up.

Half an hour later, when Melineh was calmer, Anna hugged her one more time, kissed her father and left her parent's restaurant.

On the drive back home, she was thinking only about joe.

She had started to grasp the fact of how we are born alone, we live alone with our own hopes and dreams, happiness and even sufferings, and we leave this world alone. We cannot expect those things to come from someone else. Each of us is defined by our own success through the journey of our current lifetime.

So, she had made up her mind. Her dream of being with Joe had glossed over her mother's lectures, and she was ready to give up everything for him.

What Are They Doing in Our Country?

CHAPTER 4

Anna arrived at her house exhausted. Her conversation with her mother had put her in a bad mood. To top it all off, she was caught in a web of lies. While she thought about her situation, she took a shower and got ready for bed. She concluded that if she did not act quickly, she might never be able to be with Joe.

As she began drifting off to sleep, Vasag opened the bedroom door.

"Don't you miss being with me?" His tone was expectant, gentle.

"I'm tired. I want to sleep."

She closed her eyes and thought about her life-changing plans. It was impossible to live like this anymore.

Vasag closed the door, the sound of his footsteps on the tiles growing fainter, and Anna began to drift into a dreamless sleep.

The next morning, Anna stood in front of a small apartment, her dog on his leash, a suitcase beside her, and Hashem by her side. A lady in her late seventies opened the door.

"Aunt Araxi!" Anna hugged the woman, who seemed surprised to see her niece so early in the morning and looking a total mess.

Anna's dog—Doggy—barked while Hashem moved her luggage inside. "What happened?" her aunt asked.

Araxi was a widow, with no children of her own. She had married late, in her early sixties, and now lived alone. She had raised Anna's father, and her other siblings after Anna's grandmother passed away at a very young age. Of the five children, Asbed was the youngest at only seven years old then, while Araxi was the eldest. Asbed never left Araxi, and she had lived with Anna's family until she found a husband, helping Melineh raise Anna and her sister. She had always been like a second mother to both Anna and Trivia.

Araxi was chubby, with tiny brown eyes, sparse eyebrows, and short brown hair. Her face was etched with wrinkles and marked by age spots, and yet she looked healthy and in good shape for her age. Veins were snaking up her chubby hands as she had knitted since she was young. She was an excellent cook and was obsessed with antiques. She had a soft, forgiving, and modest personality, and had been Anna's secret treasure box her whole life. The woman had a beautiful soul.

"Come in!" she exclaimed.

Anna rushed in and sent a text to an international number as Doggy jumped on a sofa with the leash still around his neck. Hashem left Anna's luggage in the hall and sat while Araxi made coffee.

Anna followed her into the kitchen.

"Did you have another argument with Vasag?"

"No. I'm leaving him." She surveyed her aunt's face. "I met someone else. I'm in love, and I want to marry him."

"But who is he?" Araxi continued, showing no signs of shock whatsoever. Anna suspected her aunt knew her all too well.

"I love him! He is the one. We were meant to be!"

"I see... and is he someone you knew before?" she asked as she poured the coffee into tiny cups, perhaps referring to Abbas.

"No Arabic coffee for me. I want instant."

"The powdered milk is in the fridge. Go get it."

"I met him in Los Angeles. I am seriously in love," Anna repeated, her face hidden by the fridge door as she searched for the milk.

"Well, how did you meet? Why are you always hasty in your decisions? Who is he? What does he do in life? What do you know about him?" Araxi asked, her face now anxious.

"Nothing about his life… but he captured my heart! And—"

Anna's mobile phone interrupted her.

"He is calling me. It's him!" Anna started jumping like a child.

"Calm down!"

"Yeah, right!" she said and flipped her phone open. "Hello?"

"Anna…" His voice was soft on the phone. "I love you. I will be there every step of the way. We will be together."

"I love you, too!" she reassured him. "I'm at my aunt's place, by the way…"

They spoke excitedly for few minutes, and she came back to the kitchen, her phone held tight in her hand, a dazed and happy look on her face.

"I said 'I love you.' I can't believe I said, 'I love you.'"

"Weren't you in love with Abbas, just a few weeks ago, before you went to Los Angeles?" Araxi asked, her eyes narrowing.

"No. That wasn't love. This is love," Anna replied.

Her aunt looked worried, perhaps thinking that Anna put her trust in people far too quickly. Anna sat and looked her in the eyes.

"I feel that maybe I should be careful and not trust him blindly… But my heart is telling me otherwise. It's like… I can't live without him!"

They were speaking Armenian because her aunt barely spoke Arabic. Hashem appeared not to be bothered by any of it, and he sipped his coffee while texting.

"I texted him that I left home, and he said he would be coming very soon to Lebanon…" Anna stood and skipped around the table, shrieking so loudly that the dog looked up from his bowl of food and barked at her. "Oh God, oh God! He is coming here!"

"Anna! Stop shouting! This apartment is tiny, and the neighbors hear every word you say."

Rather than answering Araxi, Anna hugged her.

A few minutes later, she left for work. She had a meeting with a young singer and had to prepare her for the interview.

The singer, Shaima, was already in Anna's office when she walked in. The beautiful young artist needed Anna's support promoting her album, and after watching the video, Anna agreed to help her. As she was complimenting Shaima on her talent, Anna stumbled on her words and corrected herself immediately. The singer laughed.

"I was told you were Armenian. You speak Arabic very well!" She winked at her and continued. "I heard that adorable mistake, though!"

The comment didn't bother Anna. She was having a phenomenal day; Joe was coming to Lebanon! She merely smiled and continued the conversation.

"Let me tell you a strange story if you want to laugh. I'll get us some tea if you have the time."

"Sure, I am free! My agent is taking care of some errands for me."

Anna settled into her seat and began.

"This happened when I was very young. My mother took me shopping. I was excited, singing in an annoying voice an Armenian song while my mom pulled me by the hand down the street. People in the streets were staring as we walked by—I was screaming rather than singing—but I couldn't have cared less. I'd always loved being the center of attention. I had earned that right by being a firstborn. There were no children of my age on either side of the family. All my cousins were at least ten years older; some were even married. I was spoiled, hyperactive, and extremely annoying, just like now."

"Stop it! You are wonderful," the singer replied earnestly.

"Thank you." Anna smiled. "My aunt Araxi had taught me the chorus from a traditional Armenian song. It went like this: 'Armenia, you are the source of our joy and happiness.' She always sang it with a frail, silvery voice while sewing a dress or mending old clothes. My voice was absolutely nothing like hers, but I still sang it, completely off-tune."

Anna paused to take a sip of her tea and continued. "I looked feminine but acted like a boy. I was a skinny child, with sharp features, always full of energy and with a constant twinkle in my eyes. I was talkative, always asking questions, and interrupting everyone. I was annoying."

"Well, I guess you were trained to interrupt your guests during interviews ever since you were a child," Shaima said and then laughed.

"Exactly!" Anna replied, taking another sip of her tea, this time pondering a little. "I had strict parents who tried everything to discipline me: punishing, grounding, and even slapping me. I was loud, always either dancing or singing. When I was doing neither of those things, I was plotting something that was going to end badly for myself, for my parents, or for everyone else. I was such a menace that my parents lost their patience and decided not to have any more children. My sister was a mistake—"

"That makes you a smart troublemaker!" Shaima said, still laughing.

"Melineh, my mother, was a school teacher for over twenty years. She confessed that she could discipline a whole classroom but couldn't restrain me. I was a real menace. I started walking when I was nine months old and spoke Armenian correctly earlier than most children."

"And you haven't stopped talking since you said your first word?"

"Yup!" She laughed. "Both my parents and my aunt were fluent in Armenian, and conversations were usually about art, classical music, and intellectual subjects. I listened, and I learned! So now for the exciting part of the story—"

"You let go of your mom's hand, got lost, and talked your way onto TV?" Shaima joked.

"Nope. Not that time." Anna winked at her. "This story tells you about my language issue."

"I'm so sorry about that… I meant no offense!" Shaima leaned over and tapped Anna's hand.

"No offense taken at all! I'm glad I get to tell you this story now!" She smiled and continued what was a monologue. "We entered a shop where my mom began to sort through school supplies. Suddenly, I heard a couple talking out loud in a strange language. I tried to grasp what they were saying, but I couldn't. It sounded like the words I often heard on the radio and on TV. So, I asked my mom what they were saying, but she told me she didn't know either, while she continued ruffling through the pile of school bags, looking for the perfect one for me. I yelled and insisted that she tell me. I was used to my parents answering all my questions—the whys, the whos, the whens, and the whats. Now I wanted to know why I could not understand these strangers."

"She didn't ask you to drop the subject?" the singer asked.

"No. Maybe. I wasn't actually paying attention. I was too busy racking my brain and waiting for an explanation. Finally, my mom turned to me and calmly explained that of course, I could not understand them because they were speaking Arabic, not Armenian. I was baffled and asked her why they didn't speak Armenian, like us. She told me they were Lebanese, and so they spoke their own dialect of Arabic, and that we were Armenian, so we spoke our own language, too. That made no sense to me, as I was at an age when I thought the entire world consisted of only what I knew. Everything was Armenian around me: parents, relatives, church, food, traditions. I even thought that God, and Jesus, and Mary were all Armenian."

"Okay, Anna, but what happened next in the shop?" Shaima appeared to be growing impatient with Anna's tangents.

"I asked my mom what they were doing here and why they didn't go back to wherever they spoke their language."

"Ha! You should have been in politics," Shaima added, ironically.

"No, thank you!" Anna laughed. "So, my mom laid some truth on me and burst my bubble. 'Anna, they are not in our country. We live in *their* country.' I was stunned. We bought the *Flintstones* backpack—my favorite cartoon at the time—and walked home in silence."

Anna paused and became lost in her thoughts for a minute. Melineh had purchased her first school bag that day. It was going to be with her in the new world, the world of her hopes and dreams. At the time, she had not been old enough to understand the history of her people. She had not even known that both her grandfathers were genocide survivors.

"I was not old enough to comprehend that behind the patriotism. My family didn't reveal racism or impiety, but rather the determination to prove the failure of the Turks, who had tried eliminating us as a nation and as a people. Many countries, such as Lebanon, Syria, Iraq, Greece, Iran, Kuwait, France, Canada, and the USA welcomed Armenian orphans."

"I never knew!" Shaima looked shocked.

"Well, now you do! Now you could make a song about it!" Anna said cheerily.

"I don't know a lot about your people, but I always wondered why you made mistakes in Arabic, especially as someone born and raised in Lebanon."

"I learned Arabic in school, but I think in my mother tongue, that's why! It is very different. However, I was raised to be proud of my origin, of my identity, and of my language, and I soon learned to respect and appreciate others, especially those who welcomed my grandfathers, and the place that granted me a new identity, an education, and a land to call home."

"You should tell your story on TV," Shaima said after a long pause. "Indeed, it was so moving."

"Maybe," Anna said, smiling and hugging her. "Thanks, Shaima. I have to go now. I will see you on Saturday. Please don't be late, or I will start without you!" Anna said, half-joking.

"I would never!"

As the singer walked away, Anna started collecting the papers on her desk. She was thinking about the decisions in her life that contradicted the principles she had outlined to Shaima.

True, Anna had become a star; Lebanon had given her that opportunity. She never said to Shaima that, for the first time in her life, her heart was in the hands of a person who did not speak her own language; she never told Shaima that in her life everything had come at a price.

As she reached for her phone to call her driver, it rang.

"Hi, Anna, it's me, Joe!"

Anna's heart pounded in her chest, and she closed the door.

"Hi, Joe!" she responded as soon as she heard the door click.

"I booked a flight. I will be in Lebanon in nine days."

"You know that we can't be seen together in public, right?" She was both excited and sad.

"It's fine. I do understand, my beautiful star," Joe teased affectionately. "I love you."

"I love you too," she replied, without a second's thought.

How had she reached the stage in her life when the words "I love you" would slip out of her mouth after only one night? A knock at the door pulled her out of her reverie.

"I have to go!" she whispered into the phone and hung up before he responded.

A few minutes later, she was in the car with Hashem on the way home.

Anna was counting the moments until she would see Joe. It was her first day out of her own house, and her husband had not even called her yet. Moreover, she did not care. She could not stop loving Joe.

The heart defeats the mind only by the power of true love, bursting through fear and logic. Her decision, her plan, and her love made sense to no one. Neither her aunt nor Hashem understood what she was up to. However, Joe was her world now. Anna's feelings resided in her heart, completely disconnected from her mind. She had no power over her decision.

"I am going to follow my heart!" she said suddenly, louder than she had intended.

"Sorry, what did you say, Anna?" Hashem's voice came in from the front seat.

"Nothing!" She giggled. "I was just thinking out loud."

"Yeah, and in Armenian, as usual," he added.

They both laughed.

The Milk Container is a Pee Can

CHAPTER 5

As Hashem was dropping Anna at her aunt's house, her phone rang. It was Melineh. Her parents were furious about her constant fighting with her husband, and with how she always went back to him. Trivia had told her parents about Anna's adventure in Los Angeles, suspecting that her involvement—driving Anna to the hotel and leaving the house—was partly her fault.

"It's my life, Mom!"

"Well, your father wants you to know that you are on your own with this!"

I have always been on my own, Anna thought but didn't say.

"You are doing this for the wrong reasons," Melineh continued. "You are not a teenager! You're a thirty-two-year-old grown woman, and you don't even know who the guy is!"

"What do you want to know about him? I love him!"

Her aunt appeared at the door to call her for dinner and froze. Anna was annoyed, pacing angrily in the tiny living room, grinding her teeth. Doggy was following her around. Araxi sat on the edge of the couch, waiting.

"You are going to regret it! He is not Armenian, he lives abroad, and no one knows who he is. Maybe he is married, a thief, or even a criminal. You told us nothing when we came back from Los Angeles. Even when you came to the restaurant!"

"I didn't feel the need to! I love him, and if it bothers you that much, then don't come to our wedding!"

"A wedding? Are you listening to yourself? You are a married woman, Anna. Is this a joke? I don't know you anymore! You are going to give your father a heart attack. Get serious!"

"Fine, I'm hanging up the phone now. I don't need your help; I can manage everything on my own. Now for the sake of Dad's health, I am hanging up. Good night to you both!"

She slapped her phone shut and froze.

Anna had chosen Araxi's unconditional support. Her aunt had always encouraged her to run to her, away from her parents' judgmental comments and worries.

Her aunt's voice interrupted her thoughts.

"Don't rush in with this. Try not to build your hopes up. You never know what tomorrow will bring," Araxi said softly.

"Don't worry, you will love him once you meet him," Anna replied, ignoring the warning.

Her anger had subsided thanks to her aunt, but she was not ready to face the possible risks of her decision. Araxi shook her head and headed to the kitchen. Anna sat back on the couch, her puppy at her feet and a hookah in her hand, daydreaming. Araxi returned with plates and a worried look on her face. She did not comment on any of her niece's faults, probably for fear of losing her status as a confidante. Anna knew that Araxi loved her unconditionally.

Vasag had neither called nor come by. Anna was not sad; she was actually relieved. Joe called, and they spent hours on the phone, time zones be damned.

"Anna, I know you must be living your life in luxury," Joe said after they had been chatting for over an hour. "I won't lie to you. I don't have much to offer. No fame, no power, no luxury. I can't promise you anything except my love."

"I don't care. I could live with you in a hut and still be happy."

She meant every word and yet still surprised herself. *I trust my heart!*

"I fell in love with you the moment I saw you," Joe went on, his voice soft and gentle. "You are the girl of my dreams. I want you to be my wife, the mother of my children. I want to spend the rest of my days with you."

"I feel the same way about you... and the way we make love..." she added shamelessly. "A marriage license for me will take forever, though! In the Orthodox church, it takes at least a year, even if both sides are willing to separate."

"We will find a way," he said.

"I will call my lawyer!"

"Tomorrow," Joe insisted, then whispered, "I wish I was next to you right now, smelling your skin, kissing your lips, holding you tight."

Anna's face was glowing, her heart was beating faster, and her mind was full of hopes for the future. In nine days. Very soon...

They hung up, and she started taking off her clothes to take a long, hot bath. Then she realized she had to turn on the water heater and wait awhile. Anna had forgotten that her aunt was not well off; her generator could not run around the clock.

Stable electricity in Lebanon was a daily crisis for many people, and Anna had forgotten it. She went into her aunt's bedroom and put money on the bedside table.

I should let go of my past to live the present, Anna thought, sitting quietly at the dining table. *I must not forget the ups and downs of my journey. I will be with him and shape my future to be brighter. Past misfortunes are not curses but lessons, preparing me for this tough challenge.*

She walked over to the couch where she had left her hookah before dinner, and she sat down to rest. Her mind drifted back to her younger years. It was twenty years earlier, during the Lebanese civil war, and Anna had fled with her family from Beirut to the village of Anjar in the Bekaa Valley, a village almost entirely populated with Armenians. There they were given an old house, which consisted of one room used for sitting, cooking, eating, and sleeping. It was a haunted place at night, and Anna always used an empty powdered milk container at night if she needed to pee. She never dared to step out into the evening. In the snow and cold, in the winter, the nights were even more laborious. Each morning, they emptied and washed the can. The village welcomed all Armenians from Beirut and distributed food, utensils, dishes, sanitation goods, clothing, and blankets to the newcomers. The houses, which were built between 1939 and 1940 by the French army, were given to the Armenian genocide survivors of Musa Dagh. The people of Anjar were vibrant, skilled, and strong-willed, and the area had bloomed under their care from a forest into a beautiful village with structured villas, churches, and schools.

These stone dwellings were still in the village as reminders of the hardship and the fate of their ancestors who had overcome obstacles that threatened their lives—disease, poverty, harsh weather, and even wild animals. They strived, flourished, and now they were helping families in need of shelter from the war.

At night in the chilly winter, wild animals lurked in the dark, and Anna was always scared to set foot outside the door even accompanied by her mother. They had no fridge, so any perishable foods had to be cooked and eaten right away. The only snacks they had were canned cheese, biscuits, bread, coffee, and powdered milk. Anna was the only one who needed to get up at night to pee—so typical of her to stand out from the crowd, even within her own family—so her parents solved the problem by providing her with an empty powdered milk container that became Anna's nighttime toilet.

She slept on a bed on the floor, next to her younger sister, and at the other end of the minuscule room was another mattress where her parents slept under army blankets. They were thick and prickly but warm. The girls wore thick pajamas to shield themselves from the itchiness of the blanket. Every time Anna got up to use her particular room, everyone woke to the sound of rushing liquid, first into the empty can, and then into Anna's hand when her mom helped her wash up with water. They all showered in that same room. They took turns, using a wooden chair behind a big plastic folding table that served as a door. They used a cup to rinse off the tepid water, which was achieved by mixing cold water with the boiled water on the tiny cooking stove.

They had an old heater in the middle of the room, which was attached to the ceiling with iron pillars that served as a chimney.

It was mid-January. It was cold, and snow covered the ground. They could only bathe three times a week, and they washed their clothes in a metal bin. Washers were unavailable, let alone dryers, so they hung their clothes on a rope at one end of the room. They took days to dry. A few months later, they were able to move to Zahlé, a city in the Bekaa Valley, where Asbed opened a restaurant. They rented a small apartment consisting of a single bedroom, a kitchen, and one bathroom. The two sisters were unaccustomed to the harsh cold of the mountains, and their hand-me-down clothes were not cutting it.

Anna and Trivia were always alone after school; their parents worked from morning until late at night. Adapting to a new language and mentality were the least of their problems. When they returned home one day after school there was a very bad smell in their apartment, the sewage pipes had broken and the whole place was covered with an expulsion of human feces . After having walked forty minutes from school, they turned around and walked another hour to their parents' restaurant.

"What is wrong?" Asbed asked them, surprised to see them bursting through the door. "Why didn't you go home?"

"The house smells bad," Anna answered, trying to hold back tears.

Asbed needed no further explanation. He set them up at the counter and made them dinner while they did homework. After closing the shop, they all went to see the owner, who was a rude widow.

"What do you want me to do? I will call someone to take care of it," she replied. "Very soon."

It took over two weeks to fix the problem. During that time, Anna's parents wrapped their feet with plastic bags every time they needed to go inside to get clothes or papers. They eventually moved to a nearby apartment, owned by one of their clients from the restaurant. It was a vast, empty, and cold place with no furniture. They did what they could with blankets and slept on the floor, but at least they were breathing clean air.

All the pain and suffering Anna had endured—peeing in a can at night, and having her belongings smell of sewage for what seemed like ages—had not left a trace in her memory. Fame taught her to behave in public as if she had always lived like a queen.

The anger and resentment from her childhood had brought her to a point in her life where her humanity had almost disappeared. She had been fierce and miserable. Now, suddenly her emotions were slowly breathing life back into her old self, when she had long lost her innocence, and the shattered pieces of hopes and true happiness were fading. She was not living in luxury anymore at her aunt's apartment. She was as comfortable as she could be, however, her spirits high and her heart full of dreams.

She daydreamed for about an hour until her aunt reminded her of the water heater timer, and she went in for a warm bath. Relaxed and happy, she went to bed and fell asleep almost instantly.

I am blessed, she thought as she drifted asleep. *Joe is coming to see me, and I will feel safe in his arms.*

At ten in the morning, her mobile phone rang and startled her. She did not recognize the number.

"Hello, Mrs. Anna? It's Danny Matar, the general director of the bank. We just wanted to inform you that fifteen minutes ago, your husband came in asking to withdraw all the money in your joint account. I asked him to please wait. It seems unusual. What would you like us to do?"

"I appreciate your phone call very much! Please do not let my husband withdraw anything. I am coming down right now."

Vasag had already left the bank when Anna arrived. She immediately removed his name from the account and thanked the manager again. She had nearly $117,000 saved up. That night, Vasag came to see her at her aunt's. Anna was with Araxi and Doggy in the sitting room.

"I want a divorce, Vasag!" she told him as soon as he sat down.

"What the hell happened?"

"What happened is that you went to withdraw all my money!"

"You left me, and our home before that thought even crossed my mind! You did this!"

"Are you kidding me? So, what if I left? I worked seventeen years for this money! You stole and sold all my jewelry, and now you want to take the money I made with my own sweat and blood? I want a divorce, I am telling you!"

"Sure, sure. So now, just because you are famous, I'm not good enough anymore, right? I was by your side all these years. What will people say if we get a divorce?"

"Oh yes, please forgive me," Anna replied. "I totally forgot about your social anxieties! You definitely have problems talking your way out of trouble..."

"You've become such an arrogant woman."

"Shut up! At least I'm not a thief," Anna shouted.

Her dog was clueless; he was trying to play with Vasag.

"Come here, Doggy!" All her anger was concentrated in a blasting shout, but instead of addressing Vasag she took it out on the puppy. "Go sit over there!"

The animal obeyed, his tail drooping.

"Fine. I am leaving. But you will regret this," Vasag warned.

"Am I supposed to be scared?" Anna laughed. "That's some big talk coming from such a small, petty man with no principles. I know what you've done. Don't play the innocent card!"

"You are leaving me for Abbas, aren't you? He could be your grandfather! How about I go tell him I know about you two?"

"What I do is none of your business. Do whatever the hell you want! Abbas will make you disappear in an instant!"

"Maybe. But he will leave you, too."

"Oh, just leave me alone, Vasag! You always say you want freedom. Well, now you have it. I am giving you your freedom. You keep saying you got married too young, and you wasted your younger years. You are such a hypocrite! You lied, you cheated, and you stole my jewelry and enjoyed my money. You even accepted our unholy relationship knowing I was seeing someone else." She took a long breath and continued. "I am setting you free. Go, Vasag! Enjoy your freedom!"

"Think it over," Vasag replied as if he had been barely listening. "I'll be back in a few days."

"Are you deaf? No! Don't come back!" Anna shouted.

The conversation was escalating. Araxi cleared the table of the coffee mugs and stepped out to give them space.

Suddenly, Anna remembered that the camera that contained pictures and video of her sexual exploits with Vasag from years ago was with her in her bag, and she had already deleted everything. She felt relieved and empowered. *Go ahead. Blackmail me, mister,* Anna thought. *I am safe.*

Her aunt returned with hot cups of tea, trying to calm Anna down.

"I will go to the press! Tell about the adventures of Anna. I am going to speak about the prince from the royal family who left you, and I won't forget about Abbas!"

Vasag seemed to have forgotten about Anna's aunt, now back in the room. He seemed to say whatever crossed his mind.

"Yes, please do. Don't forget the pictures and signed documents. Oh, and everyone's full name! Do you even realize what they will do to you if you try to besmirch their name? They will drag you through the mud and then you will disappear, never to be found again. However, you won't even get that far because no one will listen to you. You are no one! Go now, please. I know I caused you pain because my dreams were more important than our marriage, but you were not man enough to keep what you had. You hurt and deceived me. You are selfish and weak, and I do not care for you anymore. I'm tired of looking over my shoulder."

Anna paused again to breathe, and then blasted him again.

"You don't want me back out of love and devotion, but out of necessity," she shouted.

Anna was wondering how foolish she had been to have ever loved this man. She could not believe he had resorted to blackmail.

Araxi was now sitting on her couch in the living room.

"You will regret this, Anna. You will beg me to take you back, but I will not."

"I decided to marry you, and now I've decided to leave you."

"I made you!" he cried. "I stood by your side! But now, no one will love you! Ever! No one can!"

"You stood by my side? All you did was enjoy the money! You did nothing for me. Please go."

Vasag gave her a death stare, walked out, and slammed the door.

Anna turned toward her aunt, walked over to the couch, and collapsed beside her.

The Power of my Star

CHAPTER 6

Vasag had left, but Anna was trembling. She wanted to call her lawyer.

"Tomorrow," her aunt advised. "It's late. You are tired. Get your hookah ready and come sit next to me."

Anna agreed. She lay on the long couch with her hookah in her hand and her aunt beside her with a bowl of peanuts.

"I told Dad that I would take care of you financially. I put the money on the nightstand."

"Thank you, Anna," her aunt replied with a smile.

"I could go rent a place until everything is resolved... but I feel safe around you..."

"I'm glad you're here."

Anna was loud, angry, and she was in over her head with her problems. But Araxi loved her despite it all. She had raised her, changed her diapers, and had always been the secret vault of Anna's adventures.

"He made me! Where was he when I was dreaming of fame? I was barely a teenager."

"I know." Her aunt smiled. "Don't listen to him, Anna."

Her current struggle took her back to the first real challenge she could remember.

It was a rainy Sunday afternoon, and she was playing on the balcony. The happy sounds of children playing caught her ear. Avo, Armen, and Nairi were running down the stairs with excitement. They were all about Anna's age. She ran to the edge of the balcony, curious. The two buildings faced each other in the narrow street.

"Let's go! Let's go!" they shouted.

"Where are you going?" Anna yelled back.

"Our aunt is going to take us to the Armenian radio station! Armen chirped, we're going to sing and recite poetry."

"I want to come too! Wait for me! I'm going to ask my mom," she said as she rushed into the house.

Melineh was reading a letter from Asbed with tears in her eyes. He was working in Saudi Arabia at the time. Letters and telephone calls were their only contact.

"Mom, I want to go to the radio station to recite a poem. Please take me! The neighbors are going."

"Who?" Melineh laid the letter on the table next to her coffee, looking confused. "Calm down, don't jump, talk slowly."

"Avo, Armen and Nairi are going with their aunt."

"Okay, so go with them."

"They have their aunt. You must come with me; you are my mom! Please?"

Her aunt Araxi was standing in the kitchen, watching them through the door. Melineh shook her head, indicating a firm no.

"You will go with them, without me," she said. "I am not going to live forever. I cannot be with you until the end of time. You are a young lady now, and you can do it. If you're afraid, then you won't be able to handle it, and you should just stay home."

Be strong, Anna, she thought as she took off after the neighbors. Over twenty children aged six to fourteen were in a jam-packed room. A lady was taking them into the studio in groups of two or three. The show was live, and Mrs. Arpie was hosting the program while her husband was the DJ. Anna went in with two other kids. One of them sang while Anna waited behind the glass, quiet and careful, taking in every single detail.

Another girl entered, and she was immediately the center of attention. The host welcomed her with respect. She was Anna's age, with eyeglasses and braided hair. She sang beautifully. When she ended the song, they asked her to interview the boy next to her.

She is so dull and boring! Anna thought. *I can do better than that! They'll see.*

Anna asked around and found out that the "boring" girl had her own song playing on the radio, a song dedicated to the Armenian martyrs. She was the daughter of a very wealthy family. Anna was jealous, but she didn't want them to see it.

Her turn finally came.

"Go ahead, Lara! Ask her what her name is!" Mrs. Arpie urged the young singer.

"Please, I want you to ask me the question, Mrs. Arpie," Anna replied respectfully. "It's your program, after all."

The conversation was on the air, and Mrs. Arpie was pleased with Anna's courteous reply.

"My name is Anna, and I am going to recite, from our famous poet Barouyr Sevag, a beautiful poem."

Mrs. Arpie looked concerned. "Isn't it a hard poem for you to recite?"

"My Armenian teacher at school taught me very well, and my father has the talent to narrate. I know it," Anna reassured Mrs. Arpie, reading the worry on the woman's face.

"We are all ears, Anna!"

Lara was staring at Anna with raised eyebrows and a downturned mouth.

Anna kept hitting the microphone with her hands as she flailed her arms around while reciting, living the emotions of each verse. Her war with the microphone and her reluctance to be interviewed by the young Armenian star impressed everyone. It was an exceptional recital. She expressed happiness, suffering, and anger in equal and appropriate measures.

Anna touched the hearts of everyone in the room.

"May I ask the next question, please?" Anna felt her confidence grow.

Mrs. Arpie again looked surprised.

"Sure, sure. Next week."

Anna rushed out of the studio. For a girl her age, she was no different from any other child in that room, except for her persistence.

How can anyone know about my talent unless I show them? Anna believed that she was unique and wanted to prove that to the world. *I am special! Exceptional! I am going to be a star one day!*

At school that Monday, Anna told everyone that she was going to be a host in the new children's program the following Sunday. Everyone ignored her; even her best friend Zoey did not believe her.

"You're dreaming!" said Zoey.

No one believed in her except Araxi. That Sunday, Anna asked for her mother's permission and went with the neighbors to the radio station again. All the other children had prepared a song or a poem, but Anna had other plans. She was going to host.

When her turn came, Mrs. Arpie seemed to have forgotten all about her promise.

"What are you going to represent today, Anna? A song or a poem?"

"Neither! I am going to ask the questions to him," she responded, pointing at the boy standing next to her.

In those days, speaking boldly was not common for children, especially in the Armenian community. However, Mrs. Arpie agreed to give Anna a chance.

Anna asked him what his name was, where he lived, what his parents' names were, and which school he attended. After the interview, without waiting for any comments from Mrs. Arpie, she left.

The next day at school, all she did was brag about her interview skills. Everyone in the classroom was talking about it, and Anna spared no detail with her Armenian teacher, and they all applauded her. Since then, every Sunday, she had visited the radio station and was given a chance to ask a few questions. This went on for nearly three months. Araxi accompanied her whenever the neighbors did not go.

"I want more!" Anna complained. "I want the chance to ask more questions!"

"Why don't you tell the director of the radio station?" Melineh suggested.

"I will," Anna replied, impressed and proud that her mother had treated her like an adult.

The next day, she got home from school, took off her uniform, freshened up, and asked her aunt to take her to the radio station.

"Please do not come up with me! Wait for me here. I want to go alone," Anna told Araxi when they got to the lobby. She turned to the receptionist. "Hello, I am here to see the director."

"Wait here," he replied, pointing to a chair.

After a few minutes, a voice called to her. "You may come in now."

"Hello, my name is Anna. I want to volunteer to work for the children's program every Sunday with Mrs. Arpie."

Mr. Vartan, the director, smiled.

Anna was standing straight, her head held high, and her hands clasped. She emanated confidence, but also respect.

"Why don't you ask her?"

"I did, and she gave me a chance a couple of times. I love her very much!" Anna continued, encouraged by his reaction. "But I want things to be official! I wanted to inform you about my ambitions."

"Your words are very determined for a twelve-year-old girl; did your mother teach you what to say?"

"No, my mother only told me to tell you about my wish."

"Sure. Why not?" said the director encouragingly, taking a sip of his coffee and a puff of smoke. "If that's your wish"

"One more thing," Anna added. "When I am older and run my own radio show, I do not want a single penny to go to me! I want all the money to go to the Armenian political prisoners' fund."

The words were Melineh's idea, but Anna was the one who was up to the challenge. The director looked stunned, but he promised to talk to Mrs. Arpie.

She went back down to the lobby, pleased with herself, her yellow and pink skirt billowing around her.

Anna was growing up as she began to take her expanding opportunities. As time went by, she became the youngest speaker on the radio. Listeners could not tell that the clear and confident voice they heard belonged to a scrawny twelve-year-old.

At that point, she was satisfied with the outcome. Her next step was to land a role in her father's theater group and be recognized for her talent, for an actual performance. She dreamed big, hoping to be on the international screen someday. It was a hefty challenge; she was a tiny little girl who spoke Arabic with an Armenian accent. However, backed by her talent (inherited from her father) and a feisty personality (no doubt from her mother), Anna was full of hope.

I am not a dreamer! Anna always responded bitterly to her parents' exasperated looks. She felt some conflict—was she challenging her parents or chasing her dreams? Anna's soul had the wings of defiance and courage. She daydreamed, sure, but she spent considerable time thinking and strategizing. Every time she stumbled and got hurt, she would get back in the saddle and move on. The power of ambition was greater than any barrier. Her parents' vexation made her more insistent on proving them wrong. She made time for everything: boys, school, the radio show, and theater. Life was not an obligation to her but a field of adventures.

No one can finish the race for me, Anna thought. *I must run on my own. I might fall, but nothing will keep me down.*

"You are going to shine one day," Araxi always said, encouragingly. One day she looped a chain around her neck, and said, "Keep this necklace on you, at all times." It had a single charm on it, an ivory star. "I inherited this from my grandmother. She fled Urfa before the genocide. You were meant to have this."

"Thank you!" Anna chirped, hugging her aunt. "I will prove to you that I deserve this necklace."

I am unique, she always repeated to herself, before she even understood the power of words. She talked about stardom and fame aloud, ignoring everyone's skepticism. *Be good, be strong, and make every effort possible.* This is how she saw life. "I can't do it," and "I am afraid" were not part of her vocabulary. Everyone's mockery shaped her into an unbending fighter and transformed Anna, the dreamer into a pursuer. Everything came at a price, however, and there would come a time when she'd become a star shining for others but risking darkness for her own soul. She was a supernova waiting to happen, threatening to leave nothing but a black hole in her heart.

"More tea?" Araxi's voice came in out of nowhere, snapping her back to reality.

"No, thank you." She revisited her conversation with her husband. "He never supported me, not even once, even when Carl followed me to his dad's shop."

"Who?" Her aunt couldn't always keep track of events in Anna's life.

"Carl! It was the time when our marriage was already falling apart. On my way from our apartment to my father-in-law's shop, a well-dressed man in his late twenties stopped me in the street and asked me politely whether I cared to join his modeling agency. I thought he was making a pass at me, but part of me thought it could be true. I kept walking, and he followed me, hoping that I would answer him eventually. When I reached the shop, the presence of my father-in-law made me feel safe. Carl asked me if I wanted to do casting and gave us each a business card, completely ignoring Vasag, who was standing beside his father."

"I never knew this happened!" Araxi exclaimed.

"That day I agreed," Anna continued. "He said we'd do a photo shoot the next day, and an interview! He threw around some famous magazine names and said we would discuss my goals."

"And you didn't ask Vasag or take into consideration the presence of your father-in-law?"

"Why would I? It was my life. It's not like he knew what was best for me!" Anna paused, and after a moment asked, "Do you think that was a little arrogant? Or rude?"

Araxi did not reply, making her answer clear.

"Hovhaness, my father-in-law… I loved him," Anna said softly. "that day, I still remember how he stood there in front of the shop like a shadow, smoking his cigarette, inhaling the smoke, breathing through the anger."

"He said nothing? I mean, he was an old-fashioned man, wasn't he?" Araxi asked.

"No. I was married to his son, not to him. He was such a sensitive and a loving father, respectful of his children's choices."

Hovhaness and Anna had a strong bond; they spent many hours together. They argued, but they loved each other as a father and a daughter should. He did not live long. Sadly, he died of a brain tumor a few years after Anna and Vasag's wedding. He neither lived to hold a grandchild in his arms and nor did he have the chance to see a happy ending for his son.

the bitterness that Lisolette, Anna's mother in law had toward Anna was borne not out of hatred but rather an urge to protect her son, a defense mechanism. Whenever Anna complained that she wished to get a chance to be famous, Lisolette interjected, reminding her that she had promised to work with her son.

"Go back to teaching! Get a job in an office!" she repeated to Anna. Vasag's mother did not understand the meaning of pursuing dreams in life, especially for married women; in her opinion, married women made money to help their husbands by bearing and raising children, by cooking, and by cleaning houses. Dreams belonged to single people.

Lisolette wanted Anna to keep her promise to her precious son who needed his wife's financial assistance. Anna did not agree with Lisolette's demands.

How many promises does he break every day? How many lies does he tell? Anna thought but never said aloud. Lisolette had reasons to worry, of course. Her son was weak and irresponsible; her daughter-in-law was reckless and uncontrollable. She seemed to be in denial that her son had inherited some traits from her, including the charm in his eyes and the selfishness in his heart.

"If he were alive, he wouldn't have let Vasag do all this to me!" Anna blurted out.

"Who?" Her aunt looked lost again.

"My father-in-law!"

"Don't you have anything else to talk about tonight, Anna? Stop talking about dead people. May he rest in peace. Happy thoughts, my dear! Why don't we go to sleep?"

"No, you go sleep! I am waiting for a call from Joe."

Araxi left the room, sighing.

Half an hour later, Joe called, and the loving couple stayed on the phone until the wee hours of the morning. A loud ringtone startled her at nine in the morning. She snapped her phone open and looked at the caller ID. .it was Kareem Anna's bright lawyer, and the supportive friend.

"Kareem? You woke me up! I've barely slept all night."

"I got your message last night, but I was with a client. Are you okay?"

"Yeah. Never been better," Anna said sarcastically. "I want to divorce Vasag. As soon as possible!"

"Good morning to you too, Anna," he said in response to her grumpiness.

"Sorry... good morning, Kareem," she said, more quietly.

"You need to calm down."

"I am calm. I'm going to the station soon. But I need to get rid of my husband! I'm begging you."

"Don't you have to do it through your church?"

"It will take a year! At least. I want it now. I want to marry Joe!"

"Who? The guy you spent one night with him in Los Angeles? What about Abbas?"

He was one of the few people who knew the details of Anna's life, and therefore one of the few in a position to try to knock sense into her. Kareem could not understand her behavior, but he cared for her deeply, as a brother would.

"You do not know this guy, Anna!"

"I'm in love with him. Please try to understand."

"Give me time until the afternoon." He sighed. "I'll call you back."

She hung up the phone, got dressed, and stepped out to the car. Anna sat quietly as Hashem drove her to the station. *I was so stupid to marry him! I wish I had listened to my mom. The white dress, the wedding! It was all so wrong. Now I'm stuck.* Anna remembered how her mother had begged her not to get married eleven years earlier.

"Don't go, Anna! Take off your wedding dress. You still have time to change your mind."

Anna didn't look back; she continued down the stairs. *I'm leaving! I am finally going to be free! I will be my own boss! I've had enough of you and Dad!* Anna wanted to shout out her thoughts at the time, but she smiled at the camera. A twenty-one-year-old Anna was heading to the church, to be joined in holy matrimony with Vasag. He was twenty-three years old, tall and fit, with brown hair and eyes. He hardly made eye contact with others during conversations and had a calm yet hesitant personality.

"Anna!" Melineh shouted, this time with anger. She was still standing at the entrance of the apartment. "Take off your dress. It's not too late," she repeated.

"Are you jealous that I am wearing a beautiful dress, Mom?" Anna shouted back, her answer rude, hurtful, and illogical. She did not even look at her mother.

Anna had always wanted an extravagant royal wedding dress, and she had gotten her wish. She was in an eighteenth-century diamond-white dress with the broadest petticoat underneath. It was elegant and ostentatious, beaded with silver, stones, and pearls. However, that was not all. Anna also wore a Swarovski-adorned tiara, and a delicate veil and blusher. She looked like a snow queen, an ice princess, with her ash-blond hair, ivory skin, and gray contact lenses. The look fitted her personality, or at least how people saw her. Anna was rebellious. Vasag was not the right person for her, and her family knew it. It was not going to be a successful marriage, but no one was able to convince her.

Anna had met Vasag at a party. They'd caught each other's eye, had exchanged phone numbers, and had been together ever since. Three years into their relationship, she suggested that they get married. To Anna, the fact that Vasag was Armenian was one of the most important things. She was still too young to understand the difference between patriotism and racism, and at that point, Anna was prejudiced. Sharing her life with a non-Armenian would have been out of the question.

Before their marriage, their relationship had been going smoothly. They were both looking for freedom. They were bonded by their love of sex, nothing else mattered to both of them, and they were each other's firsts. They barely argued at that time, because they ended all disagreements in each other's arms, satisfying their physical desires. Anna never hesitated to ask and fight for whatever she wanted, and in that period her new passion in life was Vasag. She was the leader in the relationship; he was the follower, agreeing with her every wish.

Anna had no concept of dignity, logic, or future interests when it came to her cravings. She grabbed whatever she wanted, without reconsidering. If she ever heard the word no, she just tried again, and again.

Caroline, her cousin, had tried warning Anna that marriage to Vasag was a bad idea, not only because they were young but because the guy had virtually no personality, no strength of character, and would rely on Anna for everything. In Anna's mind, however, his compliance was a sign of deep affection. She was not going to learn the truth until she was hit where it hurts. Caroline knew she had to let her younger cousin have her way. Both sets of parents were worried about the young couple; they had no money and no plan. The parents helped them with the wedding, though, fearing that they would cause a scandal by eloping.

Anna's parents were more tolerant than Vasag's. His mother came up with thousands of excuses and reasons, always drawing attention to her supposed health problems every time it was time to ask for Anna's hand in marriage. Even Vasag's attempt to convince his mother by pleading and telling her he could not live without Anna was in vain, and he had to resort to asking Anna if her parents would break the ice by visiting his parents at their house.

Lisolette, Vasag's mother, had discovered a scheme to control people around her. She would have her way with guilt trips and pressure. She would complain about all the aches imaginable and could stay in bed for days. This particular behavior had broken her relationship with her husband and children, and love and affection were absent in their household. Anna, however, would not have it. Lisolette was playing games with her, and Anna decided she was going to show Vasag's mother who she was dealing with.

Lisolette was a quiet, antisocial spectator. She never spoke her mind and always gave the impression of an insecure yet peaceful person. She was in her early fifties, blond with short cut hair, blue-eyed, with the face of a weeping fallen angel.

Anna, on the other hand, was a hunter, and her dreams, hopes, desires, and goals were her prey. She was always careful not to stumble upon human obstacles. She had been a math and English teacher for a while, and after graduating university, she had found the piece of the puzzle: Vasag. Whatever trick Lisolette had up her sleeve was not going to stop Anna from laying down that last piece. Therefore, Lisolette's plan failed. Anna's tears and dramatic speeches won her parents over, and the next thing she knew, they were buying flowers and chocolate to ask for Vasag's hand.

Anna's parents were modern and educated. Both Anna and her sister were allowed to follow the latest fashions, had permission to hang out with friends and party at night. Often, however, other matters like financial difficulties, health problems, or arguments with relatives or friends put a damper on their family atmosphere. The girls were no angels, but because of the changing circumstances in their home, the parents' tolerance varied, and the punishments they dished out were not always proportional to the crimes committed. Anna felt that she was living with Mr. and Mrs. Jekyll and Hyde.They were unique and unusual, and they did everything they could to give their daughters the best life possible. Moreover, they had succeeded. Despite all their freedom, Anna had not crossed the line when it came to relationships. Only when she met Vasag did she take the extra step and go beyond the kissing and handholding, which was the limit set by social standards at the time. Their marriage was based on casual sex and a craving for freedom and lacked the thorough understanding of marital union. After much talk, though, both sets of parents decided to support the wedding. Their honeymoon consisted of a painful five seconds for Anna to officially lose her virginity. It gave her no pleasure, unlike all the other sexual experiences they had shared. That small piece of skin was left untouched throughout their relations, although no other part of Anna's body could be considered virginal.

Most mothers were more concerned about the tiny piece of skin between their daughters' legs than with preparing them for what was ahead of them, and what they should be looking out for. Sacrifice, fidelity, honesty. Surely There was more to life and marriage than cooking, cleaning, and bringing children into the world, however In that context, a girl's virginity was defined as the zenith of her values and ethics.

Feminine qualities and values are not hidden between our thighs, Anna thought. *Women should be valued for achievements, their wisdom and their personality, not by a piece of flesh.*

Anna was one of the lucky few with a mother whose understanding of virginity and honor went beyond the standard of society. When they had reached puberty, Melineh had explained to her daughters that waiting was a matter of principle and safety, not honor.

After their wedding, the couple moved into a rented apartment and began enjoying their freedom. Anna had Vasag; now it was time to chase her dream of becoming famous. Vasag was a ticket to her life of liberty and making her own decisions. She was so adamant about pursuing her goals that she did not even renew her contract as a teacher. Vasag's low income and Anna's determination to knock on every casting door for every TV show meant that the couple would soon reach a point where they could not afford rent. Anna, to her parent's disappointment, had no choice but to ask for their help. Melineh and Asbed, who lived in the family building, took in the newlyweds.

The apartments were tiny and old, but nothing could dampen Anna's spirits or get in the way of her ambitions. Her parents' flat was so tiny that they had had to leave behind most of the sitting room furniture, the dining room furniture, and even the laundry machine. They had no stable income, yet Anna was visiting every casting agency she could, hoping to be discovered.

Vasag was still working for his father and hardly making ends meet. He did not care as long as he had a place to sleep, food on the table—provided by Anna's parents—and Anna by his side. Anna and Vasag were hoping that this marriage was going to not only make them happy but also be the key to an independent lifestyle, driven by ambition and lust. It was their palace of Caligula.

During their second year of marriage, Anna's jewelry vanished from the box, including all her childhood presents. She searched and wondered until finally, Vasag confessed that he'd taken them because he'd needed the money. It had taken Asbed calling police investigators to convince Vasag to say something out of fear.

"Why didn't you ask me?" Anna cried, after getting over the shock. "I didn't care for any of it! I would have given you everything! How can I trust you now?"

"I did not want to ask because I didn't want to hurt you!"

"What kind of a stupid answer is that?" Anna shouted, through her tears.

"I promise to buy you new ones when I have the money," he pleaded.

"What did you do with the money?" she asked, suddenly interested and worried.

"We needed the money! My father's business isn't going well."

Of course not! She thought. *You're the one who ruined your dad's business with your laziness, negligence, and lack of responsibility.*

"Please forgive me. I will make it up to you," he begged. "I will buy you more beautiful things than the ones you had. I promise!"

The stolen jewelry was worth over 11,000 US dollars. The money had disappeared without a trace. Vasag slowly approached and tried to hug Anna, who was weeping on the sofa, but all he succeeded in doing was exacerbate the tightness in her chest.

"Don't touch me!" Anna yelled, pushing him away furiously. "Don't promise me anything! You sold my childhood memories one piece at a time! Where did you spend it? My mom is feeding us, and my father is putting a roof over our heads. He even gave you money to pay the electricity bill, which you forgot to do. Don't you dare repeat the words 'I forgot' again! That should be your new name!"

His head dropped, yet he somehow showed neither regret nor shame. He looked up and gave Anna a shallow stare. Blank and empty, like his soul.

She needed to stay married to keep her freedom, so she forgave him... or convinced herself so. Anna never looked at him in the same way, ever again. The pressure slowly began diminishing their sexual appetite for each other. Role-play and fantasies featuring each other became nonexistent.

Vasag started going to clubs and attending cabaret nights, surrounded by young single people. He enjoyed being with them, making up for whatever adventures he had missed out on. The money from Anna's jewelry was well spent on dinners, hookers, and gifts. While Vasag was after experiences of lust, his wife was chasing her dreams. Thanks to Anna, he had a place to stay and money—as little as she could give him—and still, it was not enough. Her marriage was the only wall that her parents could not break to interfere with her decisions, and divorce was only seen on TV, not dabbled in by real people. She struggled every day, even for simple things like medicine. However, she preferred staying poor and sick chasing her dreams over being healthy and having a steady income. The poverty, her husband's negligence, the disappointment in her parents' eyes, everyone else's mockery—none of it could trigger Anna to change her goal of chasing her dreams.

Anna always knew she deserved a chance, and her aunt's influence that gave Anna so much faith in herself drove her to be furiously stubborn and tenacious. She spent every single day going door to door, calling studios, asking for auditions, but to no avail. Anna was begging for a chance to prove her talent, to prove to herself, to her parents, and to everyone else she was destined to be a star.

When Anna was young, she saw how her parents both loved and sacrificed for each other and for their children.

Unconditional love was Anna's inspiration, and she hoped to spend the rest of her days finding out what it meant. She never knew that love had to be continuously nurtured, that it had to be appreciated and required sacrifice.

Anna woke from her reverie, still in the car with Hashem. Hours seem to have passed, but they were only halfway to the studio. *Destiny plays tricks on us,* Anna thought. *We believe that fate controls our lives, but there is a way to fight it...* Indeed, she had become a star, and she had paid the price for her success. Now she was in a new fight against all the odds—she wanted Joe. Now, after many years, Anna had decided one more time to face her parents. She was in love, but this time it was different.

Another fifteen minutes passed as she pondered, and the car finally stopped.

"What time do you want me to come pick you up?" Hashem asked, with a smile as always.

"In five hours, please," she replied.

Rape and Chances

CHAPTER 7

Anna's phone rang.

"You and Vasag should convert to another Christian sect to get divorced. A quick and easy divorce that'll take three days and ten thousand dollars between church expenses and legal fees," said the lawyer.

"That's great news!" Anna smiled broadly.

Moreover, now she had officially declared a battle against her entire world… for a one-night stand.

"Why are you always fighting something? Can't you let life be, sometimes?" Kareem asked, half-exasperated, half-amused.

"I make my own destiny," she replied. "We'll talk soon, Kareem. Thank you!"

Anna could not wait to get it done so that she could marry Joe, who was dying to have Anna as his wife. Tedious legal and religious procedures were to be avoided.

Most religious institutions purposely extended divorce procedures for years, hoping to resolve the issues between the couples and reunite them, and, of course, to cash out at the same time. So, Anna immediately called Vasag and explained the details.

"No, I will not consent for a divorce. It's disgraceful!" he answered.

At that point, all Anna wanted to do was scoff and tell him that nothing was as scandalous as his actions, but she kept her mouth shut to avoid getting on his bad side. She knew Vasag wanted something in return, which she would find out soon enough.

"I have to go now. Think about it, and I'll be in touch," she said before hanging up.

"I thought you just needed a break!" she heard right before one final click.

Joe was arriving from Canada the next day, and Anna had snagged a couple of friends for her secret mission to meet with her new lover.

It was two in the afternoon; she was in her office interviewing candidates for her TV show assistant position. The first one walked in, handed her his résumé, and sat.

"Hello. My name is Alan!" He was a young, heavyset, quirky-looking man in his early twenties. "I have a lot of innovative ideas—" he began before Anna had the chance to open her mouth.

"Would you let Mrs. Anna talk first, please?" the director interrupted from the couch.

"No, it's fine! Let him talk," Anna interjected with a smile.

He was brimming with enthusiasm and expectation, and his ambition stood out like a beacon calling out to Anna. His eyes were full of that passion she'd once emanated from every pore in her body, regardless of everyone else's opinion.

"I watched all your series before you had your show, Mrs. Anna. My favorite series were the ones written by Mr. Nidal Karam. His scripts were fantastic!"

"True," Anna replied as the name Nidal transported her back in time.

She remembered the first phone call she received after her first photo shoot and magazine interview by Carl's help, the modelling Agency owner. Nearly fifteen years had passed since then. She had answered the call as quickly as possible, excited to hear back, while Vasag sat beside her watching football.

"I got it!" Anna shouted after hanging up the phone. "I'm going to be on TV! I am going to play an office assistant in a comedy!"

"That's wonderful! How much will they pay?" Vasag replied.

"I don't care!"

It was one of the leading roles in a popular sitcom, but as it was her first time onscreen—with only modeling experience in her back pocket—she did not expect to be paid the big bucks. Not quite yet.

Her first day on set was terrifying and exhilarating all at once. Anna walked into the studio feeling as if she was stepping into her own little heaven. She was lucky to have been given this opportunity, something that hardly happened to newcomers in the business.

I am one step closer to my dream to shine.

The makeup artist working on her face, someone else helping her with the clothes, the assistant director giving her the script to review—it all made her feel like a star. The show was picked up by the network and was a hit. Anna got her fifteen minutes of fame, but the offers for other roles were not exactly rolling in afterward. Still, she kept the faith.

One day, I will have my own show, Anna told herself. Anna was dreaming, walking a snaking, winding path full of lies, false promises, and disappointments, but she did not care. She remembered how another director had dropped by one day while they were shooting, and she had rushed to introduce herself to him. Mansour was tall, with salt-and-pepper hair and a mustache.

"My name is Anna. I am so honored to meet you ."

"How is the shooting going? Is Tony very demanding?" he asked, smiling at the other director.

"Would you stop? That's how I am!" Tony replied.

"I know you, Mr. Mansour." Anna ignored the interruption. "I heard you were preparing a new series. I wish you the best of luck!"

She hoped that mentioning the series might trigger a conversation about the audition, but it did not go as planned.

"Thank you," he replied.

"I heard you were good friends with the great Nidal Karam."

"Yes. In fact, we graduated together."

"I adore him! His scripts are incredible. I am going to meet him—" Anna exclaimed.

"Well, give him my best regards," he replied and walked away.

All Anna wanted to do was meet the writer, but she had no idea how it was going to happen. After their conversation, Anna was called back along with everyone else to the continuous shooting of the scene.

Four months later, she was accepted as a member of the actors' syndicate. She often dropped by the office, hoping to meet producers or to get the inside scoop on the newest series, but her plan failed. A few weeks later, though, Anna found herself turning a fancy doorknob and standing in front of a well-dressed man in his late fifties, with a friendly face, white hair, and an eccentric personality. She had finally found a way to meet the well-known writer Nidal Karam.

"Make me a star! I want to be famous. I'm talented. Give me a chance!" Anna pleaded as soon as she entered the office.

"How did you even make it into my office?" he asked, looking puzzled.

"Your secretary…"

"But… how? No appointment. No reference. Who in the world are you?"

"I told you; I am Anna."

"That doesn't help me."

"You are the best! You can make me shine."

"That wasn't my question, sweetheart. We are talking about you, not me."

"Fine. I told your secretary that I had a message from Mr. Mansour Abboud."

"So, what's the message?" he inquired with a smirk.

"He said"—she hesitated, wondering if she should make something up or tell the truth, knowing either option was lame— "to say hello if I came to see you."

A smile appeared on Nidal's face. He began slowly applauding.

"In my whole life, I have never met someone like you. Kudos for tricking my secretary."

She was unsure if he was genuinely amused or if he was being sarcastic. *At this point, I am all in*, she thought.

"I am Armenian. But I speak Arabic fluently," she said.

"You know, the first girl I ever fell in love with was Armenian. I can even write my name in Armenian..." and suddenly he was talking like a teenager. "Look, I'll show you." He tore a piece of paper from his notebook.

She had managed to bring down his defenses, and he was now carefully writing each letter in Armenian.

He buzzed his secretary.

"Coffee, please, Rania. For my guest and me."

Coffee? No! I prefer soda, was her first thought. *Oh my God, shut up. Does it matter? This means I can stick around. Just drink it.*

"Will you give me a chance?" she asked. "I deserve it."

"Everyone thinks they deserve a chance. How are you any different?"

"Because I was born to be a star!" Anna replied with confidence. After a final sip of coffee, she stood. "Do I go now? Are you going to give me a role?"

"Amateurs go through casting. They do not burst into my office. Moreover, they are given small roles and communicate only with the director."

"But I already made it into your office!"

"I admire your confidence, Anna. I respect your people. You know, the reason I couldn't marry her was that I am Lebanese. Her parents wouldn't let it happen," he added softly.

It was a sensitive issue. Anna was perplexed. Was being Armenian going to hurt her chances here? Was he going to penalize her for what his ex-girlfriend's parents had done? She could not move. *It isn't my fault!* She thought but said nothing. She wanted to neither hurt his feelings nor step over the principles of her own people. Finally, she spoke.

"So, do I leave or—?"

"May I have your contact information, please?"

"Sure!" She wrote her number on a notepad while he watched.

"I will be in touch," he said, adding the piece of paper to a stack of documents.

"Don't you always say that when you want to get rid of someone?"

"I am serious. You caught my attention. I will fit you into a show, a character just for you."

She leaned across the enormous wooden table and hugged him like she would her father, afraid to ask more questions, and only adding that she would not let him down.

And, just like that, she had taken a huge leap.

Anna told everyone that she'd met Mr. Karam. Some people laughed behind her back, others shook their heads, and even her parents welcomed the news with a sympathetic smile. *Poor, sad Anna,* everyone thought, *living in the tiny apartment with her husband and her parents.*

Two weeks passed, and Anna was in the bedroom watching television when the phone rang.

"Hello! Is this Anna? We are calling you from Nidal Karam Productions. This is to request your presence tomorrow at five p.m. for the script reading."

Anna hung up the phone.

The next day she went to the studio.

"This way." They invited her in.

She entered a large room with a table in the middle, around which a handful of famous actors were sitting.

"I am a huge fan of literally everyone in here!" she blurted, starstruck.

They all greeted her back. The director came in with Mr. Nidal.

Nidal introduced Anna to the director.

"This is Anna, and she will be playing the character of Asma. Her personality inspired me!"

Her role was the antagonistic female lead who ruined other women's lives. *Great,* she thought. The reading session went very well, and she was overwhelmed. They analyzed all the characters to understand and truly grasp the feel of the show. A week later, they began shooting. Soon after that, she got another leading role, yet another antihero, through Mr. Nidal. She was now to be the evil jealous girl trying to ruin her sister's life. That is when she decided to ask the question that was haunting her.

"Why don't you ever write a sweet character for me?"

"It's impossible. You would either have to be reborn a different person, or I would have to rewrite all the characters of all the Snow Whites of this world. Face, it; you will always be the stepmother in front of the mirror. Mirrors will change with each script, but you will always be the villain."

"Well, you're the professional," she responded respectfully and with a smile, hiding her disappointment.

She did not wish her dreams to be colored by all the shades of her hope rainbow; she wanted to be painted by any character they chose for her. She was a guest on television shows and in magazine interviews; they were interested to hear her story. Everyone was interested but her parents. To them, she was still a disappointment. The modeling agency was just a rung from which she was hoping to climb to where she wanted, and she was taking fewer and fewer calls from them. Anna's ambitions went much further than being a cover girl.

"Are you going to the syndicate president elections tomorrow?" Anna was on her mobile with her friend Amar, a fellow actress.

"Yeah. What about you? Can you pick me up if you're going?"

"Of course. See you in the morning."

The guild was essential to her. She was still living on a tight budget, and nothing mattered more than moving forward in her career. Most actors never made it to the highest ranks, and many that did were forgotten when age caught up with them. There was no guaranteed stability in the business. The competition was fiercest among women, and fresh faces nearly always won. Young actors were much more accessible to manipulate, and their naive conception of the film and television industry gave directors much-desired leeway. Some of these girls were never seen outside of the studio, as their roles sometimes turned out to be behind closed doors.

The next day, Anna was at the office, standing in a room with Amar and some other actors, when a man approached her and introduced himself.

"Hey! My name is Jebran."

The place was crowded; famous and less famous actors filled every inch of the site—a blend of real and pseudo talent, with no outward sign separating those with delusions of grandeur from the truly deserving. Anna knew exactly what Jebran wanted.

"I don't care to know who you are. You expect me to vote for you, right?" she said, rolling her eyes and brandishing the piece of paper handed earlier to everyone.

"Yes, I'd like that," he answered politely.

"Well, I won't. Don't waste your time!" she snapped, her tone sharp and rude.

He smiled and turned slightly away, observing the crowd.

"I saw you in Mr. Nidal's series. Impressive. I was wondering if you would ever consider joining our comedy group."

"What are you talking about?" she said, after a few seconds.

"I am the writer and producer of a show for International TV station.

"Really?" Suddenly interested, she dropped all traces of arrogance from her tone.

"Yup. Here are some members of the group," he added while calling over a few people seemingly out of thin air. "Zeina, Elie, Jean, George, Rabih, Eliana… Guys, come over here and meet Anna."

"Oh my God, I love you guys! You guys are so funny. I can't wait to be a part of the group."

Anna shook their hands with admiration. She was thrilled.

"I am sorry, Jebran," she said after the group had dispersed. "I was rude. I will vote for you."

"Never mind that." He walked away shrugging.

A year later, Anna had moved up the ladder thanks to the comedy group and had started receiving offers from larger production companies.

She had retained a slight Armenian accent, and at times she made mistakes when she spoke Lebanese. They mostly went unnoticed. One evening, however, after shooting a scene, the director called her into his office.

"How do you still make mistakes? You've lived here all your life!" He laughed, mimicking her accent.

"Would you stop that?" Anna snapped.

She remembered how inappropriate his behavior was. He treated women, and especially Anna, like prey. She adopted a defensive position and state of mind. No one would come to her rescue when things escalated; even the producer was in another office working on scripts.

"Shut up, you pig!" Anna cried when he continued to laugh at her Armenian accent.

Without warning his laughter stopped, and he launched himself at her.

As she tried hitting back, he overpowered her, holding both her hands with one of his and sliding his free hand down her front. She struggled like a bird in a cage.

The door opened, and another fellow actor, Rabih, appeared there.

"What the hell are you doing, man?" he asked, shocked.

Anna took advantage of that moment of distraction and kneed the director between the legs. He released her hands and fell to his knees. Anna shoved a chair at him and bolted out of the room, in tears. She went home that night with a bruise on her left cheek, and every inch of her body was in pain. Vasag barely reacted when she told him about the incident, but that was to be expected.

The next day, the producer fired her, claiming her character's popularity had dropped. Contracts were meaningless in the eyes of power, and Anna could not afford to go the legal route.

Funny how she was now the one doing the interviewing and hiring. Alan's voice woke her from her daze.

"I am talented. Give me a chance. I swear I deserve it."

"Thank you." She smiled at him. "I'll be in touch."

Candidates came and went, and the day finally came to an end. At the top of the hour, Anna started gathering her things, getting ready to leave. Joe was coming into town, and she did not want to be late. As she zipped up her purse, a young girl with a nose ring, bright red hair, and the most revealing outfit Anna had ever seen burst into the room.

"I am so sorry I'm late! I had a fight with my boyfriend, and I had to get a cab!"

"Fine..." Anna replied. "But I don't have much time."

She pulled a piece of paper out of her back pocket and sat down. It was a crumpled-up résumé.

"Go on," the director said from behind Anna.

"I am unhappy, my boyfriend doesn't understand me, and my parents fight at home…"

She was not making any sense and was treating Anna like her therapist. Anna was uncomfortable but did not interrupt as the girl droned on and on.

"It's their fault! No one understands me… I want my name to show on the screen, so everyone can see it… I did volunteer jobs for TV shows for a brief period…"

This girl isn't here because of her ambitions, Anna thought. *She needs an easy way out.*

"You have no idea what it's like to live in a home where people argue all the time!"

"Indeed…" Anna replied.

The young woman spent the next fifteen minutes blaming the entire world for her supposed failure, complaining about the most ridiculous, insignificant details. Meanwhile, Anna sat there remembering how hard she had fought to get to where she was. This young girl had no idea how lucky she actually was.

You are so immature, Anna thought. *Clearly, you have had the chance to grow up at your own pace. I didn't have that luxury.*

Unable to stay focused on the candidate's babbling, her mind drifted again.

Anna was incapable of forgetting an incident that had taken place when she was thirteen in a bedroom of the apartment where she often went with her parents on weekend getaways.

It was the summer of 1987, and Anna had decided to make some pocket money. She wanted financial independence. It was nearing the end of July, and Anna was going to get her first paycheck. It was barely enough to cover what few expenses a teenager could have, but she was proud of it. Her parents had encouraged the idea because they were friends with the owner of the grocery shop. They wanted to give their daughter the chance to understand the value of money. As Anna waited impatiently, Harry counted the money in the register. He needed change to pay her, so he asked her to run over to his brother-in-law's house next door to change a hundred. Anna was neither old enough nor earning enough to have a bank account. She took the money and ran to the building next to the shop.

"Hi, Uncle Simon! Uncle Harry asked if you could give me two 50,000 Lebanese liras, please."

"Come on in."

"Where is your wife?" Anna asked politely.

"She went to see her mother. Come in here. The money is in the bedroom." His voice sounded off, even to her untrained ears.

"I'll wait here," replied Anna. Something felt strange, and she sensed that an invitation to accompany him to their bedroom was not reasonable. "I should hurry back to the shop. Uncle Harry is waiting for the money."

The next thing she knew, Simon was picking her up by her waist and dragging her to the bedroom. She was perplexed and in shock, and the following few minutes were a blur. He tossed her on the bed, and suddenly his hands were all over her, violating her virgin body.

"Let's see what you've got here..." he whispered in a voice that nauseated her.

Scrawny and weak, the young Anna resisted him with all her might. She was trying to push his hand out of her shirt, pushing him back, but he was heavy. She tried to shout, but his hand slid over her mouth almost as soon as she opened it.

"Be quiet! Now we are going to see how good our little Anna is!" he murmured.

His other hand was moving like a deadly snake under her shirt and trying to unbutton her flower-patterned jeans. Anna knew she could not give up fighting. The thought of having to live with the horror suddenly struck her, and Anna gathered her strength and bit his hand. He tried to hold her, but she gave him a series of little kicks in the shins and ran for the door. She grabbed the 100,000 Lebanese liras and a few seconds later was on the street. She was free. She ran through the tears and tremors, her legs carrying her at the speed of an antelope escaping a lion.

I am strong! I am safe! She repeated—her mother's wise words that had surfaced in her mind. She reached Harry's shop and handed him the money.

"He didn't have change."

"Why are you shaking, Anna? Something wrong?" asked Harry.

She realized her hands were shaking and felt her face burning.

"You can pay me tomorrow, Uncle. I want to go home. I'm not feeling well."

"Give me five minutes," he said and stepped out of the shop.

She collapsed on the chair; her mouth was dry, and her heart was pounding. Harry returned a few minutes later with Anna's pay in his hands.

"Here you go. I got some change from the neighbors," he said with a kind smile. "Go home and rest, you look like you're burning up!"

Poor sweet Harry looked genuinely worried about Anna's health; the thought of his brother-in-law being a rapist would never have crossed his mind. Anna said goodbye and started walking home.

She turned the lock, walked past her aunt and her sister, and headed for her room like a ghost gliding down a corridor. As soon as her parents came home, she dragged them into her room and told them everything. Stunned and outraged, they asked her repeatedly to describe in detail which parts of her body he had laid his hands on, trying to figure out how far he had gone and if her virginity was still intact. Her mother kept asking her if she felt any pain.

"No, Mom. I told you I didn't!" Anna finally yelled, frustrated and confused. "Why do you keep asking the same question over and over?"

Anna did not quite understand the definition of sex, let alone rape. She just knew that something about what had happened to her was abnormal or wrong. After long, torturous hours reliving those few minutes of horror and fear, she finally fell asleep.

Early the next morning, her mom and dad woke her from a deep but troubled slumber.

"Sweetie, wake up. We're going to Dr. Hanna."

"Why? I'm not sick," Anna whimpered, sleepy and afraid.

"I know, sweetie. We just want to make sure," Asbed explained.

After a much longer than usual morning ritual, a reluctant Anna and her parents drove off to the gynecologist's office. Melineh and Asbed spoke in hushed tones to the doctor, presuming Anna could hear them, while she sat in the waiting room. She was finally called in, and Melineh asked her to take her clothes off so that the doctor could check if she had any injuries.

"What injuries? I am not going to take off my panties in front of him!" protested Anna.

"Yes, you will," Melineh answered, her face stern. "Don't force me to call your dad in here."

Seeing that she did not have a choice, she took off her panties and lay on her back. The strange contraptions attached to the table were scary.

Her mom placed her legs on the metal arms, and all Anna could do was close her eyes and pretend she was anywhere but in that cold office.

The doctor started speaking in soothing tones.

"Now, I am going to check if everything is okay so that one day you will wear a beautiful white dress, just like you always dreamed, and be a bride. If you don't let me, you'll never be able to put on a veil and marry the one you love. You will live with your parents and become a spinster."

The words terrified her. She remembered similar words from her parents—about spinsterhood and marriage—when they warned her not to let a boy touch her, ever.

The procedure was short but agonizing. The doctor was using something cold and hard, and Anna was fussing, begging him to stop. She neither knew nor wanted to know what he was doing; she just wanted it to be over.

Melineh was holding her hand, her eyes swimming with tears.

"It's okay, it's nearly done, honey."

Finally, it was done, and everything was fine. Dr. Hanna told Melineh that there was nothing to worry about.

Anna was suddenly livid.

"I told you my pants stayed on, Mom. You didn't believe me, did you?" she yelled.

Asbed returned to the doctor's office. He was upset but relieved.

On their way home, they told Anna that what had happened should stay a secret.

"No one must know about it, Anna. Do you understand?" her mother said.

All was well in their world, now that they were assured she was still a virgin. The emotional scarring was irrelevant, as long as she could still be married off. At the time, support groups for rape victims were nonexistent. Either way, for a girl to receive any support she would first have to be recognized as a victim, an unlikely scenario in a world where gossip and reputation weighed more than one's well-being. She was only a girl, and he was a man. Her word meant nothing against his in a society where males were dominant.

As time went by, Asbed and Melineh eventually stopped visiting Simon and his wife. They always made up excuses, and in the end, all bonds between the two families were broken. Anna was angry with her parents because she did not understand why her father had not confronted Simon.

She felt sad, unsafe, and insecure.

The incident had taught Anna that during a crisis she would stand alone. She was too young to understand that her parents were trying to protect her reputation, for there would come a time when that is all that would matter. People were incapable of distinguishing between rape and attempted rape, between a girl who gave her virginity away willingly for sexual desire or money and a very young girl who fought for her honor and safety.

The issue was never mentioned again in the house. It was as if it had never happened. Was it a wise decision to keep such a secret? Who knows? Nevertheless, Asbed and Melineh did what they thought was right. They never bothered to ask her about her psychological state. They were busy putting bread on the table, and denial took the place of outrage in their minds. Anna was a victim, yet she did not see herself as one. The experience had taught her a lesson; it demonstrated the cruelty of society and the fear it instilled in people, even in her parents whom she had always seen as strong figures.

Years later, after Anna had heard her fair share of rape and attempted rape stories from the most unlikely people, she realized that as horrifying as the thought was, still everyone had a tale to tell in which they were either victim or hero. The difference between the strong and the weak was the will to fight back. Weak people chose to tumble down and give up, making excuses, while the strong ones stood up, dusted themselves off, and kept walking. Anna had decided to fight her own battles. Sometimes she lost, and other times she won. She chose to be undefeated, channeling traumatic experiences into the strength of will.

"I think it would be super cool if I worked on the set. They'll never know what hit them. They always say I can't do anything on my own! Well,

I will! I want my own office like yours, wear high brand clothes and shoes, a driver, and what else? Mm… let me think… oh, yes I adore first-class trips outside Lebanon."

The voice woke Anna from her daze. The redhead with the bare midriff was still talking.

Anna interrupted her. "Thank you for coming in. Sorry, I can't help you."

The girl stared, then stood and walked briskly away, and Anna grabbed her jacket and purse.

"Would you please tell Alan to come in on Saturday at four p.m.?" Anna asked the director, who also looked like he needed to shake off that last candidate.

What was that girl thinking? Anna tried to turn her reaction into mockery, but deep down she knew she could never work with someone who needed to cast blame on everyone around them. She had surrounded herself with strong, positive people, and she was not about to stop now. Courage, persistence, confidence. Those were the qualities she looked for, both at work and in her personal life and especially in women.

Women who can fight off their aggressors and stand up for themselves.

The Tombstone of Anna's Virtues

CHAPTER 8

Anna woke up vibrating with excitement.

He is finally coming to Lebanon; she thought while she drank her morning coffee.

Because she was still legitimately married to Vasag, and her public profile made it a risk for her to meet so openly with Joe, she was to wait in the car while Paul and Rida, along with Hashem and her friend Narine, had to go inside the airport to meet Joe.

On their way to the airport, Anna hummed a song.

"How will we recognize him?" blurted Narine.

"He is the most handsome guy you will ever see!"

"For you, he is!" Rida said.

"Shut up! He is!" Anna felt offended.

"I was teasing you, Anna, calm down, I am sure he is!"

They all laughed.

"Besides being handsome, what else?" Rida continued, more seriously.

"He has a goatee."

"Most men have. Can you more specific?" Paul asked. "Don't you have his picture?"

"No!"

"How come?"

An awkward silence fell, which Anna broke.

"I don't know! Stop asking me questions. I am nervous, his name is Joe, and he'll be on the Air Canada flight from Quebec."

"You are not helping us!" Hashem said evenly.

"He has a shaved head. Yes, that's it! A shaved head."

"Hopefully there aren't many shaved guys coming off that plane. Otherwise, we will be grabbing all of them for you," Narine said.

"I am in love with him; I will die for him." Anna sighed.

"Please, no one has to die for anyone," Rida said. "The war ended in Lebanon a long time ago. You should live for him instead."

"Yes, that's what I meant."

Her phone rang. It was her mother.

"Where are you, Anna? You should put an end to this circus in your life!" She sounded furious.

"What are you talking about?"

"An hour ago, four black cars double-parked in front of our restaurant, and six men got out with an old man who was not in our tiny snack bar for a bite."

Anna started shaking.

"The man, who was the age of your grandfather, came in with a suit more expensive than a car asking about you. He gave your father his business card and asked us to send you his regards."

"So, what? Probably he is one of my fans!"

"Anna, you cannot play mind games with me. I brought you into this world. I know you very well, and when a guy like that comes in, I know what he is looking for. All the neighboring shop owners came out to see the charade of so many cars in such a narrow street."

"What else did he say?"

"He said he was passing by, wanted to say hello and introduce himself. His face was familiar to me. You think I don't watch television?"

"What is his name?"

"Abbas!" her poor mother shouted.

"Abbas? Oh, yes, he is a friend of mine."

"Really?"

"Yes, I have contacts with people in high places in the country."

"I do too, but I haven't seen any of them dropping by our place, handing their business cards, and introducing themselves."

Her mother paused for a breath, then continued.

"A friend? You know if a mosquito catches my eye flying, I can identify its gender. I am neither stupid nor blind."

"I have to go, Mother." Anna hung up the phone.

Anna was trembling with anger and fear. *What a coincidence!* She thought. *The day that Joe is arriving, Abbas went to my father's shop.*

Hashem, who knew Anna's life adventures, tried to relax her.

"Don't worry; he is not stalking you. It is your fault. You suddenly avoided him when you returned from Los Angeles. Instead of avoiding his calls and messages, you should have told him you didn't want him in your life. Probably he just wants to talk."

"What if Joe finds out?"

"What will he find out? After you met Joe, you never saw Abbas."

"I meant if he knew about me having a lover."

"Just call him before we arrive at the airport parking," Hashem encouraged her.

Everyone was silent in the car.

Anna was trembling, but she dialed Abbas's number. *I will confess everything to Joe;* she was thinking when a trembling voice answered.

"Anna? I miss you so much. I've been worried about you. Where are you, my love?"

"You shouldn't be. Don't you watch my show? I am well and alive. Why did you go to my parents' shop?"

"You've been back from the USA for over ten days now, but you answer neither my calls nor my messages. Did I do anything wrong?"

"Abbas, it is over. I don't want you to talk to me. Don't call me or ask anyone about me anymore. We are over."

"Why don't we talk? What did I do wrong? Drop by my office."

"No! I'm busy. Please do not contact me again, and you are not part of my life anymore. Goodbye."

As soon as she hung up the phone, she felt relieved.

"That wasn't so hard, huh?" She was laughing, yet she was quivering.

"Everything is going to be fine. Don't worry, Anna." Rida calmed her down, without knowing the details of the whole story.

After all, it was her fault: she had encouraged the relationship with Abbas knowing full well they would never be together. In her mind, she summoned the last argument they'd had before she flew to Los Angeles.

Anna was in Abbas's office. Abbas himself—a man in his midseventies who looked far younger—was sitting in front of her. He had tiny deep-blue eyes, thin lips, a long prominent nose, and pale timeworn skin. His thin powder-white hair barely covered his hair loss, yet for his age, Abbas managed to be nice-looking and classy, with his highly expensive custom-tailored suits, his initials on his shirts' upper pocket, and his golden cufflinks. He had a calm, polite personality.

Abbas had been in Anna's life as a comfort and support. He gave her everything she needed to help her forget about her first immoral affair with a prince from a royal family, who had tossed her aside without any reason, like a broken toy, after being in a relationship with her for a year and a half.

One look was enough to realize that though time had erased all marks of his youth, the striking appeal of his aged face and body features had persisted in fighting the harshness of time. The power of his charm was determined to clash with the mortality of age that in the long run wins over the gleam, sparkle, health, and beauty of every single living thing on earth.

Time always wins the war against all human beings, celebrating the glory of its battle by crashing life's hopes and expectations.

Abbas was like an old chateau in Anna's eyes, an extensive survivor of history. Ravaged by time, yet like an enormous piece of antique art, it would quickly take any visitor's breath away with its massive construction—and although its art had mostly vanished from its internal walls, its eminent structure continued to reflect the magnificence of its' old glory days.

Abbas, a charismatic and noble-looking gentleman, a successful and intriguing personality, was then a major part of Anna's life.

Abbas was a respected person in Arab society. That day, like a teenager, he was sitting in front of Anna holding her hands while she shrieked and complained at length. He was listening to her intently.

Anna complained about how miserable and insecure she was feeling, stuck in her marriage, not knowing what to do, and needing a way to escape from this nightmare. Abbas seemed dissatisfied.

"It is not appropriate for you to get a divorce," he said. "It will not look good for your image as a TV figure. It will endanger your reputation."

Anna was frustrated; she already knew that would be his decree.

"Of course," said Anna. "I was expecting that answer. Not appropriate for you or me? I know that you do not want to marry me, right?"

Her eyes filled with tears.

Even though she had taken over his heart, and though the age differ-ence was not an issue for her, this man was not prepared to sacrifice his respectful society image. His most important objective was to protect his reputation as a powerful businessman and as a family man.

A man who had grandchildren of Anna's age was not prepared to be taunted by conservative Arab society just to fulfill his desires legitimately with Anna.

Anna had always known in her three-and-a-half years with Abbas that their immoral affair of lust had no future. Her life was so full of deceptions and devastations that in her eyes Abbas as her devoted lover was the only unvarnished truth.

He cared for her, listened to her, protected her from harm, supported her in her career, and gave her whatever any materialistic woman could want.

All her life, unable to find the qualifications of Abbas in her husband or in any other young guys with whom she had such brief teenage experience, she was overwhelmed by his personality. She had no brothers, and nor was her father able to protect her in the cruel celebrity world of fame and power.

Abbas possessed all the qualities of a man that girls require in their fathers. He was the perfect father figure for Anna.

"What do you want, Anna? A divorce?" His words had taken on a scolding tone.

"I want a life. A life! A house I can truly call home. I need to be with someone who loves me, sleeps next to me, and hugs me at night as his wife without anticipating from me any financial support. I don't want to work. I am tired of checking my looks every morning, watching my every move, every word. Challenges, extra efforts, business trips, the fear of failing my fans! Everything is exhausting me. I want everything to end. I cannot take it anymore!"

"But isn't this what you always wanted? Well! This is the price of fame."

"Yes, I did, but now I don't want it anymore!" Anna yelled.

"Don't work! I will take care of you, my love," replied Abbas. "You don't have to worry about anything. Sit home and enjoy life. Trust me. I am here for you."

Anna was not an inexperienced young girl. She knew she couldn't depend on him all her life. After all, it was a corrupt affair.

How could she ensure that she wouldn't quit loving him, or that Abbas would stop desiring her one day? She couldn't rely on him. She always feared that someone younger and more beautiful might catch his eye, or that he'd simply grow bored of her.

"I need a husband who will come home from a hard day of work to dine with me and talk about the simple things in life. I want a husband who will bathe with me following an exhausting day at work instead of someone who hurries to shower alone so he can erase the odor of his immoral daytime adventure with a paid hooker from a burlesque."

Anna was discussing her needs, the primary yet honest necessities of life that she'd stepped over on to climb into the world of fame.

"I am not a good wife either; I can't judge Vasag! I'm here with my lover. I am living in sin too." Anna felt like a drug addict who wanted to be clean again yet didn't dare to go to a rehabilitation center.

Abbas was always cautious to avoid hurting her feelings; she could tell that he recognized her agony, yet he ignored the real solution. His compensations were diamond watches, exquisite cars, private driver, first-class trips, and a beautiful lodge in one of the most luxurious resorts in Lebanon.

Abbas was reliving his past in this vile relationship while Anna was searching for a life with him. He was trying to revive his youth while she was struggling to have a future with him.

The irreconcilable clash of both their needs was clear, yet neither wanted to end this perilous relationship. While Anna was the youth and vitality that offered satisfaction to Abbas, he was her comfort in times of dire need, her provider and guide in the dark yet dazzling world of celebrities.

She lived a free life; she wasted tremendous sums, yet Vasag never interfered or asked by what means she made all her money. Vasag ignored the obvious facts since he was caught up in his own life of extravagance. Anna knew that Vasag did not love her anymore, yet he treasured whatever she offered him in return for her free lifestyle.

"I don't care how old you are," Anna told Abbas. "I don't care how many grandchildren you have, or if you are already married. Take me as a second wife. I do not care that you are Muslim; I will convert. Make me your wife and let me be yours forever."

She wanted to marry Abbas at any cost. She didn't realize that she would be publicly exposing her immorality; she was stepping over everything that was noble in her life—honor, morals, family values, and her own religion, which had brought about the genocide of her own people in 1915. One and a half million Armenians, including her grandfather's parents and eleven sisters.

Anna didn't think for a second that she didn't deserve to be called the grandchild of such an honorable man who, as a five-year-old orphan, had survived, had struggled to keep his identity as an Armenian Christian, while his granddaughter—who belonged to a proud intellectual people steeped in a history of survival against those seeking their extermination—was now begging a Muslim man to marry her.

While Anna's ancestors preferred to be martyred for their religion, Anna was prepared to convert for the sake of marriage to a man who did not even want her as his wife under any condition.

Anna's willingness to convert to another religion was not related to any doubts about Christianity; her motive was not associated with dissatisfaction with her religious faith but to her selfish interests. She was digging the tomb of her pride, destroying everything that once she had held so sacred in her heart.

Despite the fact that Anna was raised as a decent girl protecting the values of life, in front of Abbas she was a different person.

Does everyone go through these temptations? Anna wondered as the car made its way toward the airport.

Her last argument with Abbas was very devastating.

How did I arrive at a point where I lost my path in life? Did I enter a phase when I decided to give up everything that was precious to my soul just to be with Abbas? Or did I take that step because I was powerless and frightened of the future? Am I making a bigger mistake with Joe?

Her unrestrained thoughts were full of so much fear and suspicion they felt as if they were crucifying her soul!

The strength of my character should be proven during a threatening period of time, and my choices in a particular incident should reveal my principles, she thought, knowing full well she was a lost soul contradicting her own philosophy in life, her mind trying to lead her to ideologies while her heart was pondering an opposite direction, an anonymous path of passion and desire.

I am not a coward! I have values! Her brain was torturing her; while she remembered her tears in front of Abbas, she was now caught in a web of different feelings toward Joe and was prepared to do anything to be with him. Abbas made her feel needy and fragile to the point that her mind was not capable of differentiating between love and desire, between happiness and insecurity, between values and corruption. Whereas Joe gave her strength, determination, and hope. She felt complete; she was indeed in love!

"It is impossible to have any children with you, Anna!" Abbas's voice still lingered in Anna's head. "My grandchildren are your age. I already have a family. My sons could hurt you! My wife would never accept me having a second wife. It is impossible." Abbas had said this in such a calm way as if he had been chatting about the weather. His tone was low, yet his facial expressions showed no remorse . Anna knew he'd already had made up his mind.

At that moment Anna knew where she belonged: in his arms only, in secret, forever. Abbas had used the word "I" so often that Anna realized that although he may love her, but he did not want to sacrifice anything for her sake.

She remembered how the conversation between her and Abbas that day had worsened.

"You are wrong!" Anna had suddenly interrupted Abbas. "We should protect our love and fight to keep it, against all the odds; we should sacrifice everything not to lose each other."

"We are not teenagers, Anna!" Abbas had smiled, but his tone was sarcastic. "We will always have each other. I am not going anywhere. I am here with you." He approached Anna, held her face, and began kissing her cheeks as if she were a newborn baby.

Though Anna was talking about love, she knew she had become a polluted woman and that she was lying to Abbas. He never knew that her own husband knew about their affair and tolerated it.

Neither realized that love could not be true if one of them was egocentric like Abbas and the other was a deceiver like Anna.

"You are justifying your situation with nonsense, making excuses. You do not love me, Abbas!" cried Anna as she stood and grabbed her purse to leave the office.

"Please hear me out, you are angry, calm down, I beg you." He was trying to kiss her lips, but she pushed him away. "I will find a solution, Anna! I can't lose you."

"A solution? Do I look that stupid? You don't want me to get a divorce fearing I might meet someone else, perhaps fall in love, and even get married, at which point you will be out of my life once and for all. You do not love me; you just love yourself. I am not your doll. My happiness is clearly not your concern; you are terrified of changing any rules in the game, and that's why you don't want me to divorce Vasag. You are not permitting my happiness unless you are a part of it." She couldn't hold back her thoughts any longer.

"No, my love. You are wrong. Certainly, I want to see you happy..." Abbas lost track of his words like a student who forgets the lines during a poetry recital in class. He sighed then hung his head while still holding her hands.

"I am scared for your reputation," he continued, after a moment of silence. "Once you get a divorce everyone will look at you differently. TV producers, directors, businessmen, all men! They will devour you. Don't you know how they treat divorced women in our society? I am trying to protect you."

"No one can touch me or even approach me unless I let them; this is all nonsense. I am not a child, so stop playing tricks with words."

"I found the solution! Get a divorce and marry one of my single relatives. Then I can always be in your life."

"You are losing your mind. What the hell are you talking about?" Anna was so angry and shocked that she felt she could barely breathe; her heart was beating so fast that she could scarcely articulate her sentences anymore.

"I will never marry a stranger just to have you in my life. And from your family? You are exceptionally selfish."

Anna had quite a lot more to say, but she was careful to use her words wisely because she knew if she went too far there would be no turning back.

Though the agony of her recent years had turned Anna miserable, it couldn't take full control of her innocence; a part of young Anna was still struggling to be heard, the innocent part was still struggling to destroy the recent darkness in her soul, to be revealed and destroy the mask of the new Anna.

She realized that Abbas was not ready to give up on her so easily, yet he did not want to see her happy without being a part of her life. He was sacrificing nothing for her and did not hesitate to persuade her to destroy all her ethics and emotions just for his comfort.

"Fine then, let us get married at this moment by 'Zawaj El Moutaa.' The expression means 'fun marriage,'" Anna replied, her voice rising in anger. "It exists only in the Shia sect in your Muslim religion. This legal provision couldn't be applied because I'm neither a widow nor divorced."

"You know the details of our religion very well. Bravo!"

Anna understood that Abbas already had his queen in this chessboard game of life: his wife, the mother of his children. Anna was merely one of the pawns. He was playing the board using his diversion strategies, moving her wherever he wanted in order not to lose this game, a game based on fatal destruction.

Abbas was cautious and skilled, in order to avoid inevitable capture. Anna knew she might quickly be expelled from his game, either by another pawn, by a misdeed, or by his queen. She did not have the strength to resign voluntarily from his chessboard.

"I'm done with this conversation!" Evil had been unleashed in Anna's heart. "Thank you for your guidance," she babbled, still standing. She was shaking. No measure of peace remained anywhere in her mind.

The conversation ended as Anna surrendered her body to him like a hooker that a man picks up from a street corner, who yields herself willingly without recounting the painful story of her life. She gives pleasure, gets paid, and leaves, never recounting the emotional pain she carries with her like a disease that kills slowly from the inside.

As Abbas crawled over Anna's half-naked body, she closed her eyes, thinking about hookers, who also were once innocent, playing with their friends, singing and dreaming about their bright future. Were Anna's life circumstances unfair, or had she chosen to be in this situation with Abbas, as in so many other situations, out of greed? Anger? Ambition?

While Abbas enjoyed touching her young skin, she wondered why he never took the time to find out about her intellectual qualifications in art and poetry, in her university awards, her passion for philosophy and spirituality; the woman in Abbas's arms had nothing to do with the real Anna.

Abbas never cared to unveil what was hidden behind her shallow exterior image.

Am I a gem or an opportunist? Anna wondered, entirely unaroused by Abbas's touch.

"I am going to be a *star*," she always repeated to herself as long as she remembered and became one...

As Hashem approached the airport, Anna was still sunk in her thoughts.

Why do people call us stars once we are famous?

After years of struggling to be called so, Anna realized that the word might have been inspired by the sparkling stars in the sky, the ones that shine only at night, in the dark, while their glow disappears with each sunrise. Why wasn't the word *sun* chosen instead? Probably because most of us hide many dark secrets, whereas the sun is the only star that with its light reveals the truth! She was conceptualizing a theory of her own: in the end, the stars in the galaxy shine alone and die alone, while each day a new star is born.

"I want to die next to Joe!" she blurted.

"What are you talking about?" Paul asked. "Why do you look so devastated? You were happy an hour ago, yet now you are talking about death?"

"She is so romantic," Rida declared and laughed.

Everyone was quiet.

Anna saw the worry on her friends' faces after her creepy, impulsive statement.

"The ones who became legends are the ones who mostly strived; they are the most talented, and above all, they are the luckiest of them all," Anna continued.

"What are you talking about?" asked Rida. "I mean, seriously!"

"Famous people. I'm talking about them. There are so many talented people who will never be discovered, even more, talented than the ones we know, including me. They might be housewives, mechanics, bakers, strippers, or even beggars in the street."

"Not everyone is fortunate as you!" Narine said.

Probably they are petrified to use all the means to reach the top like me! Anna thought but kept quiet. She smiled and held Narine's hand.

Anna had learned that the world bears no endowments. Nothing was given to her for free, everything had its price, and she had learned to grab whatever she desired in life one way or another.

Over the course of time, she realized that those she cherished the most had disappointed her one by one. But now, Joe's uncertain love gave her new hope.

Anna had lost purpose and meaning in her life years before; she had no dreams of happiness. Thus, when Joe appeared in her life, she had not been afraid to cling to his love, though she knew nothing about him.

I have been punished for so long! She thought. Probably my own doing. *My desire for success has transformed me into a monster caught in a web of rivalry, anxiety, and insecurity.*

She acknowledged the fact that she might have a new chance of true love. Joe was her love now; she had missed so many things besides love in her life somewhere along the road to fame.

She had begun to assimilate her chosen lifestyle before she met Joe. She had been trapped in her dark way of living. Nothing brought her joy or satisfaction. She had failed in everything: unable to make her parents (who always criticized her for her mistakes rather than finding pride in her achievements) proud; wretched at finding happiness; ashamed of her errors—she was stuck between an insensitive lover and a selfish husband. Anna was not even able to have a deep, restful sleep; her conscience tormented her.

For the last few years, she had maintained a distance from people and refused to give them access to her life. She despised herself. However, now she was gradually starting to love herself again through Joe's love.

Cinderella, her favorite fairy tale since childhood, was fading from her mind. She had concluded that not only fairy tales but life itself was a big lie. *Cinderella* was a myth, a fabrication from the author in order to amuse children until they grew up and saw the cruelty of the real world that would eventually crash their hopes of happiness and for hearts full of love. She had forgotten the fact that fairy tales were inspired by real life, just as heroes from world history inspired myths.

The entire world seemed based on falsehoods and the fabrication of fairy tales, and the chance of finding true happiness existed only in fantasies. This turmoil in her mind had caused her so much pain that she was gradually dying from inside. Her pain had pushed her to the crazy risk of spending a night with a stranger in Los Angeles who was now falling for her and crossing the ocean to be with her.

Was there any hope for them? She had gotten everything she wanted, but she realized that was all vague and deceptive. Fame, luxury, her fixed outer beauty, everything she accomplished and claimed possession of had no power to satisfy her—whereas now, with Joe, she was hoping for a simple yet dignified way of life, just love.

As her friends parked the car and made their way to the airport, Rida stayed with her.

"Tell me, are you worried?"

"No, I just hope to be with Joe like all the couples embracing each other. I envy them."

"Trust me; they would die to be in your shoes!" Rida said.

"As would I wish to have their peaceful, loving life, away from complications. In place of all I have now, I want to cook for Joe, do his laundry, and hold his hand in public."

You know, the honorable yet straightforward way of carrying on with my life, she wanted to say. *I can't turn back time and get rid of the memories of my adventurous life that haunt me every time I'm alone.*

Anna's misfortunes had been lessons she had learned from, and now she was hoping to become a better person with Joe by her side.

Nevertheless, somewhere deep inside, Anna had a strange feeling that one day she would wear a white dress once again, would be a bride again; she would hear the church bells ringing for her own wedding once again. Her inner voice, however, silenced that hunch continuously, reminding her that she was already stuck in an unholy marriage. She suspected this hope was a trick played by her own imagination in order to protect her from herself and prevent her from putting an end to her own life.

Although she made mistakes, lost her way, hurt others intentionally, and paid an excessively high price for her goals, she was hoping for another chance of happiness. Even murderers are granted pardons when they demonstrate that they have fulfilled their debt to society, or are wrongfully convicted, they get a second chance to appeal.

The brutality of life had debased Anna's heart. She was on the edge of becoming a malicious person, secretly ridiculing innocent smiles and expressions of hope, and mocking every happy ending in true love stories.

"Do you think Joe can change my life?" Anna asked Rida. "It will be a miracle!"

"What? I know you're his life miracle and that fairies changed his life by bringing him into your world."

"No, I want to be in his world. He is my charming prince on a white horse who jumped out of a fairy tale into my life."

"When did you become so romantic? And what is wrong with your world?"

"I just want to live with him happily ever after. I am really in love with him," Anna replied, avoiding the second part of his question.

Time had taught Anna that people are born either evil or virtuous. Circumstances could never change the soul of a righteous person. She felt Joe was a good person and that his love was going to lead her way to the light of life. She had met many wicked people capable of evil and jealous acts as a result of their total failure and self-deception. Evil people lack the determination to pursue their dreams or cling to their hopes. Moreover, their collapse turns them into angry creatures who seek satisfaction only in the failure of others. For them, sacrifice means bargain; they do not give unless they get something in return. Jealousy, selfishness, and criticism eventually turn them into creatures living sad, troubled, and pessimistic lives full of negative energy. They cannot compete with others' success and happiness, finding comfort in competing with others' tragedies.

"He is a happy person!" Anna continued. "That means he is a good person."

"What?"

"I mean I'm not defining happiness by his smile or his words. His happiness is defined neither by his boyish performances nor by his expressions of joy. I can feel he has peace in his heart as his goodness flows from his inner peace."

"You found all this out from a night with him? Or during phone conversations?"

"I can't explain," she continued. "I just felt it. Superficial profane things cannot make someone happy; they can only offer temporary entertainment away from the inevitable reality of agony."

"Now you are my number one philosopher, Anna!"

Anna knew only a few people in her life like her aunt Araxi, who had suffered, faced tragedy, agony, and misconception in life but remained faithful to their humanity. Only a few failed to make their dreams come true yet could find happiness in the success of others. In Anna's mind, those were people whose hearts had been touched by the finger of the Archangel Chamuel, who had the strength to cure wounded hearts and give strength, peace, and purpose in life.

Her phone rang! It was Narine.

"We can't find him!"

"Where are you guys?"

"Here. The plane has landed. There's no one like you described, no bald guy with a goatee. Call his mobile!"

"No, I don't want to. Joe thinks I'm at home. I want to surprise him!"

"I swear we didn't see anyone bald coming out of the Canadian plane."

"Are you all blind?" Anna shouted.

"No, we are not blind!" It was Paul. "You are shouting! I could hear your voice standing next to Narine. There isn't anyone bald with a goatee."

"I'm coming in."

"No, someone might recognize you, remember? Vasag? Marriage? Press? Scandals?" Rida reminded her.

"You didn't even have a picture of him!" Rida continued.

"Is that him?" Anna heard Paul's voice on the line.

"No, that couldn't be him," Narine said. "He's with a woman."

"A woman?" Anna shouted into the phone.

"It's not him, the guy has a huge nose."

"Don't hang up the phone, Narine."

"Fine!" Narine replied.

"Still no one?" Anna's patience was fraying.

"No, no one!"

Maybe they lost him, she thought. *But he would have called me from his Canadian mobile. Perhaps he changed his mind. No, impossible.* The questions started torturing her, so she ran inside.

As Anna walked in, Hashem approached her; the rest were standing on the other corner.

Anna looked around frantically. A guy wearing blue jeans, a gray T-shirt, running shoes, and a red cap was walking toward her.

"Joe!" Anna shouted, forgetting she was in a public place. Her heart started to pound.

The guy smiled at her from a distance.

"It's him. Go get him!"

Hashem ran toward the guy.

The rest followed him as if they were holding a hostage.

Even with the cap, Anna recognized him immediately—his lips, his nose, his eyes. It was Joe!

It was a hard moment for Anna, seeing her love but being unable to approach him. She hurried to her car.

She walked apart while Joe walked beside Narine as if they were a couple, while the others walked with Anna ahead.

Joe got in the front seat, and Hashem turned on the engine.

"Why didn't you call me?" Anna said, nervous and happy.

"I knew you would come," Joe answered calmly.

He reached for Anna's hand and held it firm.

"I didn't give up on you; I kept on looking around for where you were."

"Don't you ever give up on me, ever," Anna replied.

Hashem drove them to an anonymous motel nearly an hour away from the city, checked in with them, and then left.

Anna was in heaven!

Joe's touch on her body was now more sensual. Emotion and desire were in every single touch.

"I've missed you, everything about you," Joe whispered, kissing Anna passionately. They made love over and over again, although they knew they had to leave soon. As they were enjoying their last couple of moments before leaving the place, Joe got out of bed.

"This is all I can offer to you for now," he said, holding a tiny diamond ring in front of her.

"I don't care. Even if it was made of stone, I would cherish it forever."

"I have nothing to offer you more precious than my heart," Joe added, gazing into her eyes.

"You don't need to; that's all I need!"

"Are you sure you could give up everything you have just to be with me?"

"You are everything," Anna replied, sealing his lips with a long, passionate kiss.

Anna and Joe rode in the car to her aunt's house with Narine and Hashem. Paul and Rida followed in another vehicle.

When they arrived, Araxi welcomed Joe like a son.

They had a great dinner. Joe had to leave to go and stay with his cousin; he could not spend the night at Anna's aunt's place. There were no extra beds; all they had were two separate beds in one room, and it wasn't safe because the divorce papers were not finalized yet. Vasag could have dropped by at any moment.

Anna's fear of Vasag was not out of respect or guilt; the only worry was that once he saw she had the possibility of happiness without him, he might never sign the papers.

Vasag's words rang in Anna's head as she said goodbye to Joe that night.

"No one can love you, Anna! No one can bear you! You will crawl back to me."

She kissed Joe goodbye and smiled as he left the building. She stayed by the door, thinking about how people take years to love each other and dream of being together—just like her and Vasag, which had turned into a nightmare.

Now she was indeed in love with this stranger whom she hardly knew; she had loved him the minute she saw him. It was not only desire or passion; Anna felt he was her soul mate, her destiny!

She was fighting any obstacles that prevented her from uniting with her true love, Joe! She was breaking the chains of a cruel society. Was it possible that she would face more complications in her life? Or that the universal balance was starting to harmonize with her destiny?

The Royal Shoe and the Champagne

CHAPTER 9

Next morning Joe came to see Anna.

Anna was still worried that Vasag might drop by, so they left in Anna's car after a quick coffee, Hashem driving them to Anna's office.

"So how will you introduce me to everyone? That I am just a friend?"

"For now," Anna replied.

Anna greeted her colleagues and accompanied Joe to her luxurious office and shut the door.

She ordered tea—Joe's preference over coffee—and while they were exchanging smiles her phone rang.

"Hello, Anna!"

It was Kareem, who got straight to the point.

"The divorce papers are ready; we just need Vasag's approval to finalize it."

"I will contact him," Anna replied.

"Relax, I'm here with you," Joe reassured her, taking a sip of his tea.

"The papers are prepared by a beautiful young divorce lawyer."

"Then let the brilliant lawyer talk to him, not you," Joe suggested, overhearing the phone conversation as he sat beside Anna on the couch.

"What difference does it make?"

"He is a womanizer; it is noticeable."

There was a knock on the door.

"Good morning, Anna. Beautiful ring!" It was her secretary.

"Thank you! This is my friend from Canada. He will be spending the day with me."

"Would you check these contracts and sign them before we publish the interviews?"

"Sure, give me an hour."

Anna stared at the papers but was unable to concentrate with Joe in her office, looking around.

"Impressive," he said.

"Nothing is as impressive as you!" She jumped and kissed him.

They spent half the day at the magazine and were frequently interrupted by Anna's daily calls and visitors. Joe never left the room.

In the afternoon, Hashem drove them to the television station.

"I've never seen those cameras and lights except in the movies," said Joe while Anna was reviewing the information for her show. "How could you leave all this behind to be with me? You are being treated like a princess wherever you go!"

"But with you, I feel like a queen!"

One of Anna's assistants took Joe for a tour of the station. Anna sat back in her chair, laid the papers on the desk in front of her, and remembered Joe's recent words.

"You're the whole package Anna, the way you talk, the way you look, the way you think, the way you love me; you are perfect, you truly are a princess."

"No, I am not."

"Yes, you are, you are my princess."

Her inner joy was scattered by a sudden recollection.

She remembered! It was the royal shoe and the champagne.

It was many years ago, and she had had her first-class ticket in one hand and her first new Louis Vuitton handbag in the other, walking to the plane from the VIP lounge.

It was her first business trip from the Gulf back to Lebanon, her blond hair down, Chanel sunglasses, a dark gray silk suit, silver rose brooch on her jacket, candy-pink mesh chemise, and light pink pointy stiletto-heeled shoes—a collective statement of her egotism.

Anyone with a sharp eye would have noticed she was trying to make a statement about her appearance: I am gorgeous, attractive, and an outstanding personality.

As she looked for her seat and tried to hold her head up, the two mobiles in her hand and her expensive handbag lingering on her arm, everything about her emphasized her show-off complex, which was becoming an everyday habit.

The extra effort spent on her appearance for a four-hour trip from an Arabic country to Lebanon was unusual. Anna was new to the world of fame, so she never missed a chance to overdo her outer appearance and bask in the attention.

Anna had been bullied at school for being tiny and thin, with her tooth braces—a rare sight in those days in Lebanon—and skinny legs; she remembered how the other children made fun of her, calling her a robot, or a billiard cue.

Those same children years later never recognized the Anna on television. The billiard cue of the classroom was now a star on Arabic television screens. Her long, thick eyebrows that met across her nose bridge and the Hellenic nose itself were later replaced by beautifully shaped eyebrows and a smaller new nose; instead of the eyeglasses with black plastic frames she was wearing colored lenses, and her brown, braided pigtails had been replaced by her long blond hair with full extensions.

At school, Anna had belonged to no group. She was not invited to any birthday parties, and whenever her mom planned a birthday party, the only two classmates who showed up came out of curiosity to make fun of the modest attendance at her party next day at school. Now she was invited to the most influential gatherings and dinners, and she always caught the eyes of men.

Once she had been sad on her birthdays; now, as a celebrity, she was always excited and others—her plastic surgeon or her colleagues at the television station—organized surprise birthday parties for her simply to see her smile.

Famous and beautiful, Anna owed a lot to those kids who'd played a significant role in helping her become a successful personality. She learned that being bullied had motivated her, that the cruel jokes had given her a reason to work harder on herself on all levels, and she had transformed her pain into success with enormous energy fueled by anger.

As many nerds did, Anna made her way up in life, while most of those bullies and popular girls ended up achieving nothing concrete.

They should see me now, she often thought, every time she was on screen—like a slave who rises to the throne while her masters stumble.

Anna never knew then that bullies revealed the anger, fear, and unhappiness in themselves, compensating for their pain by hurting others.

"Hello! I believe my place is next to you," she said politely to a guy sitting comfortably.

"Sure!" The man smiled.

He moved the laptop away, greeted Anna as she sat down.

When the plane took off, Anna turned to him and asked, "Shouldn't you be praying now for a safe trip?"

"Why? Do I look like someone who is scared of heights?"

He started laughing so hard that Anna thought he was mentally unstable. He was loud and careless as if he owned the plane.

Two women sitting in front of them turned back.

"Rasheed? Are you crazy? Hush! Everyone is looking at you," one of them scolded.

"Who cares?" he answered.

Anna was not feeling comfortable but said nothing.

The guy was wearing a long white robe with a headscarf, the two small-angled corners wrapped around his head, and he had dark skin, big black eyes, and a weird smile.

"So why did you ask me if I pray?" The guy insisted on continuing the conversation. "Do I look that saintly to you?"

"No, it is not that. It's because of your clothes, slippers, long dress, headscarf, and because you..." Anna was flustered. She did not know how to say that she had assumed he was a religious Muslim. She hesitated. Then she saw his Rolex watch. "Wow! That is impressive."

She knew she could have left it there, but her words betrayed her, spilling out anyway.

"Because of your dress and slippers! And the white fabric on your head... I don't know a lot about your traditions, but you're a religious man, am I correct?"

He looked surprised, so she continued. "Oh, and you smell like the Gulf!"

I wish I'd never opened my mouth.

"What does the Gulf smell like?"

"It smells sweet, exotic, caramelized, intoxicating like you. I meant the fragrance."

"You mean this?" He took out a tiny glass bottle from his handbag and held it out for Anna to smell.

"Exactly, yes! It is an intoxicating scent. "

"Seatbelts on, please; we will be taking off now!" the captain declared.

"I will give you a bottle once we land at Beirut airport," he promised.

She smiled contentedly. *He is such a generous Muslim sheikh,* she thought. *I wonder if the bottle is blessed like the holy water of Christian churches.*

"Thank you. May God bless you," she said out loud.

He started laughing so hard that his eyes were filled with tears.

"What? Don't you say it like that to honor your own God?"

"My God? Do you have a different God?" he continued, still laughing. "the perfume is called Oudh; it's an oil made from agarwood."

"I didn't know."

The conversation about the Christian and the Muslim gods had been eclipsed by the power of the Oudh perfume.

"So, let us return to what you were saying earlier, that I am a religious man?"

"I meant no offense, do not get me wrong. I got confused. You are traveling first class, dressed like religious Muslim men dress, and wearing a Rolex watch, and... is it a fake watch? I couldn't connect the dots."

The conversation drifted aimlessly.

"Didn't you see anyone dressed like me during your visit?"

"It was my first conference here since I became a marketing manager for an economic journal. This is my card." Anna handed him her business card.

"Thank you very much. How kind of you," he replied, giving her his own card.

Anna took it without reading it and continued explaining that she had been busy for six consecutive days, had had meetings to attend, and couldn't enjoy her time, adding that she'd seen many people wearing white like him in offices.

"I am not a religious man; I am a royal family member."

"Interesting!" Anna removed her seat belt and stood. She was in shock!

"Sit down, madam, if you please!" asked the hostess.

"Do you live in a castle? Is your mother a queen? Do you ride horses?"

"Put your seatbelt on, please," said Rasheed merrily.

The two women sitting in front started giggling again.

"Oh, forgive me, your honor, I have never met anyone royal in my life."

It was the beginning of the 2000s, and even scandals between singers and royal family members were not publicly discussed much in the press.

"I am wearing a thawb, and the thing on my head is a keffiyeh. I don't wear a crown, but I am a prince, and they call me *sheikh*."

"But doesn't that word signify a religious man?"

"It's used for both, holy people and royal family members. In our area, the royal families are known as sheikhs."

Anna looked at the card; it had a family name that she'd never heard and a sign with a crown and swords on its upper left corner.

"This is so cool. What may I call you? Your Royal Highness?" She was almost shouting now.

"No! Just Rasheed."

"You are very humble."

"Yes, he is," one of the women replied, turning her head to address Anna.

"Oh, so these are princesses, right? Your wives? How many wives do you have? Do you have a harem?"

Where does he sleep? How many secrets does he have? Does he have any servants? Do people kneel to him? Can he give orders to kill people? Anna wondered before Rasheed continued.

"No, they are not my wives, they are my friends. Saliha and Miriam."

"Hello! I am Anna."

She was so interested in these women that the trip felt like ten minutes. One woman was from Algeria and the other from Morocco.

Charming, sexy, extraordinarily beautiful, they both had long dark hair and white skin. Miriam had hazel eyes, and Saliha's were dark green.

Their clothing and accessories—diamonds on necks and hands, expensive watches—emphasized their luxurious lifestyle.

Now Anna wondered how they dared talk so candidly to the prince if they were just friends.

Fairy tales always overwhelmed Anna.

She gave her card to both women.

"We will be staying in the royal suite of the following hotel." Saliha wrote down the address.

"Promise us that you will come see us," Miriam said.

"Sure, I can't wait to tell everyone I met a prince."

After the plane landed, they were surrounded by a group of thirty people, including eight bodyguards. Some of them carried the luggage, others the handbags; they took Anna's suitcase after Miriam asked them to. Anna was entering the airport with a royal family member from the Gulf along with bodyguards and two beautiful women. She felt fortunate.

The bodyguards next to the prince had several mobiles, and one of them rang as they were still walking in.

The prince took the phone.

"Where are you, Hamad? When? Fine, I will be waiting. Confirm once you land in London. Are you going by the private jet? I will meet you there."

They were nearly at the exit when Prince Rasheed turned to Anna.

"Do you want to come with us to London next week?"

Anna did not know what to say. She was afraid they might cut off her head like Anne Boleyn if she disobeyed, but she was in no position to accept; she had responsibilities.

"I do not know. I don't have a visa. I should get permission from the TV station and the magazine."

"Yes, please come, we will have so much fun," said Miriam.

"I will call you," Anna promised.

"No! Come tonight. We are going to a private party; you come to us."

"I will think about it." Anna was walking away when Rasheed called her.

"Anna, wait! I did not give you the perfume! Here, take this one… oh, yes, this one is better, take both."

One of the guys beside him gave Anna two boxes made of carved wood with colored stones.

"Thank you," she replied. They were beautiful. They evoked in her dreams of palaces and magic lamps. "I will call you, Miriam. Goodbye for now."

She rushed to the magazine office.

She gave all the information to Walid, her boss, and showed him the prince's card.

"Oh my God! He is the one of the brothers of the ruler in the Gulf," he exclaimed.

"He invited me to go with him and his friends to London next week."

"Impressive."

"These are the papers and all the information from the conference."

"Good job, Anna. I am delighted. You may go."

"I'm tired, and I should drop by the TV station before going home."

"No, I meant you may travel to London."

Walid called the secretary to secure the papers needed for the British embassy.

"I will talk directly with one of the consulates early tomorrow morning so that you can go for your visa."

Anna was surprised that a royal name and a business card with the monarchy stamp on it in her hand had so much power.

She rushed out.

"Where do you want to go?" Hashem asked.

"The TV station; it won't be long."

She had five prerecorded episodes that were kept for an emergency so she could justify her immediate travel plans.

After going home, taking a shower, and talking to Vasag, Anna changed into another suit and went to the hotel at seven to meet her new friends in the lobby.

"Hello, Anna we are here," Saliha called as Anna reached the lobby.

They hugged and kissed.

"Hi!" said the man beside her.

"Oh my God, is that you, Rasheed? I didn't recognize you. Forgive me, it's the first time I've seen you with your clothes on."

Everyone laughed.

Anna was embarrassed.

"I meant without the white thing on your head and the long white clothes!"

"Don't worry," the prince replied.

Anna was wearing an official-looking suit while Saliha and Miriam wore short, tight, sexy dresses. The two friends had incredible taste in fashion. Saliha was quiet, with exotic beauty, whereas Miriam had softer features but a bold, active personality.

"We will dine here then go to a party," Rasheed continued. "You are coming with us, right?"

"Sure," said Anna, "just let me call my driver to give him the address."

"No need. You can come with us, and after the party, one of our private drivers will drop you off," said Saliha.

Rasheed's people—eating, talking, laughing, and having fun—occupied the whole lobby.

"The prince is very kind and humble." Anna sat and made conversation with both women beside her.

"True, he can be most of the time," said Saliha, between bites of her meal.

Anna said no more.

After dinner, Saliha and Miriam suggested Anna to change her clothes.

"Let's go upstairs; we have many dresses in our room."

Oh! They stay together in the same room? Obviously, they are lesbians, Anna thought.

They went upstairs to the last floor, the presidential suite.

"Pick whatever you want, it is yours, take anything you like," Miriam said.

"I don't know!" Anna was confused; shoes, bags, clothes, and jewelry were thrown everywhere. The whole place was a mess!

Miriam must have seen her shock in her eyes.

"We were in a hurry!" she explained. "Don't worry, Anna! They clean everywhere after we leave, and the butler will fold and hang all our clothes."

"So, have you known the prince a long time?"

"No, we met him four months ago," said Saliha.

"So, you are friends?" asked Anna, gazing at all the beautiful , expensive clothes thrown recklessly everywhere.

"No, we are more than friends," Saliha replied.

"We met him at a private party; he liked being with us, and we liked him back, so we spend time with him."

"Oh, you mean both of you?"

"Sure." They giggled.

"So you were both friends, and now you share the prince together? I mean, you are both his lovers?" Anna chose her words carefully as if she was speaking Arabic for the first time in her life. "In love with the same man? I mean, the prince?"

"Love? No, of course not. We met him at the same private party, and he liked us both, so we became friends with each other and with him."

Anna did not know what they meant by a private party, although she had heard rumors; she tried to avoid diving any more profound, but her curiosity got the better of her.

"What if he breaks your hearts? Wouldn't you be suffering then?"

"One day he might leave us for others, but he never promised us more than he's already giving us. He is generous, we even share his adventures, making love to a model or an international celebrity who comes from any place of the world just to spend one night with him; he can't resist anyone beautiful he sees on any screen. We do not mind sharing him with others," Saliha explained.

"Aren't you girls afraid of STDs?"

"No," Saliha continued seriously, "each girl is tested at a private clinic that he owns, and the results come out after a couple of hours, and even the models from Europe and other foreign countries know this rule. We are all given pregnancy pills, which are the most important part of the agreement."

So, they're bisexual, not lesbians, Anna thought. *How come they haven't made a pass at me? Probably I am not sexy enough, though I am glad they didn't.*

"Don't you work?"

"He is our work." They both laughed.

Anna, busy with all her questions, had forgotten about the dresses.

"We have our own houses in the Gulf, fully paid, money set aside for over four hundred thousand US dollars each. We have the new Bentley, jewelry, and clothes that could last us a lifetime... though out of fashion!" Miriam turned the conversation into a joke.

"Everything from him?"

"He gives us money, depending on his mood, and we shop with him in every country; the cars and the houses are a gesture of our importance in his life, aside from the diamond watches and jewelry sets we receive on certain occasions."

"You are both kidding me right now!" Anna was in shock. "What about his wife?"

"Which one? Her Royal Highness, the princess, or the rest?"

"The royal wife."

"Everyone praises her. She gave him many children, he adores and respects her, and our adventures are always outside his country to protect the feelings and the dignity of his princess."

"You are both lucky girls!"

"We are fine," they replied together and laughed.

"We're a good team," said Miriam.

Anna couldn't shut up any longer.

"Does this mean that you are lesbians?"

"No, we are not, but after meeting him we learned to enjoy being with each other first, to give the prince the enjoyment, and then the adventure became fun and pleasurable, so you might say we are bisexuals, right?" Miriam winked at Saliha.

Anna began to worry. *What if they rape me?*

Again, her heart mastered her fear and threw doubt out of her mind.

"So, he always gives you whatever you desire?"

"If you mean material things, yes. He possesses us for the time being, of course, by our choice."

When a poor guy buys his lover a rose, it's called romance, but if a prince buys his girlfriend a car, then will it be called prostitution? Anna wanted to state her opinion but stayed quiet.

"If he were not a prince, no one would have bothered about his sexual adventures, but as a powerful and wealthy personality his sexual life always attracts the interest of others," Saliha said.

"As for a prince who has everything—relationships with women, including more than a sexual experience like us—he must have feelings too. I mean love!" Miriam hesitated and fixed Anna with her gaze. "I meant taking all this from him, doing whatever he asks us to, regardless of his marital status, do you consider us prostitutes?"

"No, of course not"! Anna exclaimed. "I meant it must be hard to be with someone you know will never be yours, someone who can never marry you, even if he wants to. It is not the money but being with a married man with no love, makes me wonder how a girl would feel. I mean, having everything and being always with him, isn't it strange that you both agree that he belongs to neither of you?"

"He belongs to both of us," Saliha replied.

Anna was not satisfied with the answer. "I meant, you do not fight over him? Aren't you both in love with him? How do you manage to be with someone so close yet knowing you are going to end up not being with him in the end?"

"You are so romantic, Anna," Saliha said. "Be careful! Romance might ruin your whole life one day!"

"What? Romance?" Anna was surprised; how could love ruin her entire life? Not that she was living one now; she was with a husband who was either sitting home in front of the television counting her money or out with his friends somewhere he would not be found.

"Using your heart in every situation in life is dangerous, Anna. You should use your logic," Saliha explained.

"I use my mind for knowledge, as my heart is for feeling and loving!"

"Good luck!" said Saliha.

"You are so utopian, Anna," Miriam echoed Saliha. "No one knows if any love or relationship will last forever, or if he is faithful to you even if you are married to him. Aren't you married? How do you know he isn't betraying you?"

"He isn't," Anna lied.

"Let's say he isn't. Do you have any guarantees that you will both love each other and stay faithful until death do you part? Marrying Rasheed and living in his harem with his other wives is like being a bird in a cage; we want to be outside enjoying life!"

"Anything you buy comes with at least a one-year guarantee, except marriage and love!" Saliha added.

"We don't want to be thrown like used materials into one corner of his harem, taking care of our children while he is outside, looking for new adventures."

The girls in their late twenties, were talking about a lifestyle Anna had never encountered before; she could see that it was a tempting lifestyle that any woman could be drawn to.

"No guarantees in life. Maybe we die tomorrow."

"Don't say that!" Anna was scared.

Miriam and Saliha seemed to know the path they were walking; they were ready for any eventuality, even a fiasco, knowing that everything in life has an endpoint.

"No feelings involved—just fun, sex, exploitation, an extravagant life-style, and tons of money!" Miriam was dancing while saying these words as if they were a song.

Saliha's phone rang; it was Rasheed.

We are coming right away," she replied immediately.

They hurried downstairs.

In the elevator, Miriam whispered to Anna, "The most important thing is to stay out of public sight in their country; if the mother queen discovers his or any of his brothers' life adventures in public they will vanish us."

"What?" Anna was scared. "Come on; this isn't a movie! No one goes that far."

"Welcome to our world," Miriam continued. "How do you think movies are inspired? By the wind and the clouds? Review history."

"But that's history," Anna replied.

"One day they will be included in history!"

"Be quiet!" Saliha warned. "Miriam, we are here."

Miriam continued. "Morality, the influence of the monarchy, their traditions are a danger for both of us."

"Be quiet, I said." Stepping out of the elevator, Saliha was annoyed. "Just shut up, Miriam. You're not whispering, and they can hear you. Change the subject."

"Why didn't you change your clothes?" Rasheed asked Anna.

"I don't know. I am okay. Thank you." She had been so focused on exploring the girls' lives that they'd all forgotten about Anna's dress.

An hour later, the four of them left for one of the most famous rooftop nightclubs in downtown, High-Bar.

How can this be a private party? It is not cozy; this is a big crowd! Anna thought. *Nothing is private about here.*

Rasheed and the women sat down, and the bodyguards closed the main entrance.

Now what? Arabic belly dancers with half-naked bodies will appear, just like they do for sultans? Anna was impatient.

Tiana, a famous Lebanese female singer, took the microphone, welcomed the prince, and started singing.

When their eyes met, the singer nodded at Anna; they knew each other.

It was not like any other party that Anna had ever attended; everyone was trying to get the prince's attention, to please him, by bringing him drinks, by introducing known models to him, by whispering in his ear. His Royal Highness was delighted.

Anna remained in place as if her body had been glued to the piece of the furniture. A male model approached. After receiving no encouraging feedback, he left.

What the hell am I doing here? Anna started questioning herself. *Yes, I am going to London on a fun trip, but...* Then her imagination took her to Tower Bridge and the beauty of the city; her visionary power distracted her from the Sodom and Gomorrah of her present.

Models and celebrities were everywhere, some sitting in the laps of the prince's less feted guests, others sharing drinks with Miriam and Saliha.

Everyone was having fun.

Anna felt weird; she never enjoyed drinking alcohol, so after she ate she immediately felt sleepy. She was exhausted, and her two new friends were lost in the crowd. The loud music annoyed her; everyone was shouting to be heard.

Anna saw Saliha and Miriam walking out of the bathroom; they looked energetic, alert, and scarily elated. They began to dance and jump aimlessly without following the rhythm of the music.

Anna was bored.

Tiana started singing again but with an unusual sexy tone, moving her hips and strolling toward the prince.

Everyone was shouting, "Do it! Do it!"

Anna stood up to see what was happening.

Miriam and Saliha were next to Rasheed.

"Do it! I challenge you." It was Rasheed's voice on the microphone.

The singer, the respectful and elegant woman who embodied principles, honor, and money earned with dignity during her interviews, and who had once been a guest on Anna's TV show, kneeled in front of the prince.

It is a bizarre scene, Anna thought. She did not know whether Tiana was kissing Rasheed's shoe or performing a royal ritual unknown to her.

As everyone was laughing and clapping, a guy brought a bottle of Dom Perignon champagne.

Tiana was on her knees in front of His Royal Highness, and everyone was laughing and clapping as she slowly removed one of his shoes while her half-naked body in its super sexy tight beige dress looked like that of a sex goddess, infatuating everyone. She was leaving nothing to the imagination about how the rest of her body parts looked underneath her string panties and red transparent bra—flashes of danger beneath the nude color of her dress.

The seductive star showed no coyness.

Everyone started shouting, "Twelve thousand dollars, twelve thousand dollars…"

Anna approached and stood next to Miriam.

"Isn't this fun?" Miriam said to Anna, one of her arms wrapped around a beautiful model.

"Yes, it is," Anna responded, not fully able to hide her shock.

"Look!" Miriam pointed at the singer without removing her other arm from the young model's waist, who was standing like a statue with her short blond hair, rosy cheeks, and sad blue eyes. "Tiana is going to do it!"

Tiana took Rasheed's shoe and poured champagne into it, and everyone cheered. Most everyone was drunk.

As the prince laughed, Tiara started drinking from his shoe, still on her knees. Then she cleaned her face with the rest of the expensive sparkling liquid, which ruined her whole makeup.

It is a shoe, not a champagne glass! Anna thought but kept quiet. It was none of her business, after all.

"She won the bet." Miriam laughed.

One of the prince's guys was putting packs of money in Tiana's hand while she remained in front of the prince.

Everyone counted aloud in thousands until they reached $12,000.

Losing a bet that Tiana would not drink from his shoe had cost the prince $12,000, but he seemed not to care—he was having fun.

The whole spectacle was a shock for Anna.

What could be next?

In her favorite fairy tale, the prince found Cinderella after trying her shoe on every girl's foot in his kingdom, and they lived happily ever after, while tonight she had watched a female singer kneeling in front of a prince, drinking from his shoe for entertainment.

Tiana had drunk from a shoe to quench her thirst for greed, and to proceed further in the music industry, while the prince had had fun!

Tiana had a beautiful voice and was lovely. Her agent had taught her that drinking from a shoe filled with alcohol in five minutes could help her earn as much as she could in a show lasting for hours.

It was two in the morning, Anna was exhausted and sleepy, the music was loud, most partygoers were still hyper, repeatedly visiting the powder room, and everyone was jumping not on the floor but on each other.

Anna felt like she was watching an erotic movie, and she was a member of the cast but had no role in the film.

Though a couple of guys looked at her, no one approached her; no doubt the combination of her scowls and her business suit did not exactly invite attention.

Now Tiana was sitting on Rasheed's lap next to Miriam and Saliha. They were all laughing and whispering in each other's ears.

Miriam still had the young model next to her.

As Anna went to thank the prince and take her leave, Saliha ran to her and slurred, "I want to wish you the best of luck tomorrow at the British embassy, for your visa." She seemed to be making an effort to pronounce her words correctly as if she had overdosed.

"Thank you," Anna replied, clasping Saliha's shoulder.

"Oh! One more thing!" Saliha continued. "Aren't they both sexy? We chose them for tonight."

It's as if she's talking about a piece of furniture, Anna thought.

"What?" Anna asked, trying to avoid the conversation.

"Tiana and Anabella," Saliha said.

"Who?" Anna repeated the question as if she had not understood what Saliha was saying, trying desperately to be out of the picture and avoid the details.

The threesome that Anna had experienced many years ago was a three-minute TV commercial compared with this feature-length *Caligula* wannabe.

"The singer and the model a good combination, right?"

"Sure, sweetie, whatever makes you happy." Anna was buttoning her jacket.

"Well, it will make us all happy!" Saliha laughed.

Anna did not respond, thanked the prince for the night, and left.

One of their drivers took Anna home, where she showered and went to bed next to a snoring Vasag.

Anna could not sleep. How had she missed all this? Was there this much psychological contamination? She was not judging anyone because she did not have the wings of an archangel, but seeing the limits pushed so far was scary for her.

She started worrying about her trip to London: why had she been invited? Though excited, she could not help wondering why they would ask her if they could buy anyone they wanted. She did not know how Miriam and Saliha or even a royal prince, given their radical lifestyle, could love the company of literary and polite celebrities like her.

Anna had learned about royal families in history class, read about their tremendous values, and their unbreakable bonds with people who were devoted to them, and that their love could never be perishable.

Anna got her visa, and they all flew to England.

They arrived at the London Hilton on Park Lane. Anna was exhausted. After a shower, the three women went downstairs to the lobby to dine with Rasheed.

As usual, Anna wore another suit to make a loud statement about her education and her career standing.

In the elevator, Saliha was doing final touchups to her makeup in the mirror, and Miriam had her hand in her purse searching for a spearmint breath mint. Anna was nervous.

"I can't find anything in here!" Miriam complained, removing a perfume from her purse and gushing aroma all over her dress.

"It seems you always leave everything to the last moment," Anna replied. "Let me help you with that mint."

Anna reached into her friend's purse.

"Be careful! Try not to fall in love with Sheikh Hamad. His Royal Highness is very handsome and smart," Miriam said, looking straight into Anna's eyes.

"Don't listen to her. He doesn't pay attention to other women. He is in love with his new wife!" Saliha said.

"He's very handsome. I'm warning you, Anna!" Miriam said.

"You never know when to keep your mouth shut." Saliha looked at Miriam. "Who asked you for details?"

Miriam, talkative and adventurous, seemed to hesitate to express her thoughts.

"Think before you talk! Think, Miriam!"

"Okay! Whatever...! What did I say? I'm just warning her."

"Anna is married; she is here to be with us as her friends!" Saliha was angry.

"Fine!" Miriam sniffed.

"Girls, we are here!" Anna was glad that the door opened.

How handsome and tempting could he be that they are scared I will fall in love with him? He should be warned not to fall for me! So? Even if he is a prince! I am pretty and famous! Anna thought.

They stepped out of the elevator.

In the lounge, Sheikh Rasheed was sitting across from another guy.

When Anna saw him even from afar, she was captivated.

He is not a prince; he should be a king! She thought. Her heart started pounding so loud she thought she was going to stop breathing.

"He looks like the actors in historical movies, who played the character of a young king," Anna whispered to Miriam as they approached the two men.

"I told you," Miriam replied, beaming.

Hamad, with his real Arabic roots and his royal blood, was the king of all Arabia in Anna's eyes.

He had almond-colored tan skin and long, vibrant, chocolate hair, and his glittering light-brown eyes were visible even from a distance and held a magical power, while his symmetrical nose and angular chin with the sharp facial features were stunning.

His expensive clothes showed his impeccable fashion sense and fit his muscular body perfectly; his straight collar-length hair, styled so as to fall across his face, gave him an exotic and irresistible look.

In his mid-thirties, the sheikh was charming and extremely hot.

At their approach, the two men stood.

"Hello! I am Anna."

"Hamad." He introduced himself without a title and shook her hand. "My brother already told me that you were going to be our guest. I hope you'll enjoy this trip."

"It's a pleasure to meet you," said Anna.

"Sorry, I'm not a TV fan so that I might recall your face! My brother told me that you're a public figure."

"I'm not offended!" Anna replied, mildly upset that her effect on him had suffered. She laughed. "It's fine: you have a kingdom to run! I don't blame you!"

She winced when the sheikh didn't respond; her words had sounded more like sarcasm than a joke.

"I was impolite! I wish I could take back my words! I think I stated my response in a very unmannered way," Anna pleaded.

Although she was far from perfect, full of mistakes and secrets, Anna was courageous enough to apologize.

"I'm impressed. We rarely meet women who ask for forgiveness nowadays. It is not a sign of weakness but a symbol of virtue!"

"No, I disagree," Anna replied. "Most women do, but nowadays only a few men hear it in order to appreciate it."

Hamad laughed. "Cute and smart."

Anna relaxed.

"Enough brainstorming today," Rasheed interjected. "You two are boring."

"All right, where shall we go?" Miriam asked cheerily.

"Lunch first, then you girls take Anna with you to see London and shop," Sheikh Rasheed recommended.

After grabbing a bite, the women went out.

In the car, Saliha slipped an envelope into Anna's handbag.

"This is for you. I hope you enjoy your shopping!"

Anna was embarrassed. "From whom?"

"Sheikh Rasheed."

"So sweet of him," she whispered.

Anna had never been in such a situation before; it was a new adventure for her.

Though she had a feeling that something was not right, the excitement and the luxury were clouding her judgment and her usual ability to listen to the inner voice that was trying to alert her to danger.

"Enjoy it!" said Miriam with a devilish smile.

The shopping started. The streets were clean, the shops were glamorous, and the city was stunning.

Anna did not even count the money in the envelope.

At the end of the day she had spent over £9,000 on clothes, bags, shoes, and gifts for Vasag and all her family members.

Three young men always followed them; they held their bags and assisted them with anything they needed. Every couple of blocks, two of them rushed to the car and put the bags in, and then rushed back to their mistresses.

Exhausted, the women returned to the hotel that evening.

Is this real? Or within a couple of minutes is the director sitting behind the monitor going to shout, "Cut!"? And will the cameras then stop rolling? I am living in a dream.

After a shower, they all went out dancing; Hamad danced with Anna.

Though he did not flirt with her, she felt he wanted her as much as she did him.

Their dance involved touching each other more than moving their bodies with the rhythm of the music; dancing was just an excuse to feel each other at liberty.

He will never betray the princess, his wife? Sure! Anna thought.

After a long night, Anna returned to her suite.

"We wish you an enjoyable night," said Miriam. Both girls hugged Anna, then went to their suite with Rasheed.

Anna went to her suite, but she could not sleep; she was tired, yet she still had the musk of Hamad's body scent in her nostrils.

The way he spoke the Arabic language with his sexy male accent was enough to excite any female's emotions, no matter the meaning of the words; the sheikh's deep masculine alto was stimulating.

Anna's ears were still ringing with Hamad's simple conversations.

The Gulf district had a distinct Arabic dialect; it was so arousing when spoken by a man.

The phone in her suite rang!

Please, let it be Hamad! She thought.

"Hello, Anna? It's Hamad. Are you sleeping? I want to give you something."

"Yes, sure, come," Anna replied.

She hung up the phone and hurried to the mirror; she put on some deodorant and rushed toward the door.

He was already knocking.

She opened the door.

He had a box in his hand.

"It's for you. I should have given it to you today, but I forgot. Maybe we'll never meet again, so I thought you should have a souvenir from me!"

"You didn't need to!" Anna grabbed the box with a smile and tore it open. "Come in, please."

Hamad closed the door behind him.

"Wow…" She felt her eyes widen. "I have never seen such a watch in my entire life!"

It was a Chopard diamond watch in copper-and-gold-colored metal, embedded with brown, white, and yellow square diamonds.

"I don't know what to say." Anna was shocked.

"I did not know I was going to meet you. Otherwise, I would have brought you something that suited your beauty more."

"Are you crazy? Oh, sorry, I mean Your Royal Highness!" She was flustered.

"Just Hamad!" he said calmly.

The next words on Anna's lips were sealed by Hamad's lips. She could not believe a sheikh was kissing her. Between the desirable physical moment and the happiness of her gift, Anna was thinking, *Am I a princess, now? This is a fairy tale?*

However, by encouraging such a step with the sheikh, Anna thought she was already betraying a real princess—Hamad's wife—and felt lucky it was not an actual fairy tale; otherwise she might have found herself punished by a fairy protecting the kingdom, her kiss with Hamad turning her from Anna into a frog!

She had never experienced such a glorious moment in her whole life. However, the oxytocin hormone released by her brain was linked to the pride she felt at being desired by a sheikh. Anna's brain was activating as a response to his title more than to her sexual arousal and pleasure.

He started touching her slowly, with care, but as most supreme moments in life are brief, so was his way of lovemaking; after a couple of tender kisses, he was unexpectedly transformed from a romantic guy into a selfish monster with a slave in his arms.

Anna could not even reason that her brain was sending signals to her body to stop this. There was no pleasure anymore, no hope of sexual satisfaction; her body was being treated with swift and violent moves, far more like rape than any kind of pleasant sexual experience.

She was confused, yet she did not want to stop it. He was jamming his fingers inside her vagina, and then with monstrous impatience, his hardness replaced his fingers. She responded to all the humiliating moves, fearing the consequences of losing a guy whose heart did not belong to her in the first place; in all this confusion she was still hoping to reach her climax.

Hamad is like a savage invading a village, Anna thought.

He seemed to have no intention of giving her any pleasure; after all, he had already given her a diamond watch, so he had fulfilled his duty in another way.

After he was done, Hamad lay in bed next to her, seemingly relaxed after a hostile encounter that had lasted less than an hour.

Anna was confused and angry, but she hid her despondence.

Her pleasant smile hid her feelings entirely; she was furious, but her brain was trying to find any justification for his brutality.

Her tongue determined not to advocate for her actual state of mind, and her lips refused to speak her anguish. At that moment, there was an inner war between her current awareness and future uncertain dreams. The alliance between her soul and her self was consumed by an emotional turmoil.

She had no hopes of any happy future expectations yet lying in the arms of a sheikh encouraged her to think that feeling like a princess justified her submission to him as if she were his sex slave.

Hamad was a royal sheikh, and she was just an ordinary girl.

The smell of his body was no longer so appealing and desirable. Everything was dull. Yet she still lay beside him as she lost contact with her soul completely.

He thinks he is the Don Juan of the Arabs, Anna thought. *However, I am neither a prostitute nor a slave.*

Abruptly, he hugged her and left.

Anna ran to the shower.

Under the hot water, she used every aromatic product in the luxurious bathroom, scrubbing furiously at her body with the coarsest sponge she could find.

"I still smell bad! Why?" she said out loud. "I am still dirty."

"I am still dirty! How come? I smell terrible! Why?" She could not stop talking to herself.

She did not understand. Hamad did not smell bad; on the contrary, his body scent was intoxicating, he was very clean and well-groomed, but Anna felt that her whole body stank. The terrible odor was in her hair, on her breasts, her neck, between her thighs… Everywhere *he* had touched…

Then she realized what it was. It was the scent of corruption and shame! She was polluted…

Anna had started to want more from life!

The more that life gave her plenty to be satisfied with, the greedier Anna became, not needing but desiring more. As each chance of a glittery temptation enchanted her eyes and captured her heart, that bad odor in that hotel suite in London stayed on Anna for a very long time.

She got used to living with that corruption scent until Joe walked into her life and helped resurrect her dead conscience and every value she had contaminated with betrayal and dishonesty.

Next morning, she woke up to an annoying noise. Someone was repeatedly knocking on her door.

It was her private butler, asking if she wanted to go downstairs to have breakfast with her friends.

"No! Thank you. Just get me a cup of coffee here!" she replied.

As she lazed in bed, the diamond watch caught her eye.

The price of surrendering my body to the sheikh, she thought, but then she tried to disperse her guilty thoughts. *Am I a woman unworthy of respect and dignity?*

A couple of minutes later, there was another knock on the door.

"Open the door! It's me!"

Saliha!

Anna opened the door.

"What is wrong? Are you ill, Anna?"

"He came to me last night." Anna burst into tears. "Then he left! It wasn't how I expected it to be! He used me and dumped me, he got me a diamond watch as payment for my sexual services, how stupid of me, and I couldn't say no, I am an official hooker. Where is he now? "

A flood of tears gushed down Anna's cheeks.

"Relax, I know." Saliha hugged her.

"How do you know?" Anna sniffed to resist her tears.

"Calm down! Drink this coffee." She handed Anna the mug of coffee she'd brought.

"I'm not blind. We all saw how you two were dancing, and he is downstairs, asking about you."

"By the way, how was the sex?" Miriam asked, rushing in through the half-open door.

"Be quiet. Have some manners!" Saliha scolded her.

"It was awful."

"We didn't like it either at the beginning. You get used to it."

"You could tame him." Miriam giggled.

"Me? Tame him? Is he a wild horse?" Anna was surprised. "He got what he wanted; it's over."

"He will be back for more, trust me! But you should know how to control him."

"Didn't you say that he loved his new wife?"

"That part of the story was a scenario we created; we've rarely seen him look at other women, unlike Rasheed. Anyway, I said 'loved' not 'in love,'" Saliha replied.

"He is very selective, I think," Miriam said. "But we sought to warn you indirectly."

"But he is a sheikh!" Anna shouted. "How could I say no?"

"Don't yell, drink your coffee, wash your face. Hamad is just like any man, in his everyday life responsibilities and with his title. He is a sheikh, got it?"

"I'm trying to." Anna took a sip of coffee.

After an hour, when Anna was calmer, they went downstairs.

Hamad was looking at her with desire.

After a week playing in the private lounges of the casinos, of shopping and partying, she returned with gifts and with a beautiful diamond watch, a diamond necklace, and a closed envelope from Hamad.

Now she owned a new phone with a British mobile number.

"I will use it to contact you."

"All right!" she responded.

Without even knowing where she belonged in his life, Anna was careful with her expressions and didn't want any wrongdoing on her part to ruin her relationship with Hamad.

When she reached Lebanon, she went directly to the bank. She gave them the envelope, which included £35,000. She had not even known there was so much money in it.

Her bank account was piling up, but so was her guilt.

The relationship continued between Sheikh Hamad and Anna.

Their conversations revolved around jokes, the funny incidents of daily life, and their plans for which country to meet in. He avoided any serious discussions about personal worries or the expression of emotions.

The very subjects Anna needed to talk about most did not interest His Royal Highness.

They met two months later in London again. This time they were heading from there to another destination in the Gulf by private jet.

Anna had never been on a private jet in her whole life.

It was comfortable, ample, and luxurious. Though from outside it looked smaller than other planes, it was extended for only two people, with an entire flight crew. It even had beds, a bar, and a shower.

They enjoyed the Gulf together for only four days.

Anna's visa in her passport had come via an invitation from the royal family, so she did not have to wait in line for any check-in policies at customs, which made her feel special.

The sheikh did not accompany her; she had to go through customs with two bodyguards; despite this, it was evident that she was with him, yet no one dared even to gossip in public. No one wanted to get in trouble.

Employees even controlled their facial reactions; they were just the ordinary class, and the other party featured royal family members!

Anna was not the first guest of a royal family member, and she was not going to be the last.

During their relationship, Anna was introduced to many powerful and wealthy people in the Gulf, England, and even in continental Europe on the sheikh's behalf. Regardless of their interest in Anna's show, they all promoted their companies on the television screen during the show itself, merely to see an appreciative smile on the sheikh's face.

The income of those contracts brought more success to her show and her bank account. Her viewer ratings skyrocketed, and that year she recorded the second most-watched television show in the whole Arab world.

Anna was growing more and more successful in the world of celebrities; she was grateful for her persistence and education, which would have meant nothing if Hamad's prestige had not existed in her life to highlight her hidden and valuable talents.

Soon they became more intimate in bed.

Now she was enjoying every single touch from Hamad; she did not feel she was being treated as a sex slave anymore. She climaxed with her eyes closed, thinking of happy future plans rather than enjoying that excellent moment in which all a woman's senses meet at the apex of complete pleasure, where she is lifted spiritually to heaven via the utmost physical and emotional satisfaction.

Anna could not be sure whether she'd succeeded in taming the dominant sheikh in lovemaking or she would become used to be his sex slave. Nothing was clear.

Anna and her sheikh started meeting more often in different countries.

Their trips were always short in duration, but she traveled with him all around the world.

They met in whichever country Hamad decided on, and each returned alone; often they took his private jet, which was always a joy for Anna.

Anna grew used to this adventure, and her husband never bothered asking; though he was not stupid, his love for her was replaced by a greater love defined by money, dependence, and a casual lifestyle with no dignity. Those were Vasag's greatest desires, which led him to places in his heart as dark as Anna's.

The difference between them was that Vasag only cared for money without ambition, while Anna, on the other hand, wanted her dreams to come true, and her adventures came with the package.

Nothing is free in life, so besides what was discussed in public during interviews and conversations, every celebrity hid behind a different mask.

The phone was ringing. It was nearly seven months since the first time Anna had met Hamad.

"Saliha! I am worried. I've been calling Miriam, but she isn't responding."

"I know," Saliha answered sadly, "I can't find her either!"

"What? What do you mean?" Anna's heart started to race, and her entire skin went cold.

"She had a huge argument with Rasheed. While we were together, she called him, but it was Her Royal Highness who answered the phone. I do not know how she got her hands on that phone, as he used to hide it in his office drawer!" Saliha sighed.

"Then?" Anna was tapping her foot quickly.

"The princess asked who it was! I didn't hear Her Royal Highness's voice because the mobile wasn't on speaker, but I was next to Miriam, who yelled, 'I am Miriam, and I am pregnant! He will have another heir from the royal blood and my own common blood! Get ready!' Then she hung up the phone. It was a disaster, Anna!" Saliha was crying.

"Calm down, please! I wish I were there."

"Rasheed called back two hours later, and they had a big argument over the phone. Miriam kept repeating 'No! No! No! That is impossible, I am not going to get rid of my baby, and you do not decide it!' I tried to calm her down, but she didn't listen to me, and she kept on shouting on the phone!" Saliha stopped talking.

Anna could hear her weeping; she could not find the words to reassure her.

"Please tell me what happened then." Anna insisted on knowing the rest of the story.

"Then?" Saliha sighed. "She left my place. Next day she didn't come back, so I still waited a couple of days hoping she would appear or answer my phone calls. Rasheed didn't contact me, so I packed everything and returned to my country. I kept this phone number, in case she ever needed to reach me, I checked her villa before leaving, and four days after her mobile was off. She was nowhere to be found; her clothes were all there, jewelry, car, everything was still in her house. I asked the servants, and they said they had not seen the madam."

"What? Oh, my God!" Anna was crying.

"Yes, they started arguing when he wanted to get rid of the child, and she wanted to keep it."

"Didn't she use birth control?"

"I think she fell in love with Rasheed and wanted to be in his life forever; she probably thought a baby of his royal blood would be the shield to protect her love. She wanted neither to live in his harem with her child nor would she agree to an abortion. She refused both choices given to her by the sheikh. Now, with the five-month-old baby inside her womb, she has disappeared; she is nowhere to be found."

Anna was shivering.

"Miriam knew the road she was walking, yet after some time she could not bear to be controlled by the sheikh's orders, and she did not accept being subject to his decisions or under the control of his conditions, or his money. Everything Miriam had was not enough for her anymore. She was no longer an ordinary girl, quickly dazzled with a diamond ring; she wanted more from her life with Rasheed, which was a hazardous dream for an average person like her. She thought the path would be easy, but the sheikh holds his political reputation, his royal family, and his duties to maintain the image of the monarchy higher than anything else in his life."

Rasheed had been born with royal blood running through his veins—defined in Europe by the term "blue blood"—but Anna never believed in this, thinking, *they are also human who love, care, fight, and bleed red not blue blood when they are wounded.*

Time had changed the lifestyle of members of the monarchy in the Gulf; education, degrees in the best universities had established highly educated royals, but the modern lifestyle did not distract them from clinging to their royal duties and strategic and family decisions.

Miriam was never found again. The national police forces were never involved, and neither the embassy of her own country nor her family members interfered with the matter.

Did somebody hurt her? How could she disappear on her own? And pregnant! Or had Rasheed's wife found her and ordered her death in secret? Was she taken by force to Rasheed's harem for the sake of the baby, who had royal blood in its veins? Anna did not even dare ask Hamad.

No one knew anything.

Anna was devastated.

A couple of months later, Anna received another call from Saliha.

"I am traveling to France. I met a guy, and we are getting married and will be living there. I will text you my new phone number. You take care of yourself, Anna, promise me, and if you need anything, anytime, call me!"

Anna called her a couple of times since, but Saliha had found a new life, and Anna felt that she wanted to forget anyone, or anything related to her past and that Anna herself was part of Saliha's luxurious yet painful memories.

A couple of months later, while Anna was still with Hamad, they had a straightforward argument on the phone.

Anna was sad, suffering from the loss of her precious uncle, her mother's brother whom she loved dearly, while Hamad kept making jokes without sympathizing. She told him she was not in the mood, but he kept on joking. After telling him that what mattered wasn't being royal, was not a title written in a passport and inherited from parents by bloodline, it was being human and having compassion for others; Anna hung up the phone.

He never called her again.

One month later she called him, and he never responded.

Anna called him again, but after getting a response from a girl who asked her who she was, she stopped calling him.

Outrageous responsibilities, laws, and political duties gave Hamad burdens in his choices, Anna often thought after their argument.

Any ordinary girl in a royal relationship realized that such unions hardly ever endured.

Princes and kings had their princesses or queens officially, in social media, whose names went down in history as the mothers of the heirs of the new generation and the loving wives as their partners for a lifetime, while Miriam's name disappeared along with many others.

Beyond all the luxuries they owned—eagles, horses, palaces, harems, race cars—they also had other sports: the destinies of women.

Heavy is the head that wears a crown, Anna thought. *Yet how heavy should the burdens be on those hearts that must obey that weight so orders can be applied in the name of duty?*

Did Hamad ever love me? Anna often wondered.

After suffering alone with this thought for a couple of months, she called Saliha.

"He dumped me!" she said.

"Anna, I warned you: feelings are not accepted or understood as they should be when matters of the heart conflict with the rules and the doctrines of monarchies."

"Why did he leave me? Have I no right to say anything?" She felt like a used toy tossed aside by a toddler after he'd grown bored of it.

"We don't know if he left you because he was bored of you or because he was falling in love with you. Maybe that argument was just an excuse for him."

"Nonsense, how could he leave me if he loved me?"

"He loved you as a man, but he thinks like a sheikh when things get complicated."

"Why? Sheikhs are not men?"

"Sure, they are," Saliha replied, "yet they have the power to rule not only over their people but also over their own hearts when things become a hazard to them."

"I wasn't a danger!"

"I know that, but he doesn't," Saliha replied. "Hamad is a wonderful person, we both know it. Maybe he didn't want to be involved so deeply with you. He was aware that you could never be his, you are married, successful in your career and ambitious; you wouldn't have accepted living in his harem like the other girls. One way or another, it was going to end."

"Did he love me?"

"Anna, stop asking questions like a teenage girl."

Anna's heart was unable to understand how doctrines were written on paper, related to obligatory and political royal rights, how rituals devised to protect the royal families, could take Hamad away from her.

"He bleeds red when he is wounded, just like me." Anna's tears were falling freely.

"You're now very dramatic, Anna."

Many are unfortunate to be deprived of education, success in life, or any political power without inheriting royal blood, and do not have the opportunity to fulfill their fantasies. Simply, they do not have the resources to carry out their dreams.

Justice? There is no justice! Anna thought. *There are only rules to be obeyed. Duties to be executed, roles to be played, and life will go on.*

"It is easy to judge, blame, and punish, but Hamad did what should be done for your sake," Saliha said.

"It was hard to say no when temptation came…" Anna had run out of words.

"You can't judge a life you have heard about or seen but never lived yourself! One can never know the taste of the honey by its description;

it should be tasted not read or seen to sense its sweetness. Maybe Hamad loved you, but he loves his country and his family more."

"The only difference between them and the rest of us is not their perspective on life or their feelings, but the way they control their pain and hold it inside," Anna replied.

Anna saw Hamad's human side, his fears, struggles, disappointments, hopes, and joy, but she needed time to learn how to monitor her heart once more after such anguish.

"The secret of overcoming all is a power inherited by the royal blood!" Anna concluded.

Joe came back into Anna's office, and she snapped back.

"The tour was cool," Joe said happily.

"The definition of being a princess should be based on virtues! Not bloodline and power!" Anna muttered.

"What are you talking about Anna? Do you always jump from one subject to another?"

Anna sighed. "I am giving my opinion on the topic of the princess subject you mentioned earlier."

"Why do you bother yourself with such superficial issues?"

"Superficial?" Anna drew a fake smile on her face. "Never mind." She did not argue.

She'd never felt like a princess with Hamad, and she never felt unique around the wealthy and powerful Abbas, and yet Joe had the heart of a king that was beating honestly and nobly for her.

Joe interrupted her thoughts again.

"Aren't you hungry?"

"Do you want to eat? I can order pizza!" Anna said.

"No, thanks, I don't eat tomatoes!"

"Well, what then?"

"Hamburger."

"Fine, let me order."

"No ketchup, no tomatoes, please. How about you?"

"I eat everything," Anna said and laughed.

While eating, Anna could not stop staring at Joe; she was in love to the degree that her eyes were seeing him as the most handsome guy that had ever existed in the history of mankind.

As they were leaving the office, Kareem called.

"The lawyer will meet you tonight before she talks to Vasag tomorrow."

She'd previously informed Vasag about meeting him tomorrow.

Though Anna and Joe had plans to see her parents, they had to change them.

"I can't take you with me to a public place, Joe! Why don't you go meet my parents? Then I'll finish the meeting and come and join you."

"I don't think it is a good idea." Joe looked perplexed. "Your parents don't want me, and I have a weird feeling about this. Let us postpone it."

"No, please!" Anna squeezed his hand.

"Fine, but I'm telling you, this is not going to end well!"

Before Anna and Hashem dropped Joe at her parents', they stopped so Joe could buy a bouquet of flowers and a big box of baklava—Armenians' favorite sweet.

Anna phoned and informed her parents that he was coming.

They dropped off Joe and left. Half an hour later, as Anna reached the location of the lawyer's meeting, her cousin Tila called.

"We are in trouble, Anna."

"Why? Did my parents humiliate Joe?"

"No, though they weren't pleased having him around; you know your mom and dad are respectful enough not to disrupt anyone who enters their house."

"So?" Anna was in a panic.

The lawyer sitting in front of Anna understood nothing of the Armenian language, asked for two coffees, and waited for Anna to finish her phone call.

"While I was in the kitchen making coffee, Joe said he wants to build a loving home with you, and Mom replied that he should not be the reason for your own home to be destroyed because you are already married."

"Then?"

"'I'm not ruining anything,'" Joe replied, adding that if your home weren't already being destroyed, he wouldn't be in your life."

"Then what?" Anna was agitated. "You could have told me this when I returned."

"Listen!" Tila continued. "He said he wants to marry you! Moreover, he would not lie about anything because if he did, he would destroy his own life too, binding his faith to yours with marriage. Your father interfered, asking him how he could ask for someone's hand who's already married, and the conversation continued when the doorbell rang, and Vasag walked in."

"What?" Anna was in shock. "Where, there? Now?"

"It's okay. I handled it!"

"What is that idiot doing there?"

"He had come to make an attempt to stop the divorce."

The lawyer looked at her watch. "Do you want to delay our meeting for another time?"

"No, give me five more minutes," Anna said apologetically. "This is an emergency."

The lawyer nodded and took a sip of coffee.

"I went in," Tila continued on the phone, "and told Joe to come to the kitchen."

"So? Then? Where is he now?"

"I took the coffees in, and Joe is in your parent's bedroom. Vasag thinks he's my boyfriend."

Anna called Hashem. "Please go get Joe!"

Once she told Tila she was sending over her driver, she continued her meeting with the lawyer.

Anna and Joe met later that night. He told her that he was not mistaken about his weird feeling and filled in the details about how he saw Vasag—the arrogance of her husband, the way he talked to her parents as if he owned the whole world, a cigar in his hands, dressed in such fancy clothes. He added that her parents had told him they did not interfere with Anna's decisions and that she was mature enough to decide what is best for herself.

"I told that idiot not to annoy my parents!" She ground her teeth.

Anna called and thanked her parents later that night. She and Joe spent the night at a hotel till the morning light.

Next day, while taking her morning coffee, Anna thought about the coincidences in her life. Her past and present loves had been in the same room yesterday!

As she stepped into the shower with Joe, she knew he was not her present but her future.

Joe was leaving two days later, and Anna was trying to spend every precious moment with him.

While they were on their way to her aunt's house, Kareem called.

"The divorce lawyer talked to Vasag to sign the divorce papers. He wants you to give everything you own to him; otherwise, you have to wait for the procedures of your church, which will take over a year. He wants the house, all your money, the two cars, and you are going to pay for all the expenses, which will be overvalued at eleven thousand dollars," Kareem explained.

"I just need one car. Let him bring my books and the rest of my clothes and give him everything!"

"Are you sure?" Kareem sounded shocked. "You have worked so hard for everything!"

"I don't care for material stuff! I will give away everything just to get rid of him. Let her prepare the papers, and I will come sign today, in the afternoon."

Anna signed the papers that afternoon, giving away everything she'd ever worked for, including the maid she had ordered.

She paid for everything with Joe's help, who withdrew money from his credit card. She asked for an advance from the TV station, and they paid her.

Three days later, everything was done! She had her divorce papers.

Joe had already gone back to Canada to prepare everything and return after a month for their wedding.

Anna was living at her aunt's house continuing at her job; except for her salary at the TV station, she had no income. Joe had left his credit card with her in case she needed anything extra. She had resigned from her post at the magazine because she intended to leave everything for good, and she could not make business trips anymore.

Joe was poor financially but rich in his heart.

Vasag had gotten everything Anna had worked for in her life, but in return, she had gotten the most important thing back from Vasag: her life!

The Alphas of the Living Kingdom

CHAPTER 10

It was a warm afternoon. Anna was sitting in the waiting room in Dr. Richy's clinic drinking hot cappuccino. Joe had returned to Canada early that morning promising to be back after thirty days.

Lebanon is crowded with beautiful women; they adore fashion and nightlife, and they love their families. However, as a small country with the highest rate of Christians and the most religiously diverse society in the Middle East and its fashion and free nightlife, Lebanon inspires the rest of the world to be the idealistic place of diversity, cohabitation, equality and women's rights .

An elegant woman entered Dr. Richy's waiting room. Anna recognized Dina—early thirties, mother of two children. Dina was one of those women like Anna who were always insecure about their outer appearance.

"Doctor, do I need this? Doctor, do I need that?" were Anna's usual questions, while she held a mirror in one hand and pinpointed small details on her face with the other. "Look here, Doctor... I mean when I smile... when I cry... when I frown..."

Dr. Richy's personality with his patients was one of calm, positive energy; he was a respectful, honest, and generous person, and one of the best plastic surgeons in the Middle East.

He had won many awards, and he had participated in numerous international conferences as a guest speaker presenting his latest accomplishments as a specialized expert in the world of plastic surgery.

"Hello, my precious," Dina greeted Anna.

"My beautiful Dina," Anna replied. "Seems we should wait because as usual I came without an appointment and the doctor is busy. He has two consecutive operations, one liposuction and the other a face and neck lift."

"That's all right, me too," Dina replied. "My kids are with the nanny, and my husband drove me here. I just have to call him to inform him that I am going to be late too."

Dina called her husband while Anna sat admiring Dina's beauty and luck.

She has everything. I wish I were in her shoes, Anna thought. *Beautiful kids, a housewife, a loving husband who spoils her.*

"It isn't worth going home then returning because we will be spending most of the time in traffic," said Dina after hanging up her phone.

The two women occasionally met at the clinic and had short conversations.

"Being at Dr. Richy's clinic is my soul spa," said Anna. "I couldn't let a week pass without seeing him."

"I agree," answered Dina with a smile. "So, what is new with you, Anna?"

"Nothing especially new, although every week there are new stars to interview on my show. But at least I took a break from attending conferences; I hate traveling," Anna replied, hiding the fact that she wanted to spend more time with Joe.

"I adore traveling the world," Dina responded with a sigh. She rested her head on the back of the sofa and took a deep breath as if she was in an open field smelling the scent of the roses.

"You must be kidding me," said Anna, laughing.

"No, not at all," continued Dina. "I can be free. I can do whatever I want."

"Free? Why? Are you a prisoner in jail? You have everything any woman desires in life."

Dina was silent; she looked down at her wedding ring.

At that moment Anna felt that Dina's ring told a story of pain, lies, and fear as if the story of her sad life was written on that tiny diamond ring.

"Look at me, Dina. Did I say something to offend you?" asked Anna. She realized she did not even know Dina very well.

Anna was thinking about changing the subject when Dina pulled her head back abruptly, took a ribbon out of her Chanel handbag, tied her hair up, and continued.

"No, you said nothing wrong, Anna, but I wish I had your life."

"My life?" Anna giggled. "Yes, sure you do; a world of frustration, responsibility, and competition."

"That is how you see it? I see it as a world of power, independence, fame, and money."

"But you have a comfortable life, children, and a great husband; you have things I do not have," Anna replied.

"True… but as I see your world, that's how you see mine." She sighed.

"What do you mean?" Anna was curious; leaning forward she balanced her elbows on her thighs and rested her face in her hands. "Now tell me why you are so sad?"

"Nothing you can solve," said Dina with a deep sigh. "Let's go out to the balcony. Do you mind? I want to light a cigarette."

"Sure." Anna stood up quickly. "Let's go. I do smoke hookah like a train," she said in an attempt to make Dina laugh.

They walked to the balcony.

It was a cloudy afternoon but not very cold. Dina lit a cigarette.

"Do you know that my husband has other women in his life who dare to call him anytime, even if the children are at home? He takes the phone and goes to another room; he has no respect for my feelings."

"What?" Anna was shocked, though she had a similar life with Vasag. "But he does not look that type at all," she continued, thinking of her own story.

"He is a sociable person, a loving husband, a perfect father," Dina said bitterly, raising the cigarette to her lips as if she was inhaling with the nicotine her pain. "I have no luck in life. He beat me a couple of times—"

"No way! Why?"

"I faced him and said that if he continued his adventures with other women, I would leave him. He hit me!" She lowered her head.

Anna realized that Dina was suffering, that though she did not know Anna, she had swiftly started talking about such details.

"I wish I could exchange my life with yours, Anna!"

My life is full of lies. I don't have your courage to confess it, maybe, and if you were famous you wouldn't have dared to talk, Anna thought. "Where did he hit you?" she asked in a gentle voice.

"Here!" She showed Anna her lower back. "And here"—she showed her thighs. "And here"—her waist.

"Oh, my God!" Anna was in shock. "He is a beast. Tell your mom, take the kids, and go."

"Go? How? I have no education. I married him at a very young age, my parents depend on me financially, my other sister has five children, and her husband can hardly afford to bring bread to the table. My younger brother is always partying, and my other brother who lives in the United States with his family sends money to my parents only on occasion."

"So why did you say you will leave him? Where were you going to go?"

"I don't know. I thought he would be scared. Then there are my children—what will happen to them? I could live on the streets, but I can't hurt *them* with my decisions."

"So, he hit you because he didn't want to lose you?"

"No, he was angry because he said to make such a decision I must surely have a lover. He asked for my forgiveness after he saw me cry, said he was sorry, that he couldn't bear to see me with another man. He wasn't like this when we first got married. Through the years his violence escalated."

"But he is betraying you too."

"I told him. He said that he was a man, and I was a woman, and I would destroy the family honor if I left him."

"Sure, "Anna said and sighed. "He is a man." She felt lucky that she had Joe in her life.

"I am to be blamed too—I love shopping, do plastic surgeries… He is generous, but the alcohol is affecting him…"

"Stop it, Dina, are you crazy? These are stupid justifications; I saw him here with you! Give yourself some credit. He is nineteen years older than you; he has a sexy, loving wife."

Dina was smiling, but the pain in her eyes seemed like a virus that, once it struck somewhere in the body, needed time to heal.

"I can't even travel. Do you know that he can stop me at the airport? If he doesn't sign my passport, I can't leave the country," said Dina.

"Divorce him!" Anna shouted.

"Sure, you think it is easy? You do not have kids, and you have a loving husband."

Anna was ashamed of herself, but she kept quiet.

"It will take years; how will I pay the expenses? He will win the case, he knows influential people, has money, and he would say that I am a hooker and take my children from me forever. He already threatened this."

"No way, he can't, he has no proof."

"He doesn't need proof—he is a man, and he controls everything, even our sexual life. All men disgust me; I hate them… except for my baby boy!" said Dina, wiping a tear.

"Do you know the difference between duty and humiliation? Between lovemaking and rape?"

"It's my duty to sleep with him, that's my spousal duty. He tells me if I'm divorced, men will treat me as a hooker!"

"Let's go inside," said Anna, seeing Dina's pale face. She didn't know how to respond. "I will get you water."

"Women want equality? No, we just need respect and appreciation," Dina continued as they went back in and sat together on the sofa.

"True," Anna responded. "Nature created us differently, and we respect this difference. However, what women seek is to be taken into consideration as humans, and that our honor and feelings cannot be used as tools to keep us from asking our rights."

"Thank you! I don't want to be equal to men," Dina answered. "Tell me, how come if a man betrays a woman he is called a womanizer, yet a woman betraying a man is known as a hooker? Therefore, all womanizers should be called male prostitutes."

They both laughed, and Dina continued after drinking some water.

"'Don't get a divorce, you will destroy your family,' my mother told me when I told her about my husband. For her, divorce is the definition of the destruction of a family; for me, it's the declaration of the destruction that the unhappy marriage already is."

"No woman wants a divorce if she has a happy marriage. All girls dream of being a bride in the same way boys of a certain age prefer playing with cars or fighting with each other."

"He gives me money when I want," Dina continued, suddenly distracting Anna from her thoughts, "but he makes all the decisions over household resources because he tells me he works, and I don't."

"I beg your pardon? Because you don't *what...?*" Anna was angry. It reminded her of her own situation in the sense that even though she was the money supplier, Vasag always asked her about every penny. However, Anna did not bring up the subject, and she continued speaking. "But you take care of the children; you are a full-time mom. He doesn't own you like a car; you are a human being."

Dina was quiet; she stood up to get a cappuccino from the machine.

"He wants me to be elegant, Anna, I swear. He takes me shopping. He says I'm sophisticated. He even asked me if I want to go back to school."

"Yes, of course, he did, after or before hitting you?" Anna said, more as if she was talking to herself than addressing Dina. "He knows in Lebanon how people look at women over the age of thirty going back to school. He is telling you to do things he knows are impossible. He is smart and evil."

"Why do men think that nature has given them blessings to be wiser, more successful, and better leaders in every field?"

"They are not. They confuse the word *quality* with a superiority complex!" Anna laughed.

"You know, Anna?" continued Dina. "Jesus said when someone hits you on your right cheek turn him the other."

"But he isn't hitting your cheek; he's hitting your body and soul." Anna was shocked that Dina's heart was broken to the extent that she used verses from the Bible as justification for her self-destruction. "It is for being humble and not for being hit, raped, and abused. I am shocked that you think that way."

"Why, don't you believe in the Son of God?" Dina sounded surprised.

"Whether I believe in God isn't the issue; it's your logic that is irritating me."

"What can I do? This is my destiny!" continued Dina.

It is not your destiny, Dina! It's your choice. You are afraid of the consequences; so, what if you are going to be poor, not be able to live with your children, and might have to struggle in court? Who cares what people think about you? What matters is what you think and know about yourself. Don't you have self-determination? You fear to lose your comfort, but to choose deception, humiliation, and imprudence? Nothing is achieved without sacrifice. You do not deserve freedom. You are selfish, Dina. Anna didn't dare say any of these thoughts out loud because she too had been selfish, scared, and lost.

"Hundreds of years ago, countries were led by many powerful queens like Elizabeth I of England. In the Middle East, history glorifies the power and the strength of Cleopatra, the queen of Egypt. Regardless of the mistakes made in history, which are nothing compared to the ones made by male leaders that led to the destruction of countries, queens were not perfect, but with their love, passion, and patriotism they ruled countries. Many powerful emperors in history ruled either by the inspiration or the support of their queens. While ruler queens led their countries even as virgins—without the need of a man either on the throne beside them or officially in their bed—they were complete."

"I wish I were a queen," said Dina.

"You are with your heart." Anna hugged her.

Men in Lebanon are absolute; even their God has a male gender. The tension between men and women is a result of the non-recognition of female abilities, and the lack of equality commensurate with their gender differences—rules in Anna's society were applied according to religious and political laws, assessed injustice, based not on conscience but on gender.

Anna always questioned why religious men in the highest positions in the Christian religion were not permitted to marry.

Dina was correct in her way of thinking; she was scared not because she was selfish, as Anna thought, but she knew that regardless of her husband's behavior both Christian and Muslim courts would award custody of the children to the father, and the mother would be stripped of custody rights after a certain age, according to the gender of the children.

Dina was Catholic, a church that did not accept divorce, only separation. Christian men can convert to Islam and are able to remarry or have three more wives without getting a divorce, while Christian women do not have the right to enter a new marriage without the termination of their first marriage. The high costs of religious courts—which often take years—accompanied by the inherent psychological and social abuses are all aspects of the manipulation and barriers used as tools to destroy a woman's will. These burdens banish a woman's hopes for a happy future, not only as a mother or as a wife, but even as a respected member of Lebanese society.

The theories of true love that stem from female brain neurons are beautiful fantasies, elaborate scenarios of happiness and joy that play games with the hopeless minds of women, that result in soul-destroyed women like Dina, destined to share a lifetime with a man who owns her as a piece of furniture in his house rather than share a happy life with her.

Some women react differently; some fight evil with evil, justifying the concept of "The end justifies the means," but during this struggle, they risk losing their way. In their helpless effort, women who resort to using any weapon to fight back for life and rights unwittingly become vicious and merciless creatures.

Men brag they are the head of the family, as is mentioned in stories. Therefore, they are the brain. On the other hand, women are the neck, so they move the head toward the direction they desire. So that is why Anna believed that the only way to capture once and for all any human being, even from ancient times, was execution via the neck; her own theory was that the best tactic to destroy a life was by cutting the neck.

A woman like Dina could keep quiet and live in deception and sorrow as a victim for the rest of her life, or she could transform her pain into power and rise back to her feet to regain her hope for happiness. But at what cost?

A cost that Anna had paid many times in different ways to her success and freedom. As she rose from the level of living fantasies to become an achiever by following her goals in her business life, she thought she deserved to have a chance of true happiness away from lies, deception, and dishonesty.

Dina did not know yet that Anna had left Vasag and was already preparing to marry her new lover.

Dina's pain contained a memory for Anna; she recalled one of the worst situations in her own life that hadn't brought her honor, yet she had gone through with it at the time just to reach a goal.

It was a period in Anna's life when she had been no more a part of the comedy group, and though she had made a name in the world of celebrities, she needed a new hit to keep her fame.

During this time, she had heard from Amar, her actress friend who did casting for a company and who'd taken a small role in a huge drama series. Anna wanted the major part; she would never have agreed to go for any role.

A few weeks later, Anna paid a visit to the company with a box of chocolates and met Olivia, the producer, a beautiful lady in her mid-forties. Anna never mentioned anything about wanting a role in the series.

Jawad, the CEO, had inherited the company from his father; he was newly married, a tall, fetching guy in his early thirties with eyeglasses and long hair. He was classy and educated.

The director Olivia was a kind woman. Anna was thrilled; she had no work then, so she often went to have coffee with her, hoping they could be good friends and that Olivia could help her land a role in the new TV series they were preparing to broadcast on an international television station.

Anna often waited in her room for hours while Olivia met with her boss. Olivia would eventually emerge with a smile free of lipstick, with her beautiful silk blouse all wrinkled.

Olivia had a dominant personality; she had a beautiful body and a charismatic brunette beauty.

"Come on, Anna, let us have some coffee!" Olivia always welcomed her with a hug.

Whenever she came out of her boss's office, Anna smelled men's cologne on her.

After a couple of meetings, Olivia told Anna that the CEO was interested in seeing her alone.

"Hello, Mr. Jawad. You wanted to see me?"

"Yes, please take a seat. You are a lovely young girl."

Suddenly Jawad approached her and started to kiss her neck.

Anna was in shock.

Her brain could not process what was happening. The shock paralyzed her body, and she could not decide what to do. Run? Shout? Hit him? However, he smelled so good, Vasag's love was vanishing in her heart, and Jawad was very tempting. A couple of minutes later, and Jawad was kneeling before her.

She spread her legs voluntarily, and he began to taste her talents.

After half an hour, she left his office. She did not know what to tell Olivia.

"Is everything okay, Anna?"

"Yes," Anna replied, rushing downstairs to the new silver BMW that she was leasing, her first car.

Did she know what had happened in there? Was she trying to get words out of her mouth? Anna was embarrassed.

Next day, same time, Anna was on the couch with Jawad who appreciated her talent more thoroughly.

Why not? Anna thought while his hands were discovering her senses with delicate touches. *He's an attractive chestnut-haired guy. I can't refuse the temptation; maybe he will help me.*

A couple of weeks later, Jawad asked Anna for a weird favor, out of the blue.

"Now I want to see you with Olivia!"

"What?" Anna was in shock.

"Yeah, I want to see you with her."

"Are you crazy? We are girls."

Anna argued, but that night she left with Olivia. They drove to Olivia's house where she was alone, her children with their grandparents and her husband overseas.

Anna lay naked in Olivia's bed, waiting for her to come in after her shower.

"Are you sure you're okay, Anna?" Olivia asked from the bathroom, almost as if she was checking if Anna needed anything else from the kitchen before they started dinner.

"I'm fine," Anna replied. "Thank you."

She lay still under the sheets, totally naked, like a victim waiting for her executioner who was getting ready with her ax to come and decapitate her.

It was an execution with no interrogation.

"Relax! Just look into my eyes," Olivia whispered as she entered the room and crawled into bed.

"Okay, I am fine."

Anna felt Olivia's soft body on hers; she had never felt a woman's touch before, never known how it felt. It was sweet and arousing.

Oh, my God, am I lesbian? Anna was worried. *I'm enjoying this. I am not going to enjoy a man's touch after this.*

Anna was inexperienced—she did not know that a woman's touch is desirable by both sexes, regardless of whether one is lesbian or not.

Olivia kissed every inch of her body.

Anna was stressed.

"Relax, Anna, let it go. See? The phone is open, Jawad can hear us, and he is on the line."

Anna did not know how all this had been planned; was she a victim, was this a scheduled game or was she becoming a prostitute just to get a significant role? Yet she was enjoying it.

What kind of life should someone with Anna's strong character face after falling on her knees in front of her new destiny? Wasn't she someone who'd fought her whole life? Wasn't she high, glorious, and fearless? What had happened to her? How had she ended up like this? When had life struck her? Or had she decided to hit herself?

Olivia knew where to touch her, how to please her, even better than Vasag and Jawad.

She is older than me; she has experience. No, but she is married! Anna thought. *Oh, maybe because she is a lesbian.*

Anna was enjoying it because Olivia knew when and where to touch her to arouse all her senses, how to kiss, how to breathe on her body, how to make her tingle and stimulate her with her soft, feminine finger.

They were both moaning. Anna was satisfied, and so was Olivia. They took a shower together, and they hung up the phone. They went out for dinner late that night, and Olivia brought Anna back to her place.

Two days later, Olivia and Anna were in a great hotel suite with Jawad. He was very turned on watching the two women kissing and touching , rubbing their bodies against each other. Then Olivia invited Jawad to join them, and he could not get enough from both women.

Anna was younger than Olivia, and Jawad was more taken by Anna. Both Jawad and Olivia tasted every inch of Anna's body with lust, like wild animals.

It was an adventure. The suspense that had started with fear, disgust and a sense of obligation ended with pleasure and satisfaction for Anna.

The pain haunted her when she returned to her little apartment where she did not have hot water. She heated it on the stove and took a hot shower to clean away the dirt off her body, but as much as the water was hot and as much as she used soap to scrub at her body, she felt dirty.

She needed more than soap and hot water to clean away the shame. Also, she did not care; she wanted a career.

After a couple of months, Anna's new series was playing on international television screens. She was shining again.

Jawad had given her a vital role in the massive production.

A year passed by, and one day Anna met the owner of an economic magazine in another entertainment magazine office during an interview. Walid offered her a post as a marketing manager, promising her that she would have her consultant and a good salary.

Anna took the deal.

That was the time when she had met the sheikh.

Walid followed through as promised and gave her an office, her secretary, and a high salary. After a couple of months, she placed a down payment on a luxurious apartment.

She was now a marketing manager for one of the most eminent economic magazines in the Middle East, and she was traveling once a month to attend every conference held for Arab businessmen.

She attended seminars and met influential people all around the world, interviewing them. Her trips featured first-class VIP treatment, and the best hotel suites and butlers—all the luxury one could dream of.

Meanwhile, she also started her own TV show, owned two cars, a great apartment, a summer chalet, a servant, and a husband who served hookers at cabarets with her own money.

She was excited in the beginning, traveling all around the world, her work life hectic, with significant responsibilities. She loved it. She was in contact with politicians, influential people, and diplomatic personalities around the globe, interviewing them, dining with them, having fun, feeling special, and admiring herself.

Her success had overpowered her grace. She did not cry anymore, she had no time for people, and she had her own world.

A new Anna had been born. Everything she wore, every diamond watch she fastened to her wrist, every piece of gold she chose, every car she drove, all were expensive, far more valuable than her soul and her conscience.

The television station was owned by a prolific and a famous journalist in the Arab world, Mrs. Minwa. She taught Anna the competence to shape her objectivity and to increase her conceptual speed.

Anna's ability to connect with the audience through effective communication made her famous.

She worked from nine a.m. to seven p.m. at the magazine; afterward, her driver took her to the TV station, where she worked until the early morning hours.

Soon her show was ranked one of the best live television shows in the Middle East—it was daring, featuring celebrity scandals. Anna's marriage, like most marriages, lacked the actual concept of the marital union: devotion, love, respect, sacrifice. None of these qualities existed except their lovely pictures in the magazines standing in front of the press, hand in hand and smiling for the cameras.

She rarely talked to Olivia or Jawad anymore. But if they met at galas, at invitations, she barely greeted them.

At the time, Anna knew that if she wanted to take, she must give in return. Some were unlucky—they gave and received nothing, while others gave and eventually got back so much more than they offered. The most unfortunate ones ended up with nothing, left chatting idly with bored strangers about their past glories, covering for their present failures with the hope of a future miracle.

I was lucky, Anna thought. Though she had given away a lot to succeed, she had reached her goals slowly, and by giving away value and dignity had collected in return fragments of inner satisfaction in her pursuit of fame, which had crushed many of her valuable qualities.

Anna's thoughts were distracted by Dina's voice.

"Where are you, Anna? You look distracted."

"No." Anna snapped back to reality.

Then she realized she was still in front of Dina at the doctor's clinic, and those experiences were just memories now.

I could give hope to Dina to motivate others.

However, Anna knew that she was only able to do that with words since she was so often stuck in a Gordian knot.

She never thought about what price one might pay to start a revolution like that for the whole society.

Anna was living in a world of men, but soon she was going to create her world: Anna's world!

The secretary, Talar, came in. "Yes, the doctor will see you now, Dina."

"Okay." She stood and turned to Anna. "Thank you, Anna, for listening to me. I know it will be our secret."

"That is your secret, sweetie. I have no right to share it with anyone," replied Anna.

"I adore you," said Dina and rushed to the doctor's clinic.

After forty-five minutes, it was Anna's turn.

"What is wrong?" Dr. Richy asked when he saw Anna's unsmiling face. She neither approached nor hugged him as she usually did.

"What is wrong with *you?*" Anna replied. "You men! You are you so rude! Why? I mean, why do you think you are wiser and superior to us?"

"No one is superior to anyone," Dr. Richy replied.

"No, I do not mean you as one man. I'm talking men in general." Anna started to calm down.

Dr. Richy laughed. "Is this a new episode of your show? I mean you, did you come here to see me and check your face or to attack men through me?"

"No, no, not at all. I didn't mean that at all, but I don't think you men see how passionate and energetic we women are," continued Anna.

"You are wrong, Anna. Not all men think the same. Do I ever underestimate your intelligence and abilities? As a man, as a doctor, or even as your best friend?"

"Men have justifications for their every wrong path, whereas women must be punished for any misdeed. If a man does something wrong, a woman must be patient. But if a woman commits an evil deed, he has the right to let her go. If any woman is sick, a guy has the right to let her go, but if a woman leaves her husband after he is diagnosed with an incurable disease, the whole world will persecute her. A wife should follow her husband until the end of time, but the husband has the right to stop at any exit along the way."

"Come on, Anna! You know I always say, 'Behind every great man, there is a greater woman supporting him.'"

"I know," Anna said. "I'm so sorry. I am not sure why I suddenly had to throw all my anger at you."

"Why? Because I am a man, or because I am your friend?"

"Maybe both."

They laughed.

"Let's check what you need." He approached her face, checking every detail. "Perfect, you need nothing."

"When will we do a curl lift? Don't I need anything here?" Anna persisted.

"No, you are still too young, and no more Botox for you. You should have some expressions on camera where you won't look like a statue. Let us grab a bite. By the way, what is going on with you? Did you leave Vasag? You had a fight? Are you okay staying at your aunt's place?"

"I'm fine. Don't worry about me! It's a long story."

"I have all night," replied Dr. Richy, grabbing his jacket. "Let me wash my hands, and we will go."

"Okay. I am waiting," Anna replied.

They went to a restaurant downtown. They entered and asked for the menu.

"I am opening a new chapter in my life. My whole life is in turmoil; it will collapse, I know, and will be shaken up in so many ways only to be repositioned, shifting my entire destiny in an utterly mysterious spine-chilling direction. However, I have you by my side, right?"

"My dear Anna, I am always there for you, don't ever doubt it. So, what is his name?"

"Joe. I met him on the internet, had a one-night stand with him, and will marry him."

"So typical, Anna." Dr. Richy laughed. "You know, anything you need, I will always support you?"

"Thank you, my friend, I know… By the way, about our conversation before…"

"Anna," said Dr. Richy, laying his fork and knife on the table, "I was thinking about what you were telling me at the clinic. I believe that not all men see women as inferior—on the contrary, they are scared of them because women are so competitive. Although men are more rational, the passion and the strong will of women make them great leaders without the compulsion to dominate the world. Maybe if women had been given a chance, the world would have been a better place than where we are today."

"I'm impressed." Her eyes lit up.

"I am a man. I am telling you, so see?"

"I am so happy you are my friend," Anna replied, gripping his arm.

"Your hands are smeared with ketchup!" Dr. Richy said.

"I am so sorry!"

They continued eating.

"The biological imperative of only women being capable of pregnancy, of childbirth, along with the fact that only men are able to impregnate them gave males the idea that they should be treated proportionately differently without observing the fact that the biological structure of both species applies not to a competition between the superiority and inferiority of differences but to the union between both women and men that holds the balance of the whole human species—not by competing but by completing each other," explained Dr. Richy.

On their way home in the car, Anna was quiet.

"Are you happy, Anna?"

"I will be with Joe, and you will one day have your own luxurious hospital."

Dr. Richy laughed. "You dream a lot."

"No, I don't, I live with hopes alone, and you will because you're the best."

"When is Joe coming back?"

"Thirty days from now; you will get to meet him."

"I am here for you, Anna, anything you need!"

"I just need you to be in my life as my friend and be at my wedding!"

"Of course."

In bed that night, Anna thought about all the things that had happened in her life, and that there was one more thing left to do before binding her destiny to Joe's.

She texted him; it was after two a.m. in Lebanon and after seven p.m. in Quebec.

Joe, I need to travel somewhere, alone.

You can do whatever you feel you should but be in Beirut when I am back!

It will take only three days. I can't be later than that for my TV show anyway.

I love you. Sleep now. You can use my credit card if you need extra money.

I will be okay. Thank you. Love you," Anna texted.

He neither asked and nor did she tell him where she was going.

As secretly as Anna's wedding dress was being prepared and all other arrangements were being made by her friends and assistant at the TV station, Anna would board a plane and leave Lebanon for three days.

I Hate You, Armenia!

CHAPTER 11

A week had passed since Anna told Joe she needed to make one last trip before they got married. The plane departed Lebanon. After long hours, they were finally landing.

Anna's heart started to pound; it was the first time she had traveled to meet her longtime lover. She was so anxious that Joe's image disappeared in her mind; she recalled pictures that had never been erased from her memory, from long before any men had walked into her life.

The fear of disappointment was worrying her; seeing him with her own eyes was bringing thoughts of anger and blame, yet she knew she had to come.

This lover was unlike any others she'd had—bold, unconquerable, and noble. Anna was stunned by his magnificence and charm, even in her dreams.

Ever since she became aware of her existence in the world, she had loved him. Since she started to distinguish varieties of love, Anna realized that her love for him was idiosyncratic and irretrievable.

How could I long to be with a lover and have the patience to wait thirty-two years to meet? How could I be in love with someone for so long and fall in love with other men? How am I in love with Joe now?

Why am I so hesitant of being loved back yet persist in appearing in front of him? I probably shouldn't have come; he already has other lovers. Will he even recognize me? These thoughts tortured Anna as the captain announced, "Welcome to Armenia."

It was a cold afternoon in February when Anna stepped from the plane, and she found herself surrounded by snow. Everywhere was white. The plane had landed in the field of the airport, and she had to walk with the passengers nearly two miles to reach the gates.

The lover who'd been imprisoned for seventy-one years had his freedom. He was free, out of jail, with no handcuffs on, and he was waiting to be with her!

She knelt, bowed her head, rested her hands in their leather gloves on the icy terrain, and kissed the snowy, freezing ground.

Instantly, Anna's imagination came to life!

The wind was blowing; it was a cold and stormy afternoon, but the sun as a faithful witness was faintly shining in the sky, illuminating with its rays this remarkable moment of destiny between the two lovers.

"Hello! My love! I am here finally to see you, be with you, and feel you!" Anna said softly, whispering, "I promised myself I'd kiss you the second I met you."

As she stood, her knees and hands were wet from the snow, and a couple of snowflakes were still on her face. But she didn't care!

The passengers were hurrying to get inside the airport.

Everyone was cold, yet Anna's heart was burning with fire.

She had only three days to spend with her lover, the lover who was unaware that Anna even existed. The lover separated from his only brother and left all alone, defenseless in the world. Yet he had had many lovers long before Anna was born.

The bold lovers had fought battles for him, rebelled against his jailers for his freedom, and died on battlefields trying to unite the two brothers. They were thrown in jails and had to work in camps seeking to defend the rights of their lover and his precious brother.

The brother was kidnapped at a very young age, captured by the enemy and raised against his will. The memory of his origin, roots, and language slowly vanished in his brother's mind.

Gradually, the faith of his ancestors as the first Christian country in the whole world was swept away in the brother's heart, and to survive, he converted to another religion.

Many of his brother's children escaped this inexcusable injustice and stayed alive, multiplied and became stronger, known to the whole world for their love and fidelity.

The compassionate love of so many for Anna's lover and his brother was inherited like crowns in royal families, from one generation to another.

The lovers are known as Armenians in the diaspora, and the fighters for his captive brother are called *fedayis*, a word derived from the Arabic *fedayeen*, meaning "those who sacrifice." They belonged to Armenian irregular units who voluntarily left their families, forming armed groups out of self-defense to protect their families and their loved ones from the Ottoman Empire and any other foreign forces that endangered the royal family of their lover.

Anna's lover is Armenia. He is old, born in 860 BC. The brother is named Cilicia.

Anna wept and ached for once-magnificent Cilicia, the homeland of her two grandfathers—Urfa, which was considered to be a holy place since it is believed that the Armenian alphabet was invented there, the legend tells that King Nimrod was going to set fire to Abraham, but God transformed the fire into water and the coals into fish. Seeing a white fish means going to heaven, as eating the fish of the holy pool of Sacred Fish in Urfa will cause one to go blind, as Musa Dagh is a mountain that consisted of six main villages, where Armenians resisted for fifty-three days against the enemy in 1915 when they received a deportation order from the Ottoman empire— those lands did not belong to Armenia anymore. Anna had long dreamed of seeing the liberated part of Armenia.

Armenia is the love of all Armenians everywhere. The passion for visiting their homeland is in each and every Armenian in the diaspora. Armenian poets, singers, writers, celebrities, actors, and even comedians in their own way describe their love.

"Armenia our love!" says every Armenian.

In Anna's heart, she saw Armenia, her lover, her Armenia.

As she headed to the hotel after her arrival, she was exhausted and sleepy.

I am breathing the air of my motherland, she thought; it filled her heart with joy.

The weather was frosty and bleak; The wind snapped at her face, Anna could no longer feel her nose, but she was content inhaling the irreplaceable breath of her lover.

Anna had made the reservation of the plane ticket and a hotel room so she could see Armenia alone before she bound her destiny to a man who was not Armenian.

Why did I never make the time to come and see you? she looked around as the driver stopped in front of a hotel and helped her with her luggage.

Was it the guilt of marrying someone who wasn't Armenian that had pushed Anna to make this trip, or was it a lonely period in her life after losing so much and not knowing what the future held for her? She did not know, but she was glad she had made this short but essential trip.

She had no clue what she could do in only three days. She had no relatives, no friends, no one.

It was just Anna and Armenia.

She went upstairs to her room, took a shower, and dressed; then she went down to the lobby, with no plans.

Even with no purpose or any plans, being there in her spiritual homeland gave her inner contentment.

A girl with skin white as snow, beautiful black eyes, and a friendly smile approached her.

"Hello, my name is Ani. What is your name?" the girl asked in English.

"Parev!" Anna said, meaning *hello* in Armenian. She jumped up from her chair. "I am Anna."

Though they spoke two different dialects, they could understand each other.

"You have such a beautiful accent," continued Anna. "It is like music to my ears."

"Thank you, so is yours. Where are you from, Anna?"

"I was born in Lebanon," Anna replied. "I am pure Armenian. Both my parents are Armenian, and my grandfathers are both survivors of the Armenian Genocide—one is from Urfa and the other from Musa Dagh."

"Welcome to Armenia. I'm pleased to meet you."

Ani spoke warmly, but she likely didn't know that Anna's heart was pounding vigorously with enthusiasm and excitement.

"I'm from the hotel's tour department," Ani continued. "Is there anywhere specific you would like to visit?"

"Yes, of course."

For Anna, everywhere was worth treasuring. Unfortunately, she had only three days.

"On Sunday we have a journey to Khor Virap, next Tuesday a tour to another monastery, on Wednesday the museum of ancient manuscripts, and the opera—"

"No! I can't! I only have three days. What can I do, what can I see in three days?"

"It depends on where your favorite place is. It is concise, your visit," Ani replied with an edge.

"Don't get me wrong: I wish I could live here forever, but I must go back very soon. My vacation is short, but I must return quickly to my TV show, and..." She stopped before she mentioned Joe.

"Oh, how exciting." Ani smiled.

"Yes, I have my own television show, but now I am here." Quickly, she changed the subject; she wanted to be the one asking questions rather than being asked how it felt to be in front of the camera and how she had made her dream come true.

Weird, I love bragging about my achievements, and now I'm avoiding talking about it? Anna was surprised at herself. Her priority was Armenia now.

She was talking more to herself than she was addressing Ani.

"I want to see the memorial monument. On my way, I will buy flowers for the memory of the victims of the genocide."

"No problem; that could be arranged, but it is going to be just you. Tomorrow at ten a.m. Is it fine with you, after breakfast? I will meet you here in the lobby, and the driver will take you."

"Sure, of course," Anna replied. "Thank you very much."

Ani left.

The lobby had red velvet embroidered sofas, mahogany pedestal tables, and colossal porcelain vases. Exquisite historical paintings decorated the walls, and the floor was covered with colorful handmade Armenian carpets. Anna listened to a young pianist who was playing a piece by the great Armenian composer, Aram Khachaturian. Then she ate her dinner and went to bed early.

Anna decided to stop by a flower shop the next morning and buy a big bouquet of mixed red, blue, and orange roses.

I am going to use the colors of my Armenian flag, she thought.

Her phone rang; it was Joe.

"Hello, my love, you worried me. Why didn't you call me when you arrived?"

"I'm sorry," she replied, wondering how she could have forgotten to call him all of a sudden.

"I am in Armenia." Anna giggled.

"I know, I thought that now you've seen Armenia, you forgot all about me."

"But how? I didn't tell you."

"I know you more than you know yourself," Joe replied with confidence.

"You're my love, how could I forget you?"

"Where are you? Are you going somewhere?"

"Tomorrow, my love."

"Well, then I'm going to hang up, get some rest. It's your last trip alone since from now on we will always travel together. Enjoy! Love you."

"I love you too. Bye."

In Anna's eyes, Yerevan was a patient; it had been bedridden for years, suffering from an acute disease, and after its recovery, it needed time to regain its strength. Like the patient with weak, trembling limbs from the effects of the illness, the city needed a chance to regain its strength in every way—spiritually, physically, and financially.

She believed in her people, and she was sure they would recover in time all that was lost. *With their determination they will overcome all difficulties and will defeat poverty and stand still once again,* she thought.

She was touched; everything held meaning for her. She was trying to see everything with her mind and not with her eyes in an effort to keep all the memories in her head when she returned to Lebanon.

She realized she missed Lebanon. She was born there; it was her homeland.

She was exhausted; she took a shower and went to bed.

Next morning Anna was in the car. After buying the flowers, the driver took her to the destination.

Buildings, shops, cars, the churches—everything was unlike anywhere else she'd ever traveled.

They reached the place. It was quiet. Anna asked the driver if he could wait to take her back to the hotel.

"Of course!" he replied. "Take your time."

She took the flowers and walked to the center of the monument. Although it was in the middle of winter, the place was decorated with all types of fresh roses and flowers.

The bright fire in the middle was impressive. It warmed Anna's face. The snow that covered most of the ground calmed her heart; though the wind penetrating her coat reached her skin and made her tremble, she did not care—the fire in her human heart was stronger than the winter cold around her.

This was the place I needed to see, she thought. It was a whimsical feeling, a combination of love, sadness, and excitement.

It was a feeling that cannot be described by words; it was a flash of the moment where the human heart shows its greatness and conquers the mind. Logic disappears, and tears of joy and sadness meet at the same time in the eyes of any Armenian who stands in front of an enormous scene as "Dzidzernagapert," the incredible monument.

She put down the flowers and knelt. Anna felt as if the gloomy, phantasmal voices of her ancestors mixed in the cold breeze were welcoming her.

The twelve imposing pylons around the fire represented the twelve provinces where Armenians were massacred, surrounded by the eternal memorial flame inside the fortress.

"What a unique piece of art; it is the altar of my soul," she whispered to herself.

She was on her knees; the enormous place had touched her heart so keenly that her tears had started to fall down her cheeks involuntarily. Rage interfered with her sadness, and a feeling of blame conquered her sensations.

She looked around her. A couple of people were wandering aimlessly, a family with young children were standing on the other side, teenagers gathered behind one of the pylons on the other side, and she was alone. Suddenly she felt the need to shout, slander, and protest.

"You can't pray, Anna; you are full of pain and anger in your heart." An inner voice was controlling her emotions. She let the questions come.

"Why did you leave me?"

"Why did you deprive me of you?"

"Why wasn't I born here?"

"Why did you leave your people to be adopted by other countries?"

"Why should I clarify each time someone asks me why I don't speak Arabic in my house with my family members?"

"Do you know how hard it is to be proud of a language when the people of the same country don't even understand it?"

"People laugh at my Arabic accent because I am used to speaking Armenian all the time; it is your fault."

"How can I hold a passport of a country and make mistakes in their language?"

"I hate you. I never even took my baby steps on your ground."

"I hate you for not letting me take my first breath in your arms."

"I hate you for not giving me back the lands of my grandfathers."

"I hate you because you never searched for us."

"I hate you for making me feel that I do not know where I truly belong."

"I hate you because rather than holding the flag of my homeland with pride I held the torment of my people's past."

"I hate you because I inherited living the grief of the genocide from my parents."

"I hate you for not giving me my true identity."

"Why didn't I have the chance to live on the soil of my forefathers?"

"It is all your fault. You left me!"

"I hate you."

"I have no land."

She felt as if the whole land had come alive, and its aching woe had touched her soul.

Armenia was sad!

She felt strange guilt and regret at the words she had uttered, the words she had spit out so loudly.

"No," she continued. "I don't hate you; I love you. That's why I hate you."

"Each day of my life I dreamed of seeing you."

"Answer me."

"I love you so much. You are not my lover; you are my father, my spirit, my identity, my existence."

She was sighing like an actor in a drama series, but this was a real moment, one of the most honest and authentic moments Anna had ever experienced.

"Do you know how hard it is to think in Armenian and talk in another language?"

"Answer me!"

She realized she was weeping. Another thought tortured her: Joe! He was not Armenian. She was raised to be married to an Armenian—not as a mark of disrespect to other nations but to multiply to prevent Turkey from reaching its aim: the vanishing of the Armenian race.

"I love him. Please forgive me for marrying him; I love him with all my heart! I paid my dues to my people and country. I did it the first time!

How can an Armenian be a good husband to me if he does not bring you pride as a human being in the first place?"

"Forgive me!" Anna was speaking out loud every single thought, as she kneeled in the freezing cold.

"Joe didn't choose to be born not Armenian any more than I decided to be born Armenian! Not that I am sad; I am proud!"

Anna's voice was raised, her head was bowed in front of the fire, and she was rubbing her face with an already used tissue stuffed in her coat pocket. Suddenly a hand touched her shoulder.

She jumped.

Her tears were mixed with mascara and the rest of her makeup.

"Are you okay?" asked a guy in his mid-fifties, while a woman standing next to him handed Anna a clean tissue.

The man held her arm, and she stood. She didn't know what to say; she was embarrassed.

It felt like an enormous moment.

Without any hesitation, they began talking to her in Armenian.

What a sensation! Someone is not knowing you at all and approaching to ask if you are okay, in your language.

"Yes, I am fine, thank you very much," she replied, trying to draw a smile on her face.

"We are all touched; it is okay, my daughter," the woman said. "It's okay to have such emotional moments filled with tears. We all share the same pain and have the same attachment and loyalty to our beloved Armenia and Ararat, our glorious, sacred, yet imprisoned mountain."

"We are from Australia!" added the man.

They shook her hand.

"I am from Lebanon." Anna smiled.

Their eyes were flashing with rays of pride, contentment, and gratification.

Anna had found her answer. She could see Armenia in their eyes, hear it in their language—the same historical pain and destiny they shared with her.

"We are all Armenians." Anna laughed.

Anna saw her pain in their eyes, as if the strength, the persistence, and the willpower of her whole people had been captured in this couple's Armenian chestnut-colored eyes.

Anna felt elation and relief.

Is it magic? No, it's the power of living and the sensation of patriotism.

At that moment, she realized that Armenia was not only the country itself, with its location on the world map, but it was also alive in every Armenian's eyes.

She hugged the strangers and left. On the way back to the hotel, she was happy. Though she did not have the time to see and explore all of Armenia in this short three-day trip, she went to buy souvenirs—tiny glass bottles filled with the soil of Armenia—and she dined in a beautiful traditional restaurant. But she was not alone; she was spending her time with her beloved Armenia.

All Armenians are vaccinated with the loving Armenian soul, she thought on the last night in her room. She was glad she would come.

Next day, Anna packed and left the hotel.

Stepping onto the plane, she promised Armenia she would come back. "I will bring Joe with me and introduce you to him. You will love him."

As the plane departed, Anna thought again that Armenia was the biological father of her existence. She felt Armenia was pleased, and serenity filled her heart.

"I am going to Lebanon to my other father who adopted me, loved me, cared for me, and gave me the chance to be who I am. We will never abandon you, we believe in you, you never left me; I was taken from you by force. Forgive my anger."

Extraordinary nations are challenged by extraordinary difficulties.

Armenians rose from the ashes to power. Scattered like so many other nations, yet they are strong, united, and patriotic.

When the plane landed, she called Joe.

"I arrived in Lebanon."

"I hope it was a good trip," Joe said in a low voice.

"Why are you talking like that? Are you okay?'

"Yes, I am. You woke me up."

"Oh, I'm so sorry. I always forget the time zone difference."

"No worries. Soon we will be waking up in the same time zone every day."

"You're so romantic. I love the way you talk to me."

"As I love everything about you, Anna... even your Armenia that I can never know about."

"You're too good to be true."

"How was it? Tell me."

"Go back to sleep, I will tell you later."

"No, tell me, I'm awake."

"I know no nation is perfect, but my love for my Armenia is perfect."

"You're so racist; how are you going to marry me?"

"I'm not racist, Joe, please correct your words: I'm patriotic."

"Okay, sweetie, whatever you say."

"Patriotism teaches the soul pride, respect, and gratitude, whereas racism fills the heart with hatred, denial, and an inferiority complex."

"Too much information to digest at such an early morning hour."

As Anna left the airport and Hashem drove her to her aunt's house, she felt happy to be back. She was grateful for Lebanon.

When Hashem asked about her trip, Anna told him she'd once thought she belonged nowhere, but after discovering the profound meaning of gratitude and patriotism, she now resided in both Armenia and Lebanon.

"I did not choose to be born in Lebanon, though I love it. If I am given the choice where to die, I wish to be buried in Armenia."

"Die? What kind of talk is that? You are getting married."

"Yes, you're right. I'm so excited." Anna smiled.

She texted a long message to Joe's number in Canada.

> I should like to see any power of the world destroy this race, this small tribe of unimportant people, whose wars have been fought and lost, whose structures have crumbled, literature is unread, and prayers are no more answered. Go ahead, destroy Armenia! See if you can do it. Send them into the desert without bread and water. Burn their homes and churches. Then see if they will not laugh, sing, and pray again. For when two of them meet anywhere in the world, see if they will not create a New Armenia.

She received a reply.

> Though I'm not intellectual, the words are powerful. Did you write it, Anna?
>
> Of course not. I wish. Those are lines by the great Armenian poet and writer, William Saroyan.

Joe texted her a kiss emoticon.

"Three was just my lucky number, but now I see it has other meanings..." She continued her conversation with Hashem as they neared home.

Hashem was used to nodding at Anna about subjects that didn't interest him much.

"I reached three important conclusions after my visit to Armenia. First, we rose from the ashes, so we won. Second, Armenia lives in every Armenian heart. And third, patriotism isn't about the bond of marriage to an Armenian guy but is about my pride and devotion to my Armenian roots."

"The third one is justification for your decision to marry Joe?" Hashem arched an eyebrow.

"I don't know. No, it isn't." Then she paused and sighed. "Yes, probably. I love Joe."

"I know, I was joking. I'm happy for you, Anna. You deserve it."

"So, do you," Anna replied.

Inside the apartment, her aunt welcomed her with a warm hug, and Doggy jumped for joy.

Hashem left.

"I have prepared for you a delicious lunch—chicken with rice, your favorite. Change your clothes, then come and eat."

They both sat down to eat.

"So how was Armenia?"

"Awesome. I wish I'd visited it before."

She told her aunt about her trip, finished her meal, and got up to prepare her hookah.

"Though I'm marrying Joe, I will teach my children their mother language and our history."

Araxi hugged her niece with tears in her eyes. "I'm so proud of you."

"My blood is Armenian, but my heart is Phoenician now, beating for Joe's love."

"Very poetic." Her aunt laughed.

Joe returned a couple of days later. Her parents were not happy with her new marriage, but she didn't care.

"You don't know him!" her mother exclaimed.

"I don't need to! If it bothers you that much, do not come to the wedding," Anna snapped.

It was Friday night, two days before the wedding day.

Anna was in a hotel room, sitting on the bed, hugging Joe.

"Joe! There are things you should know about me before we enter the church together."

"What things?"

Anna told him briefly her life story, how she'd avoided having children with Vasag to succeed in the TV business, her relationship with the sheikh, the orgy, Abbas, everything. She told him every single detail.

"I don't want to build our life together on lies and secrets," she said. "We rushed things, and I didn't have the guts to tell you before."

Joe didn't interrupt during her confessions, but his eyes showed shock, sympathy, and love.

"Are you done?" Joe asked in a soft voice, while Anna wiped her tears. "Everyone has secrets, but not many dare to confess and judge themselves like you just did."

"I did it because I love you," Anna replied.

"I know, so do I. Most people are cowardly and debase their marriages, have children, grow old, and even die with secrets. Strange how they share life but live a lie."

"I don't want that; I cannot, this is my chance to live my life with a clear conscience with you. Are you going to leave me?" Anna asked though she felt the empathy and love in his voice.

"No, I want to be with you more than ever. You're brave and honest, and I have no right to judge your mistakes in the past, but now that I'm in your life I don't tolerate betrayal."

"I promise." She kissed his lips.

"This is a new chapter in your life; we are responsible for both of us," Joe continued. "A kiss on another man's lips ends my love for you."

Joe looked straight into Anna's eyes as if searching for an honest spark.

"Why should I? I love you," Anna replied, her voice steady.

"Enough not to go again into any temptation?"

"Of course. Don't you have anything to tell me?"

"Compared to your adventures, my life is like a children's bedtime story."

"The day you stop loving me, or if I stop loving you, regardless the bounds of marriage or children or society duties, we will tell the truth and let the other go. I do not want a relationship based on duty, social fears, or obligations."

"I agree," said Joe. "Our marriage will be based on love, nothing more. If we have everything else but lose our love, then we walk away."

Anna held him tight.

"You love me very much," Joe added. "No one ever loved me like you, Anna, not even my own parents. Your love is unconditional!"

"You are my most precious treasure," Anna replied.

They dived under the sheets.

The Boy with the Lazy Eye

CHAPTER 12

It was Sunday, early in the morning, and Anna was getting ready at the designer's place. Her inner circle was there: Dr. Richy, Rida, Hashem, Kareem and his wife; and Narine with her two TV assistants.

The cameramen from the television station were not there yet. Anna was already exhausted because the television had made her shoot a short video clip of love the day before, which was to be added alongside shots from the wedding video and broadcast on television.

"I am going to declare my love for him today," she told Rida while he fixed her makeup and while Paul was busy with his assistants getting her dress and all the accessories ready.

"We will declare you have one eye in the wrong place," replied Rida, "if you keep on moving your head and talking with facial expressions."

Everyone laughed.

"Guys, let me tell you a real story about a girl and a lazy eye."

"Now?" her doctor asked. "Be careful! If you move a lot and hurt your eye, there is no time for plastic surgery."

"Let her speak," Rida said.

"When I was young, I was hyperactive and annoying."

"Only then?" asked Hashem.

"Let me finish, please."

"Silence!" Hashem was smiling. "Anna is telling a story. Go ahead; we are listening."

"I was talkative, asking questions, always interrupting adults during conversations. My parents tried all methods to discipline me—punishments, depriving me of things I loved most—but nothing worked."

"You are describing yourself today!" Hashem said and laughed.

"Let her talk," said Dr. Richy. "She is stressed; stop pushing her."

"My parents told me many stories about me, but this one is one of the best. I was a tomboy with a thin, girly, flexible body. I was very active, continually planning devilish pranks while my mother—a school teacher for more than a decade—confessed that she had disciplined classrooms of thirty-five children yet was unable the to instruct her daughter. I was a brat.

"One Sunday afternoon, when I was only four years old, my parents took me to a family wedding. For those of you who remember, few couples with financial means back then had the ability to afford a wedding banquet in a restaurant or a church hall.

"The wedding was held in the church, and afterward we went to the groom's parents' house; the catering consisted of homemade sandwiches and cake served with juice. There were no banks to borrow money from, neither credit cards nor cash in envelopes from attending guests. People celebrated their weddings living in the moment of the occasion and not waiting for comments on social media pages to cheer them up later. People lived for themselves, whereas now they live for others.

"My mother spent most of her time that day in the churchyard running after me, and after the ceremony, we went to the groom's house. The place was crowded. On one side of the apartment, chairs were arranged while on the other end of the room a table was placed, covered with a white quilted table runner, and sandwiches wrapped with colored napkins at one corner of the table. A white cake sat in the middle of the table decorated with colorful flowers made from sugar. Atop the cake were two doves.

"My father was on the balcony smoking a cigarette with men, my mother was sitting in a corner next to other women, and I was on her lap.

"'Don't touch the wedding cake; when the bride and the groom cut the cake, then you may eat. Otherwise, if you make your dad angry he might take us both home, and you will enjoy neither the juice nor the cake,' my mother warned me.

"I was looking at the cake. Then my eyes caught the dress of the bride, who was sitting close to us.

"'I want to wear a dress like hers. Why don't I have one like hers? I want to wear her crown. Please let her lend me her veil,' I asked my mother. I was overwhelmed by the white bridal dress, which didn't match my boyish character.

"'No, Anna, you cannot. That dress belongs to the bride, and you are still very young. You will grow up like the bride,' my mom warned me. 'Get a good education, and then, if you are a good girl and you listen to everything your mother tells you, you will be a bride like her.'"

Everyone was listening. Rida had finally finished her makeup and had started to fix her hair.

As Anna continued to tell her story, the cameramen came in, and Hashem asked them to take pictures quietly.

"My mother was caught in conversation with other women, and I got up from her lap.

"'I am here, Mom,' I comforted her."

"One question." Kareem interrupted her. "You were so young. How do you remember all these details?"

"Honestly, I don't, but with the many times I've heard it from my parents telling others, I now tell the story with the same details.

"So, as I was saying, my mother was watching me and asked me to stay close to her. I promised her, but after a while I probably got bored, so I decided to look around. When my mom next checked on me, I had disappeared. The apartment was big, with many rooms, and the front door was open. My mother got up and started checking the rooms; she couldn't find me, so she told Asbed I was lost.

"My mother never permitted me to play in the street where we lived.

"'Children aren't born to be left playing in the streets,' she always said. 'Mothers should raise them in the house, and they shouldn't be allowed to play alone in the streets while they have gossiping circles with neighbors over a big pot of Arabic coffee.' There were no parks in Beirut, so my only playground was our long and narrow balcony.

"That's why my parents freaked out, worried that I had run into the street from the main entrance door to enjoy my forbidden freedom. As my parents decided to go downstairs to search for me in the street, my mother saw me standing in the corner of the dining room, at the very end of the room, facing the wall. My mom rushed to me with relief, but she found herself standing in front of a shocking scene. I was standing on a tiny handmade wooden bench—used in those days during bath time as a chair—and a boy a few inches taller than me was stuck in the corner in front of me."

Everyone laughed, and Anna continued.

"The boy was held like a captive. My mother told me that I was using my index finger on his face, and the boy was groaning, trying to shut his eyes. I was insistent not to let him go. I don't entirely remember how long it went on, and neither did my mother, but she said I was poking my index finger into his right eye, and the boy—who was whimpering—couldn't keep his eyes closed because of the force I was using with my finger.

"The scene was so terrifying; my mother was traumatized and angry and immediately jumped and tossed me on the floor like a small bag of potatoes.

"'I am going to break your fingers one by one! Do you know that Anna?' she shouted at me.

"I was surprised, like a person who is shocked if a third party interferes to prevent a nurse attending to a wounded soldier on the battlefield.

"'Why are you screaming at me?' I asked.

"All this time the boy stood there like a statue, not making any move, but his face had the expression of a caveman who sees the light of the flashlight for the first time in the night.

"'You still dare to answer your mother? Such a naughty child. We are going home right now.' My father had appeared, and my mother told him that I had tried to blind the boy.

"'Mom, look! I swear, look at his eye; it is still in the wrong place. I gave him my word that I would fix it.' I pointed to the boy's right eye while still on the ground where my mother had tossed me. My mother approached and checked the boy's eye, asking him politely if he was all right. His eye caught her attention. I wasn't lying.

"'Tell her that I was fixing your eye. Didn't I promise you that I can put your eye in the right place?'

"'Let me see if Anna hurt you. You are not in pain?' The boy didn't answer my mother.

"'The boy has a lazy eye,' I said.

"His right eye was very naturally turned inward. The misalignment , I mean seeing one of his eyes not in its right place had gotten my attention. I kept on explaining to my mother that I was using my finger to put his eye back in its place, and he was repeatedly closing it, resisting me. But that was not the deal.

"We left the celebration."

Back in the designer's studio, Hashem asked, "How did you find the chair, convince the boy to fix his eye, and squeeze him in a corner among all the guests?"

"I don't know."

"The boy is lucky your mom found you on time; otherwise you might have blinded the poor kid," Dr. Richy cackled.

"I know, right? People laugh when my mom tells them the story."

"It astounds me," said Kareem. "How could a four-year-old child have such a vivid imagination? The consequences could have been dramatic for that boy, but your intention was virtuous."

"Anna has believed in beauty, perfection, and glamour since she was a child—everything around her must be pretty, correct, and beautiful. She's never considered for a second that she lacks the power to make the world more beautiful," said Dr. Richy.

"I think I never knew the limitations of my abilities to succeed in making things perfect."

"There is no perfection in the world, my dear," Dr. Richy continued. "You made an effort to make a change, risked blinding that child trying to relocate his eye, and rather than playing with other children at the wedding, you decided to help someone you thought you could."

"I was not able at that time to understand that beauty doesn't lie only in appearances but within the beating heart of the human body; I didn't know then that sometimes the most beautiful people by appearance can be the ugliest inside."

Paul was looking at Anna's dress. "So which dress is prettier? The one I designed for you to wear today? Or that bride's dress?"

Everyone laughed, and Anna winked at him.

"Come give me a hug." She was astounded by her dress, hair, and makeup. Rida and Paul both hugged her.

"Don't move. Let me take a picture of this," the photographer said.

The two besties smiled at the camera, their hands around Anna's waist.

It was time to go. Anna left in the car to meet Joe to take pictures before the wedding; she thought that all that is loved by the eyes as outer beauty will eventually disappear with time, while the inner beauty loved by the heart and the mind will endure forever. The eye will ultimately betray its fidelity toward external charm; all of it is vague and temporary. With time it will diminish ultimately. However, the mind stays faithful and never betrays its love and admiration for the true exquisite beauty of the heart.

"I was in love with everything that my eyes saw as beautiful," she told Hashem as he drove, "and anything I saw as ugly I thought I could change."

"Why don't you leave that part to Dr. Richy?"

"I do now," Anna replied, and she continued. "I was not competent enough to understand that the only everlasting beauty is the kindness, honesty, and virtue that lies in the heart."

"You know, as you were telling the story no one interrupted you, not even me; everyone was impressed. That is a lovely story."

Between the divorce, the trip to Armenia, losing all her financial assets, and her parents' disagreement, and so many other things, she was too stressed to attend to the details of wedding preparations, so her friends had taken mainly over. She was lucky that all the professional people around her had helped, and that she had not had to pay for anything. Everything had been offered as gifts: her dress, her makeup, the cameras, and the decorations.

They reached the park. Anna saw Joe from a distance and rushed to him.

"Be careful!" she heard Hashem shout behind her.

"You look gorgeous," said Joe to his bride. "I love you."

"Me too."

The photographers started taking pictures; Anna held Joe's hands and thought how lucky she was that she would found the love of her life and was blessed to have friends who supported her not for what she could offer them but because they loved her for her heart.

The First Kiss Chewing a Gum

CHAPTER 13

Once the photographers had finished capturing enough pictures of the couple in the park, the bride and the groom headed to the church in separate cars, to be united officially after the ceremony.

"Hashem, do you have any gum? I drank a lot of coffee." Anna was worried.

"Don't forget to throw it once we reach the church," Hashem replied, handing her a stick of gum.

"Yeah, I know. I'll swallow it. Now we're both going to church in separate cars, Joe and me? He just saw me in my bridal dress in the park already."

"Tradition."

"Sure, as if anything we're doing is related to any culture we know." Anna laughed and chewed her gum.

They reached the church, and Anna entered holding her father's arm. The decorations were white and fuchsia, the latter one of her favorite colors.

As Anna walked down the aisle, photographers took pictures of the bride with the groom who had appeared in her life so mysteriously. The media knew nothing about Joe or his family background; Anna herself did not know and nor did she care—she just wanted to marry her lover. She knew no one in his family, not even his parents.

Joe's family had flown with him from Canada for the wedding. When Anna looked to the side allocated to the groom's guests, she felt uncomfortable at their curious stares and looks, but her worries faded when she turned back to Joe, whose eyes were filled with love and honesty.

As the priest started the ceremony, Anna realized that she was still chewing the gum. As they stood in front of the priest joining hands, Anna's mind rewound to an earlier adventure.

Anna was only thirteen when, on their way home from watching a basketball game in the neighborhood, her friend Aurora greeted a boy.

"Who was that guy?" Anna asked.

"Didn't I bet that Anna was going to ask?" Alice said to Aurora, and the entire group laughed.

"What does that mean? It was just a question. Be a good girl. I am one of your group, girls!" Anna was happy belonging to a group of being alone and bullied for so long before Zoey had come into her life.

Zoey rested her hand on Anna's shoulder. "Calm down, Anna, they're teasing you."

"So, Aurora, who is he?" Anna was impatient.

The boy was nearly fifteen with long, straight brown hair worn back, heavy-lidded green eyes, a broad forehead, a rounded nose, and a protruding chin. He was stylish and nice-looking.

"His name is Shant; he's my cousin."

"I want him to be my boyfriend. Get me his phone number, and tomorrow afternoon I will meet him in front of the basketball park."

Next day, after Anna called him, they met. Zoey went with her.

After Anna changed schools, Zoey had become her best friend; they were inseparable. Before Zoey, Anna had never had any close friends.

She was a nerd in her classroom, alone and bullied. Zoey was different; she was popular. Zoey was Anna's cousin's neighbor, Silva. They had met a couple of times on the building's stairs when Anna visited Silva, her cousin, and the two girls had played together, but there was no particular bond between them at the time.

Zoey had an independent mind; she was ferocious, while Anna was simply a nerd.

The first day of school, Zoey walked into the playground where Anna was waiting for her.

"Hi, Zoey. Your neighbor, I mean my married cousin, Silva, who lives in your building, told me you were coming to my school. You will be in my class." Anna was hyper and excited.

"Come, put your bag next to mine." Anna was gesturing that by putting Zoey's bag next to hers, she was committing to bonding as best friends, and Anna certainly needed a friend.

As Zoey looked around her, she seemed to realize that she was stuck with a geek in the school playground.

"Let us walk," Anna suggested.

"Wait, why are you wearing your school uniform like that? It's too long from the waist down. You look like a tiny weird nun." Zoey fussed over Anna's uniform.

"Really?" Anna was surprised.

Zoey's mission started at that moment.

Anna, a shy and insecure type of girl, had a controversial personality full of energy, but a terrible taste in fashion. Anna had double French braids and wore dental braces and eyeglasses.

Zoey was Anna's opposite, in both appearance and personality. She was slightly overweight and shorter than Anna, with green eyes, thin light eyebrows, full lips, a tiny nose, and short blond hair.

After working on her school uniform, Zoey encouraged Anna to listen to English music, buy famous weekly magazines like *Smash Hits* and *Seventeen*, which were the only ways to follow the world of pop music at that time.

People then were not able to access world music, news, and celebrity scandals with one click of a technological device. The landline phones in people's homes were the only communication system.

Slowly, Anna started changing her style outside the school. Whatever Zoey had in mind, Anna was up for the challenge. The school discipline was essential to her, but outside of school, she was so different now that she had Zoey in her life. She retained her nerdy style in school because she was convinced that one should separate duties and fun time.

During gatherings such as basketball games, theater, Armenian festivals, and birthday parties, Anna started making an effort to look her best beside Zoey.

Life was less complicated, even in a country at war; young girls and boys had freedom and fun, and the people they lived among were peaceful in their hearts and had no violence on their minds.

Zoey and Anna lived as teenagers in an era when sexually transmitted diseases, psychos molesting young adolescents, drugs, and social media addiction were not threats to them. They had no mobiles or internet websites with which to meet boys, but nevertheless, they had the chance to experience life through direct human contact.

Most parents in the city were somewhat tolerant and gave their teenage children the chance to live their lives to the fullest.

They hurt themselves, yet the stones of life on the ground were less piercing than today; they made mistakes and learned from their adventures rather than being imprisoned in front of screens, which today's parents think is safe because the teenager is surrounded by four walls in a room under their surveillance.

Anna and Zoey never knew what they were missing in the world of technology; they did not have it but were satisfied with what they had in life.

They learned about the quest for life through their experience of reality rather than being trapped behind screens that impair creativity, imprison minds, and paralyze social skills. Their mistakes molded them into strong-minded women with the willpower to make their own choices in life.

Anna's preferred look—colored leggings like her icon Madonna's, short tops that showed her belly, one-sided high ponytail, and a half bottle of gel on her hair, tied with a colorful piece of fabric—was unpleasant to her mother. Cross earrings, long shirts, and shiny lipstick with black sunglasses drove her mother crazy. Anna felt as if she was one of the coolest girls in Lebanon.

"Getting ready to clean the floor, Anna?" her mother would mock.

"You don't get it. It's fashion, Mom," Anna responded.

No one understands me like Zoey, she thought.

Through Zoey, Anna became friends with other girls. She started talking to boys on the phone or dancing with them at parties, but once she saw Shant, all other boys became invisible to her.

There were no cyber relationships to transform Shant and Anna into prisoners of technology; they expressed their emotions out loud to each other rather than using emoticons on screens.

There was no danger of a misunderstanding about sexual activities through devices to haunt their young, inexperienced minds. Anna and her friends had few worries about society or of discovering another type of private life through computers, cybersex, cozy talks, and Photoshop pictures that can play with young minds, encouraging them to live with illusions.

Shant! The first love of her life! Anna was happy with him; every time they met, her heart beat like a hummingbird, and she felt butterflies in her stomach.

The relationship started with holding hands, smiles, dancing at birthday parties, and long hours sitting under their building's stairs talking about simple irrelevant matters, but soon Anna wanted more.

Four months after they met, encouraged by Zoey, Anna called Shant.

"I am going tomorrow to my cousin's house, Silva, where Zoey lives. Come at night. We will be alone." Moreover, she told him the address.

It was Saturday. Melineh dropped Anna off, and the young girl ran to her cousin's apartment, threw her school bag to the floor, and rushed downstairs to Zoey's house.

The girls had planned to meet with Shant, although their parents thought it was a night of reviewing their exams.

Zoey's parents left after a couple of hours, and they told the girls that if they needed anything to go to Anna's cousin's house.

It was already eight at night, and Anna was getting ready to greet Shant at the door,

"Oh, my God! I forgot to put on perfume!" Anna shouted with frustration.

"I have roll-on deodorant," Zoey said. "Use it under your armpits."

"I want to smell good. He will hug me and kiss me."

Zoey giggled. "Try it."

Anna smeared the roll-on all over her neck.

Charles, Zoey's boyfriend, was sitting in her parents' bedroom, already with her, when the doorbell rang.

"It's Shant!" Anna shouted.

"Rather than jumping, go open the door." Zoey's voice came from the bedroom.

"How do I look?" She ran into the bedroom.

"I'm sure you look great, Anna; go answer the door."

She opened the door. It was Shant.

"Come in." Anna held Shant's hand and took him to the balcony, where they sat on the swing gazing at the beautiful view of forest under the moonlight.

Neither spoke for a while; they had never been so free and alone. Anna could feel the anxiety in the air, and a couple of minutes later she broke the silence.

"Kiss me!" She did not want to miss the chance on such a romantic night. *I want to feel his lips on mine,* she thought.

Shant caressed her hair, and their feet brushed the ground as they swung back and forth.

"I'm waiting. Don't you love me?"

He held her close, moved her body on the swing mattress underneath him. Her nervous heart was beating fast, yet she continued talking.

"Kiss me like they do in the movies."

As he touched his lips to hers, she felt the warmth of his mouth, the heat of his breath, and his saliva on her lips.

"Open your mouth," he whispered.

I never heard him speak in such a beautiful tone.

"Do not close your mouth," he said, trying to dive his tongue inside her mouth. "Anna, open your teeth too, not only your lips."

"Yes," she said, like an obedient student.

Anna felt his tongue touching her upper gums.

Her eyes were open, but as she felt stimulated by his kiss, they slowly closed.

Both with their eyes closed, holding each other close, Anna felt strange with another tongue in her mouth. She felt like she was in a sea cave, waves crashing against the cave walls and the water slowly swallowing her.

He smells so sweet, she thought, but then she felt another intruder inside her mouth beside his moving snakelike tongue, something soft yet tasty.

His chewing gum!

She was so excited that she did not want to ruin this first-time experience of a French kiss. She involuntarily swallowed his gum.

Shant moved his lips from her lips, going down to her neck. She felt like a patient given an electric shock, and her skinny body surrendered itself to the passionate, unforgettable experience.

"Yuck, there is a bitter taste on your neck." He moved up, rubbing his lips with his sleeve.

Anna pushed him away, jumped up, and ran into the bathroom.

"Zoey, I need you!" she shouted.

"Be quiet, stop yelling!" Zoey ran into the bathroom with her wrinkled blouse and ruined hair.

"He said my neck tastes bitter," Anna complained.

"No way? Why so?" Zoey looked shocked. "Let me check." She licked Anna's neck.

"So?"

"It smells and tastes like the roll-on deodorant. Did you actually put it on your neck? Wash it off."

"You didn't have perfume."

"Who says you should put perfume where he will be licking you?"

"Shut up, Zoey."

"You shut up! Wash. Charles is alone; I'm going back to the bedroom."

"Okay! We both shut up. Go."

Anna cleaned her neck and rushed back to Shant.

Can't waste another minute of my movie kiss, she thought. She jumped back on the bench, and the kiss continued.

Anna's body was responding to this most intimate situation, with Shant moving on her slowly and rubbing his body against hers.

Now the kiss was more intense and more prolonged. Her first teenage physical yearnings scared her. She was afraid that her curiosity had led her to learn that human instinct cannot be completed without emotions, and this was simply the need of her body lusting for sexual experience.

Anna was not ashamed of her physical turmoil. The need to explore her teenage adventure had awakened her curiosity about her own body. She knew her body was responding to his touches. It was the awakening call of being transformed from a child to a teenage girl.

Anna was discovering her femininity through Shant's gentle caresses. The inquisitive touches were fulfilling her hunger for this new experience.

The kiss continued. Anna was being touched, stroked, kissed on her lips and neck, and slowly he started fondling her breasts under her blouse.

Nervous and scared, she felt that she was on the top of a mountain, and suddenly she was pushed down. As her arms stretched, she surrendered herself to this new physical exploration without hesitation; slowly the fear started to dissipate, and a strange feeling of pleasure and desire flooded her.

Her body was releasing enormous bursts of physical and emotional energy. Her eyes were closed, yet the excitement was so enjoyable that she felt like the dispersed mercury of a broken thermometer moving in every direction, free of any physical control.

When Anna opened her eyes, she was safely on the ground in Shant's arms. Relaxed and happy!

The hour was late, and after some time Shant left.

Even after he was gone, Anna thought about him, and her body released an explosion of desire mixed with excitement and tranquility. She explored her body, and the fulfillment of the quest was a secret between Anna and herself.

I have discovered a secret, which is a shame. I must keep it a secret that no one else should know about, except me, Anna thought. An alliance was made between her mind and body to maintain this secret forever.

She was totally in love for the first time. She was in love with Shant, and she started loving her body and how much pleasure she could explore.

She had discovered the astounding existence of physical pleasure aroused by her feelings toward Shant.

Anna had found her first love with him through thinking about him. *No one will ever know what my body wants as I do,* Anna thought.

The next few weeks, whenever she remembered their first kiss, she felt an increased blood flow rushing into her head. Her heart beat fast as if she could feel her pulse in every part of her body. She craved his touch. The throbbing sensation between her thighs aroused a yearning to be touched in every square inch of her body.

She could never get enough of repeatedly falling from that mountaintop. Phone calls, words, gestures, written letters, meeting in the theater, or birthday parties... all became pointless. They met only to be together, to enjoy their first teenage sexual experience. They called it love.

Fondling ears, lips, neck, passionate long kisses, the slow friction of their young bodies stroking against each other, even with their clothes on, was not a hindrance to give them both what their young bodies desired.

Then again there was the fear of the unknown and the risk of being caught in an unforgivable sin.

Fingers and gentle tongue movements always satisfied their needs, leaving no fear of sin or banishment from their parents' Garden of Eden.

Anna and Shant were very young, and unlike future generations, they could not learn to flirt from sources like the internet and electronic devices; instead, they learned their first sexual experience together, from each other.

Shant gave her a new understanding of life; she discovered with him that her heart needed to feel emotions as much as her body yearned for his touch and that the harmony of the two desires fulfilled her whole system, body, and soul.

Anna started exploring the world around her as soon as she learned how to explore the closest and the most private world of her own: her own body.

Shant and Anna lived their teenage years in an era of innocence.

Two years later, she lost her interest in Shant; she stopped loving him. She was not excited to meet him as before, didn't want to jump off the top of that mountain, and she knew she was pulling away from him.

Everything about him began to agitate her—his walk, his talk, his clothes, and even his touch.

One day Anna told Shant she did not want to see him anymore. He did not fight to get her back. They both realized they were falling out of love. They never said the words "I do not love you."

Shant left.

Anna was growing up, and like all teenage couples who think they are unique sweethearts and will stay happily together forever, Anna and Shant had felt the same at the beginning of their relationship.

In the church, the priest was still praying, but Anna was still swimming amid the memories of her past, standing next to Joe.

I'm glad I didn't rush to marry Shant, she thought, in an effort to forget about her mistake with Vasag. *I could never live in the shadow of my past; only cowards build their lives on the memories of the past.*

She heard her name.

The priest was talking to her directly.

"Anna, do you take Joe to be your husband? Do you promise to be faithful to him in good times and in bad, in sickness and in health, to love and honor him all the days of your life?"

It was so sudden that she said her "yes" rapidly, swallowing her gum.

Joe noticed, and he smiled.

This time Anna was not falling in love but was rising in love.

They headed to their wedding reception. As the newlyweds got up for their first dance as husband and wife, Joe whispered in her ear.

"I saw you chewing and then swallowing the gum in the church."

"It was a sign that you will be the last person who kisses my lips." Anna squeezed her arms tighter around Joe's neck, and her cheek brushed against his face.

"Of course, I will be, though I don't get the connection between a kiss and gum."

"I will tell you one day. Don't forget; I have a lifetime with you. I have all the time in the world to talk about my life chronicles."

"I love you, Anna."

Rather than answering, she sealed his lips with a slight kiss, knowing she was in the arms of the one she loved most in the whole world.

God is Death

CHAPTER 14

Anna was at Beirut–Rafic Hariri Airport.

She did not head to the VIP lounge as she usually did; she wore no fancy suit or business handbag—just a shirt and a comfortable pair of jeans.

She was with Joe, her parents, her doctor, and some close friends were surrounding the newly wedded couple. The press was taking pictures before she left.

"I give you my blessings, Anna! Be careful! Do not worry; you are a strong woman, I know you," Melineh was continually saying while holding back tears.

Dr. Richy was smiling, but underneath his smile, the agony of parting from his best friend was obvious in his eyes.

Joe was quiet, yet he looked worried; although he was the only person boarding the plane with Anna, he was lost in deep thoughts. He was holding Anna's hand as if someone was going to kidnap her.

Anna was his prize.

He repeatedly checked his phone.

Suddenly it rang, and he did not even wait for a second ring.

He let go of Anna's hand. "Yes?" he answered quickly.

Anna looked at him.

Joe's brows knitted, he drew his lower lip between his teeth, and terror overtook his face.

Anna knew that the call was making Joe uncomfortable; he was nodding without interrupting the caller. After some minutes of listening, he hung up the phone.

Joe lowered his head and let out a harsh breath.

His face was pale, and his eyes were gloomy; without explanation, he held Anna's waist and moved her away from the crowd.

"It was the doctor. He called with our test results," he whispered. "He apologized for the delay but… he said…" He could not continue the sentence; he was speechless.

"It is okay, my love!" Anna replied. "It wasn't his fault. I mean, after a hasty marriage in twenty-one days I am glad we got time for this test. So? What did he say? Did he give you the results? What did he say?"

Anna was talking recklessly as usual. Her voice was loud and high-pitched, and she kept repeating herself.

"So? What did he say?"

"Anna, I am so sorry."

"Sorry? For what?"

"There is no hope. Anna! I cannot give you any children. I can never make you a mother. You can marry someone else and have kids of your own."

He whispered the words in her ear, his arm still around her waist.

"You cannot give me children? That is nonsense."

Anna had never seen him so sad; she was in shock.

"Forgive me; I did not know I was sterile. My family was worried that you were barren, being divorced and not having children from Vasag. They insisted that we do this test, and I thank you for doing it, but…"

"But what?" asked Anna. "That's why we did the test, right?"

"I did it too, to be on the safe side because I really know that I've waited my whole life to be with the one I love and to marry her. I've never been married before, Anna; this was unexpected. I have no money, no education, and you gave away every penny you had to your ex-husband for a fast divorce, leaving your career and converting to another sect in Christianity. And you are following me someplace where you will be a simple woman, not a star anymore. But this? I will never forgive myself! I cannot give you a family, Anna. My aunt was at fault when she thought you might be barren. The problem is with me. I am shocked, just like you."

"So, you are leaving me now? Joe?"

"I cannot let you get on that plane with me. This is not a movie or a fairy tale; it is a fact that I won't permit myself to involve you in."

Anna's parents were standing aside with everyone else, waiting for the couple to finish their secret conversation and join them because time was precious.

"Anna, you should stay here, I cannot take you with me. I know I will put you through a lot, and I cannot see you suffer."

It was as if the universe had collapsed and Anna was stuck under its vast implosion.

"Forgive me! I swear I did not know this before. Please stay here. I am sure once the results of my test are sent to the committee of the Catholic Church they will immediately grant us a divorce. I am not a man who believes in adoption or going through artificial medical treatments. Maybe this is how God wants it to be, so let it be."

"What?" Anna's eyes were huge, and she did not blink for a few seconds.

"Don't worry. I will send you the divorce papers from there. In this brief period, the love story that we lived together will stay in my heart forever."

He knew he had no right to deprive her of being a mother. He was devastated, and the disrespect and the negligence of his own parents and family toward him and his decisions were painful.

"They never understood the meaning of true love and honesty because they neither truly loved nor chose a life with integrity," Joe stuttered.

"Who are you talking about?" Anna was confused.

How dare they put us both through so much disgrace and pain with their ignorant and ill-mannered attitude, never mentioning to me once that I had an operation when I was very young? I do not even remember it. The doctor said something about orchidopexy. I am so lost, he thought but said nothing.

Anna's parents had never wanted him to marry her because he walked into her life while she was already married to another, and because he was a total stranger, had no financial stability, and lived abroad... and yet they had never kept any secrets or treated him once with such bad manners as his parents had shown toward Anna in the short period of time that Anna had met them after the wedding!

For Anna, everything had happened so quickly, and she was so much in love that she had believed that this was the happy ending, her true love story, her fairy tale that she'd almost lost faith in until these last few weeks.

The press, her parents, Dr. Richy, and everyone gathered there realized that Anna was standing like stone, unmoving.

"Forgive me, Anna! I did not want things to end this way! I know your heart is breaking. So is mine, but we have no future together!"

However, this is just the beginning, Anna thought. *Why is this happening to me?*

His words were coming out of his mouth so slowly, but Anna felt his heart beating so strongly it seemed as if it was going to come out of his chest.

Was it true? Or it was just her imagination?

"You might love me today, but tomorrow you might blame me for my problem," he continued. "My parents were reckless not to inform me of this fact; they hid it from me even when we reached the church gate."

This was a new nightmare for Anna, a new sad chapter in her life story.

She had been through many difficulties, but she had never expected to face such a catastrophe at the moment she had let herself dream of a new beginning.

Now Anna had to make a big decision; she had played all her cards of chance on the table of destiny except one card still holding in her hand, The card of love!

Destiny is playing a cruel joke on me, she thought.

The plane ticket in her hand and the wedding ring of her love on her finger. Anna's mind was in turmoil.

They called the flight number to Canada.

"I must go now," he said.

"What?" Anna had no other words.

The shock paralyzed her.

"It is the will of God!" Joe answered and started to walk.

Slowly he headed toward the gates.

Joe was walking away, the voices on the intercom were calling out names, announcing flight timings, and passengers were rushing through the gatehouse.

People hugged each other, and families gathered; some were crying, others were talking out loud, giving comments about luggage weight problems, advice, and encouraging words to each other.

Workers with their empty carriages were looking for passengers who needed assistance; children with their tiny backpacks cavorted, jumping and shouting while mothers tried to keep them quiet. Police officers and security guards patrolled the periphery.

In all this chaos, Anna was immobile in the terminal while Joe walked away toward the baggage reclaim area.

Joe looked at Anna with sad eyes then nodded toward her parents and friends and kept walking.

He began disappearing into the crowd.

Asbed and Melineh approached Anna.

"Anna, why are you still here? Why don't you follow your husband? Did you fight?"

Anna's mind was blocked like a huge stone hindering the entrance of a mysterious cave in the middle of an enchanted forest, yet her heart was like a magical butterfly—a mere caterpillar before she met Joe and now ready to fly free and full of hope.

All her desires, hopes, and dreams were wrapped up in one person: Joe!

Smiling, Dr. Richy joined the conversation.

"They wouldn't fight. I know Anna! They love each other madly. They are still on their honeymoon."

"Anna, go! Why are you here? Are you scared? Are you regretting this decision?" urged Melineh.

Anna was twisting the thumb of her left hand, reaching the end of her ring finger where the new diamond ring and the wedding ring were placed.

The will of God? What has God to do with the matter of children? Anna thought. *No one prays to God; they pray to Death!*

Thoughts rushed through her brain. So many answers are required in life: why corruption, disease, wars, and injustice?

Where is this God? Anna thought. *Most people are cowardly and blame it all on a male creation sitting in the clouds.*

Her thoughts arrived like thunderbolts.

God—a word that had been the subject of debate since the existence of humankind—was now an obsessive concept for Anna.

She never blamed or saw flaws in people of faith; she had no business judging others. However, those who used their religious ideas to blame others, or used the word *God* to manipulate others, gain wealth, or create differences between equals according to their belief had always annoyed her.

The human mind needs a mysterious force outside itself that can be answerable for all the good and the horrific events in our lives. So, God is responsible for everything in life—the cause of all pain, the answer to disappointments, the justification for our choices, and the adjudicator of our destiny.

In fact, people never make pledges to God with conviction; they simply bargain with him.

Humans decided to create a god floating in the sky—invisible, loving, mighty, and compassionate, yet vulnerable, merciless, and deaf.

Whenever Anna tried to grapple with the issue of God, people looked at her as if she were an atheist. She, however, felt it was better to be known as an atheist than to believe that humans had the capacity to crucify their own creator or the son of their God on a cross.

This was not only illogical but in Anna's mind, it was a sin against the human conscience. The ability to crucify whoever created them! How could she believe in the existence of a God who permitted the crucifixion of his own son? Humans are stronger than their own God?

All mortal qualifications that humans bear they ascribe to their god, as written by other humans many centuries ago.

In Anna's mind, religious rituals, fearful obedience, and the obligatory human traditions for avoiding hellfire after death were a circus.

Fear overruled the human mind so powerfully that rather than helping the poor and feeding the hungry, religious faith mostly concentrated on indulgence, celebrations, exchanging gifts, and declaring faith in rituals from bygone eras.

Logic and conscience had been silenced, and declarations of faith were shown only through shallow rites and surface convictions.

Wasn't it terrifying to see how so many humans made efforts to develop their terrible habits rather than unlearn them?

Godly spoken words did not matter to her; what mattered was how people touched others' lives through good deeds, with no expectations in return.

It is said that God allows evil but does not cause it—a very interesting quotation that made Anna question the love of the creator for his creations, specially the innocent babies, the sick and the weak, who pray for his help, or his followers who have been burnt at the stake or slaughtered with the swords of others.

The question was how the fear of a power that can throw Anna into hell—and all the horror of that everlasting punishment—can make her a better person.

The terror of becoming a sinner in the eyes of this mind-created God never controlled her thoughts. People had been brainwashed for centuries by religious fictions, tortured so much by the religious men in history in the name of their god, that in time generations were born already believing in the myth of what their ancestors had taught them and even created militias today that killed others. They used the name of their god complete with their conditions and expectations!

People were so busy living that they did not have time to ask about the misconceptions that had been shaped by other humans and were unable therefore to control their lives. Others were scared that their questioning might prohibit them from entering the realm of heaven after death.

Who would dare question the phenomenon of a god who had performed so many miracles? He had created the world, and he'd also created all the dangerous animals, like alligators and sharks that could devour humans.

Anna found it funny when people came up with answers for tragedies in their lives; the sentence that always got her attention was "God always tests the ones he loves."

She could never understand how a creator could torture, cause pain, and even kill to test someone's faith. How wise was this God? Humans, who are meant to be so inferior compared to their God, do not test the love of other humans by going to such limits, yet the one who created them even dared to kill to test their faith, obedience, and love for him.

Anna recognized that this God must be as wise as his followers; after all, he was their creation.

Although peace and forgiveness should have resided at the core of every believer, those things were hardly ever found within those who prayed, wore religious symbols, decorated their houses with saint sculptures, or kneeled in front of statues in substantial luxurious places called the houses of their God.

Anna did not need religion; she needed to have faith in her conscience.

She always thought that the human mind had not yet reached the level of understanding needed to comprehend the true power that harmonized all living things, and it indeed couldn't ever discover this fact if death was inevitable and no one understood the cycle of life and death.

However, once the mystery of death is solved, humans do not need to pray again. Finding the secret of death means finding the true God because all religious convictions and doctrines are created from the fear of the unknown, which is death.

Some people who learned to believe in a god only through doctrines and without using their minds do not understand that the true relationship with God is through death. The created God in the human mind is the manifestation of death. So God is death.

If God has given life, how does he permit other creators to take away the life of his loving creations?

Anna did not deny the existence of the universal power, but she did not believe a person could be happy based on books written thousands of years ago.

The heart was not just the organ used for pumping blood through her body but was also the conduit between Anna and the universal divine power. She believed that the heart was the source of mercy, righteousness, and integrity and could lead her to live with godliness—through her conscience, without the fear of being punished, but by choosing to live so because the choice would bring her serenity.

Joe's news, his confession, his decision, his terror of an unhappy life with her, his distress at his disability, which was not his fault... all this was altogether too much to be borne for one more minute.

Anna had left everything behind, had given up everything to be with him, to be happy with him, yet now he was walking away from her, leaving her just to protect her from unhappiness for the rest of her life.

From her standing point in the middle of the terminal, Anna was observing Joe with love and compassion.

She was penniless, divorced, and in love with someone who was leaving her in the name of a god he held responsible for whether they had children and stayed together.

You are my everything! She had left everything behind for the love of her life, challenged the whole world, broke all the rules, yet he was walking away from her.

"Anna, why are you still here?" Melineh gazed steadily into her daughter's eyes.

Anna's lips were trembling, her palms were sweaty, and she could hardly breathe.

Melineh tried again. "Apparently you're not listening to me."

"I don't know," Anna mumbled.

Melineh reached out and placed her hand on Anna's shoulder. "What's wrong?"

"I was thinking about God."

"You? God? ... Now?" Melineh rolled her eyes skyward.

"I'm scared, Mom."

"Scared of God?"

"No, you don't understand!" Anna cried.

"I want to, but there isn't any time left if you want to be united with the one you love. We can discuss your God complex issues once you're in Canada."

"I'm lost." Anna's voice was filled with panic.

"I can see that you're worried." Melineh sighed. "But if you value your love for your husband more than your fears and worries then don't let him go."

"I do, I really do."

"Love is your strongest weapon in life to fight all obstacles, Anna."

"God is death, but Joe is life, Mom."

"Now you're uttering absurdity; may God forgive you." Melineh crossed herself quickly, touching her forehead, navel, right shoulder, then left. "Amen."

"I'll tell you later." Anna hugged her mother. "Thank you for teaching me how to love."

"But I didn't teach you to be agnostic." Melineh kissed Anna's forehead. "Go follow him," she continued with a wobbly voice.

Anna had left everything in the name of love, yet he was leaving her in the name of life! He was barren.

She saw him turn his head one more time before departure.

Even from that distance, she saw that his eyes were filled with tears, and she felt as if in his silence his heart was shouting out for her. •

Anna felt as if he'd said what he had to say in order not to deprive her of being a mother, but his eyes and his heart were calling out for her:

"Are you coming, Anna? Do not give up on our love! Come with me! Anna, do not leave me! Love conquers all! Come, Anna!"

She realized she couldn't let him go. He was her love!

"Stop, Joe! Wait for me, I can't live without you!"

Dr. Richy was smiling, and her parents and friends were in tears, urging her forward.

"I don't care about anything else; I want you! Only you!" she was shouting.

"That's a love story to write about," said one of the journalists, scribbling in his notebook.

Three hours had passed.

On the plane, Anna gripped Joe's hand.

"Sorry, Anna. I couldn't afford two first-class tickets as you are used to."

"I don't care I am in economy class because my heart is in first class! You, my love!"

With nothing but her love, Anna began the next phase of her journey into a bright new foreign country.

It was enough.

Her love was one of the few true loves that still existed in this false world.

Acknowledgments

This novel is the culmination of a long process that would have been very difficult to complete without the guidance, assistance, and care of a number of people.

To my fantastic editor, author David Antrobus, whose patience, humility, and expertise have helped me grow as a writer: thank you for guiding me with such passion, respect, and wisdom over the goal line.

David, you have shown me that an actual editor not only edits but also coaches writers through the whole process.

You challenged my thinking, writing, and storytelling skills and served as my mentor.

Words cannot express my sincere gratitude toward and appreciation for my dear friend Marina Nigoghossian, who helped me blast off and sustain this journey. She followed the entire process from the start, reviewed all the drafts, and never hesitated to offer me help with her professional skills and ideas.

I'm grateful to the professional and compassionate team of people with whom I worked at TellWell publishing company, who helped make my book a reality.

You are fantastic, guys.

I thank my loving parents, Leon and Marina Restokian, my precious baby sister Nancy Restokian Zalaquet, my one and only brother in law, Dr. Marcel Zalaquet and my most prized nephew in the whole world baby Marcelino for being a part of my life. I Thank them for their love, concern, and pride in my work.

My Family; your help and assistance played a significant role in the completion of this book, you were always a major source of strength to me. Your advice, encouragement, and personal sacrifices have made an everlasting impression on my life.

My most precious cousins, Lena Zilifian Damerian, Houry Kazanjian and Agat Hergelian my life coach. You kept me sane through the whole process and gave me a shoulder to cry on from oceans apart. Your unconditional love, understanding, and confidence gave me the strength to believe in myself.

I am the luckiest cousin in the world to have the three of you in my life. I cherish your love.

How could I forget my adoring departed aunt, Araxi Restokain, May her soul rest in peace. She always believed in me long before anyone else did. My aunt lived each day believing that one day my hopes and dreams would become a reality. Although you passed away, your memory is in my heart.

Thank you for instilling in me the values of positive thinking, affection, and persistence.

I will never forget you.

Special thanks to my photographer, Kamil Maksoud, who deserves recognition for the beautiful pictures he has taken and who has always offered me his full support, patience, and service.

I promise you I'll be less hyper next time during the photo shoot and will listen to your advice when choosing the image for the back cover of my book.

Special thanks to my talented make-up artist, Arminee Oulikian, and my hair stylists, Maria and Eve Oulikian in Canada. Your exceptional care, kindness, and incredible service are highly appreciated. I know I can be very exhausting and demanding, but what can you do? You are all stuck with me.

How could I forget my amazing friends in Lebanon: my plastic surgeon and friend Dr. Hratch Saghbazarian; my TV makeup artist, Rabih Hmede; my fashion designer, Joe Yazigi;my friend and the lawyer, Rabih Jaafar. The distance didn't have the power to destroy our friendship. Thank you for always being a part of my life and never letting me go.

Your encouraging words, confidence, and assistance in every way taught me that honest and long-time friendship with no personal benefits is an everlasting blessing. I will always treasure your friendship.

My most precious TV fans in Lebanon and the Arab world; the media and the virtuous journalists in my life I salute you all; You taught me a lot, I adore you all. I can't thank you enough for your continuous support, encouragement, and love. You never let me down. You helped me become who I am today, a woman with courage and confidence.

Quebec, Canada. I thank this beautiful country that welcomed me with open arms—a land of serenity and new opportunities; with its beautiful cold winters but warmhearted people, Canada gave me a once-in-a-lifetime opportunity to make this dream come true.

In the end no matter how many people will try to hurt you, crush you, or betray your confidence, there is always a bigger crowd who will encourage, love, and support you and set high standards of excellence for your accomplishments.

Never stop believing in yourself and accomplishing any goal you set your mind on.

You are more significant than you think.

Life is beautiful. Choose to enjoy it.